Max's grin fell away and his gaze sharpened, zeroing in on her face. "Are you okay with all this?"

Kira blinked. "Why wouldn't I be?"

Then realization hit. Oh. Right. Max thought she had a jones for his brother Elan, and she hadn't corrected that misconception for him over the years. She might even have done a few things to encourage it. The more incentive he had had to keep his distance, the safer it had been for her.

Despite being the ranking officer in the King's Guard, Max was still a freaking *prince*, and Kira's father had been his father's butler. She might have played with Max and Elan as a child, but her father and theirs had made it very clear she would never be the equal of a Delacourt. She was a servant's kid, and her father had expected her to be a servant as well. He'd been pissed as hell that she'd gone off to be a cop. Then she'd returned to San Amaro to serve the king. She might do it with a gun instead of a serving tray, but a servant was a servant. Too bad her father hadn't lived to see his wish come true.

Max had ditched all the trappings of royalty and joined the Marines when he turned eighteen, but when he came back to command the Guard after his brother's coronation, he'd still had to deal with being a prince. Which had made him not only royalty, but her superior officer.

Off-limits on every possible level.

Until today.

# Between the Sheets

## CRYSTAL JORDAN

CJ BOOKS

# CONTENTS


Between Lovers

Chapter One — 3

Chapter Two — 10

Chapter Three — 17

Chapter Four — 27

Chapter Five — 32

Chapter Six — 41

Chapter Seven — 45

Chapter Eight — 50

Chapter Nine — 57

Chapter Ten — 65

Chapter Eleven — 71

Chapter Twelve — 75

Chapter Thirteen — 81

Chapter Fourteen — 89

Chapter Fifteen — 97

Taken Between

Chapter One — 110

Chapter Two                                          113

Chapter Three                                        121

Chapter Four                                         129

Chapter Five                                         138

Chapter Six                                          147

Chapter Seven                                        150

Chapter Eight                                        160

Chapter Nine                                         177

Chapter Ten                                          184

Chapter Eleven                                       191

Epilogue                                             204

About Crystal Jordan                                 211

Also by Crystal Jordan                               212

Excerpt from Reclaimed by the Immortal Viking Wolf   214

# Dedication

For Michal. Just because.

This book is particularly dedicated to Dayna Hart, critique partner and editor extraordinaire, who not only critiqued the first version of this book before it came out from Kensington Books over a decade ago, but also helped me brainstorm the new content (almost 40 extra pages) and then edited the new independently published version. This book has been on quite a journey, and she's been along for the ride, helping me make it a better story the whole way. Never doubt that you're the best, Dayna!

**~Crystal**

# BETWEEN LOVERS

## THE BETWEEN, BOOK I

## CRYSTAL JORDAN

CJ BOOKS

# Chapter One

"Who are you?" Rhiannon asked the question for the millionth time since she and four other women had been stolen from a campground in eastern Oregon. Her words were slurred, her swollen tongue and bruised lips unable to form the words properly.

"I'm the man who's going to kill you." His response was always the same, always delivered in that chillingly calm, almost cheerful voice. Sometimes he said the words out loud, and sometimes they echoed in her mind as a telepathic thought. She'd heard the Between could do that, but she'd never experienced it before now. She wished she never had, wished she'd never organized an impromptu all-women camping trip at the health club she owned, wished she'd never crossed paths with this shape-shifting monster who'd beaten her, drugged her, bitten her, and made her into a monster just like him.

Made her a Between.

He approached the large dog kennel he had her locked in and ran his taloned fingers over the tight mesh covering the bars. She'd learned quickly that was to keep her in, no matter how small the animal she shifted in to. Mouse, finch, she'd tried everything she could think of.

Now, she was the last one left to suffer his torment. The other women who'd been taken with her had disappeared one by one, their dead bodies twisted and grotesque, half morphed into beasts.

Pain seeped into every molecule of Rhiannon's body. She shrank back on her hands and knees as far as the cage would allow. It was no use, and she knew it. That he'd let her resurface from the mind-numbing drugs he shot her up with only meant one thing. He was going to beat her until she lost control and shifted again. So far, she'd moved completely from one form to another without the distorted partial shifts the other girls had gone through. She prayed she could be fast this time, too. The disgusting half human, half animal was what he wanted, what he waited for, what he killed for. She had no idea why or what he did with the mutilated corpses, but she knew he'd keep her alive until she gave him what he wanted.

And there was no way in hell she'd willingly give this asshole what he wanted. As long as she lived, there was hope of escape.

She didn't know how long she'd been here—only that she was always cold and naked, and the drugs made her waver in and out of consciousness. Her muscles shook with tension as she watched his every move.

The silver light that signaled shifting haloed his hands until the talons disappeared. Then he flipped open the lock on the cage and her stomach revolted. She swallowed hard and braced herself for the lightning-fast grab he made for her neck. The mesh pressed into her legs and buttocks, but there was no getting away.

His grip closed around her throat, choking off her air. Panic ripped through her and the heated rush of change exploded in her veins. Silver glowed around her and power that was so foreign to her made her body tremble. No matter how hard she fought, he'd win, but it didn't stop her. She shook her head, jerking back. It didn't break his hold on her neck.

An explosion rocked the side of the old building, and the man whipped his head to the side to try to see what had caused it.

Rhiannon didn't hesitate. Willing herself to shift into something *big*, she launched herself forward. In the blink of an eye, her body was gone and her mind controlled the limbs of a tiger. She screamed, making the tiger roar. Slashing at him with fangs and claws, she felt the heat of his blood cover her paws and face.

Then it was over, and he was as dead as the girls he'd killed, and Rhiannon was surrounded by men and women in black. The guns in their hands pointed at her, and a few beastly predators prowled just beyond them, which sent warnings straight to her brain.

She tried to speak, but only a low roar rumbled from her. The sound of guns cocking made her blood chill and she shook her head, tried to plead for help. In an instantaneous flash of silver, she was on her knees in human form, her body healed from her kidnapper's abuse as it always was after she shifted. "Please don't kill me."

"Weapons down." A cool female voice sounded from behind those who'd trained their guns on her. The woman glided up, planted her foot on the kidnapper's chest, pointed her pistol at his head, and fired two quick shots.

Rhiannon shoved to her feet and scrambled back until she was sitting on the cage she'd been in. Her voice sounded stunned and reedy to her own ears. "He was already dead."

"Just making sure." The other woman gave a tight smile, flicking her short blond locks away from her face.

"Kira likes to be sure about everything." Turning to see the man who'd spoken, Rhiannon saw another figure dressed in black fatigues, boots, and bulletproof jacket. As he drew closer, she saw that he was tall and broad, with dark hair and pale amber eyes that swept over her in a quick inspection. The intense soldier disappeared as he offered her a wide, friendly grin. "Hi, there. I'm Max."

The woman—Kira—rolled her eyes. "Was anyone talking to you?"

"No." He turned the smile on her, and his expression heated to something both flirtatious and wicked.

She rolled her eyes again, faced Rhiannon, and holstered her weapon. "You're Rhiannon Reid?"

"Yes." Rhiannon blinked and pulled her long hair forward to cover her nudity, crossing her arms over her breasts. She wasn't shy, but a lot of people with guns milling around could make a girl feel more vulnerable than normal. "How did you know my name?"

"That's my job." The blond nodded and moved to extend her hand, but paused when she took in Rhiannon's folded arms. "I'm Kira Seaton."

Rhiannon hugged herself tighter and some kind of *knowing* filtered into her consciousness. "You're Between."

The other woman dipped her chin in another quick nod. "Yes, and so are you."

Rhiannon shook her head. There had to be a way to undo the damage her kidnapper had done. She didn't know much about the Between except what she'd seen on the news, but someone had to know how to fix her. "What are you?"

"I'm one of the King's Guard. His personal security staff." Kira's pale brows drew together for a moment. "Or maybe you meant what kind of Between? I'm an arctic fox."

Confusion filtered through Rhiannon. Kira could only shift into a fox? She didn't get to pick? That didn't make sense. Then again, as exhausted as she was, she doubted her ability to make sense of anything.

Kira tilted her head, but when Rhiannon said nothing more, she just gave that small smile again. Spinning toward the people that still ringed them, she issued quiet orders. "Let's get this place cleared out, and take care of Arkon's body. I want to be out of here within the hour."

"Yes, ma'am," they chorused and faded away to do as they were bid. Two hefted the kidnapper's body to carry it away.

She looked back at Rhiannon, her voice kinder than it had been so far. "I know this may be difficult, but I'd like you to tell me what happened here, Ms. Reid. Anything you can remember."

So she did. In fits and starts, she told Kira and Max how and when she'd been taken, what had happened to the other women, how she'd managed to avoid the same fate. Everything she could think of. She didn't tell them of the way a lead weight settled in her belly when she thought of the women who'd followed her into the wilderness, or the looks on their faces when they'd cried, when they'd died. No one needed to know that but her. Max and Kira stayed quiet through it all, only asking the occasional question, but Rhiannon got the impression that they didn't miss so much as a single inflection she put on a word. Not even her kidnapper had examined her that intensely. She rubbed her hands up and down her biceps. "That's all I know. I don't know what he did with their bodies."

"He took them back to the city and left them there to be found." Kira pivoted to walk away. "I'm going to check on everyone and get you something to wear. Thank you, Ms. Reid."

Max leaned against a nearby wall and folded his arms. "How are you holding up?"

"Okay, I guess." Rhiannon jerked her chin in the direction they'd taken her tormentor's carcass. "Did Kira say his name was Arkon? I asked, but he'd never tell me. Just that he was the man who was going to kill me."

A low growl unlike anything a human could produce rumbled from his throat. "His name was Raymond Arkon."

"Thank you." She swallowed and let out a shaky breath, still unable to believe she was safe. "Since you're being so informative, can you tell me what the hell this is?" She brushed at a mark on her arm, but it didn't rub off, didn't even smear. It hadn't the entire time she'd been here. It looked like shiny silver body paint had been applied to her upper arm in a ragged spiral. She flexed her bicep and the silver glowed around the edges as though lit from underneath.

"It's the mark of a Between." Max pushed up the bottom edge of his shirt and body armor to reveal a similar silver spiral on the muscled planes of his lower abdomen. "If you're born Between, you come out of the womb with one. If you're changed, it's where you were marked."

She shook her head. "Not all Between have fangs to mark someone, right? Like birds?"

"You don't need fangs to break the skin with your teeth." He flashed his straight white teeth in a smile. "And it's really the magic in our souls entering the humans' that matters. You can't be turned unless we *push* the magic into your body. The point we push the magic in is where the mark is. Biting isn't necessary to mark someone, and most Between don't do it that way anymore. That's old-school claiming."

"Barbaric, you mean." She sniffed, hugging herself again to ward off the ugly memories of Arkon's fangs sinking into her flesh. She just wanted to get away from here, undo what Arkon had done, and get back to her old life, her old self. Or as much of her old life as was left, considering four of the women who'd come to her gym every day for years had been slaughtered before her eyes. The lead ball in her belly expanded and her heart twisted.

"Call it what you want." Max tugged his shirt back into place. "This isn't *our* way, just the way of a twisted fuck who happened to be Between."

"Whatever." She wasn't interested in the ways of the Between. She looked away from him and caught Kira's eye as she came back.

"Put this on." She handed Rhiannon a long leather duster. It was obviously a man's—it wrapped all the way around her like a black leather robe that trailed across the floor when she stood.

Her legs wavered underneath her when she took the first few steps she'd had upright in a long time. She felt no pain, the shifting had taken care of that, but reacquainting herself with the movement took a few moments. Anger pumped through her and she clenched her jaw. She couldn't even walk naturally anymore. Arkon had stripped even that from her. Hell, he'd literally ripped away her humanity and left her a stranger uncomfortable in her own skin. And she was the lucky one. Frustrated tears welled in her eyes, but she blinked them back. They wouldn't help her get through this. She just...had to find someone who could make her better again. A doctor, a really powerful Between. Someone.

*Please, God, let there be a way to make her better again.*

Max straightened from the wall. "Kira, take her back to the helo, would you? The king will want to see her. I'll wrap things up here."

"Follow me." Kira took the order without question, without protest, which seemed out of character, but Rhiannon hastened after her, more than ready to get out of this hellhole.

The huge black helicopter dominated the clearing outside the building. Kira held Rhiannon's arm, guiding her out into the sunlight. She took her first breath of sweet, clean air—of freedom—and smiled hugely. The motion felt stiff, but it didn't matter. She was free.

"You can sit in here while we finish up." The fox-shifter easily boosted her into the back of the helicopter even though Rhiannon outstripped her both in height and weight.

She slid into a corner and rested her head against the window. "Thanks. I'll be fine by myself. Go do your thing."

Kira nodded and retreated, leaving Rhiannon to stare at the building that had been her prison. It looked...like a cabin in the woods. Nothing sinister or menacing about it. Something loosened inside her chest, snapping the fear and rage that had owned her for so long. The cabin blurred before her eyes as sudden tears welled and fell. Closing her eyes, her head dropped back against the seat as she cried. Exhaustion crashed around her like a great wave, and she let it claim her.

Her lashes fluttered a few minutes later when the helicopter began to rumble, and she watched the cabin grow smaller and smaller as they lifted off. When it disappeared behind the trees, she shut her eyes and let sleep claim her again. She had no clue how long she was out, but some internal instinct said it had been several hours.

Sitting up groggily, she shoved her hair out of her face as they circled an island in the middle of the ocean. "Where are we?"

"San Amaro Island." Max sat in the seat across from her, and though he didn't shout to be heard over the loud *thwap* of the helicopter blades, she could still hear him clearly. "Home."

Home of the Between king, the lion-shifter Elan Delacourt. Her stomach flipped at the thought. For most people, the Between were a mysterious race that had only made themselves known to the human world ten years ago. They were powerful and scary. From what she'd seen, people tended to want that power themselves or they wanted to destroy it. Rhiannon just wanted to go back to knowing next to nothing about them or how their magic worked. Her mind scrambled for what she'd heard on the news about this place. The large island was one of the nine Channel Islands off the coast of Southern California. It had been annexed as its own sovereign nation when the Between came out.

From this height, she could see the island was rocky, with snaking canyons and rolling mountains. Houses dotted the sides of the sloping canyon walls. She shoved down the realization that she could see far more detail than she should be able to. They came over a final rise and a small valley opened below them.

The palace was massive. The gleaming white building looked like a cross between a European castle with turrets and spires, and a Spanish-style mission with thick stucco walls and red tile roof. It was as beautiful as it was intimidating. She doubted the effect was accidental.

Lush green lawns surrounded the palace. Palm trees were scattered across the grounds and lined the gravel driveway that lead down to a marina and docked boats of every imaginable shape and size. It was nothing like Portland—a world away from her real life. The life she desperately wanted to get back to.

She clenched her jaw and straightened her shoulders, determined to face whatever came next with the same boldness she'd always been known for. A Between had done this to her, and the Between king was going to have to fix it. Now.

"Out of the fire…and into the lion's den."

# CHAPTER TWO

Elan watched the woman walk across the lawn between his younger brother and Kira. So, that was the one who'd survived Raymond Arkon. She wasn't what he'd expected. Max caught her arm when she stumbled on the gravel path. She looked far too soft to have lived through what she had and come out victorious. All the information she had given to his Guards had already been transferred to him, and it would seem implausible, if his people hadn't been hunting the man for years. Arkon's pattern had remained the same, though he'd moved around the country—kidnap women and take them deep into the wilderness, turn them into Between illegally, murder them, and dump their mutilated, half-changed bodies where humans were most likely to find them.

Arkon had had to be stopped, and quietly, or all the peace Elan had fought and sacrificed for would have evaporated like mist on summer day. It was a bit anticlimactic that when his Guards finally tracked down the rogue shifter, they'd found someone else had done their dirty work for them. Elan had taken no joy in giving the order to have one of his own killed, but he would take whatever precautions were necessary to protect his people. As their king, he owed them that kind of vigilance and ruthlessness. He owed his father that after he'd taken the man's throne. There was no making up for what he'd done, but he had a lifetime of servitude ahead of him as penance.

Clenching his jaw, he shoved his hands into his pockets and ignored the bite of guilt. He sighed, closed his eyes, and turned away from the window to await the three in his private study. He'd decided to forego intimidating Rhiannon with his formal office and bustling royal staff—Arkon had already put her through enough.

So much damage caused by one man. Arkon's actions could thoroughly fuck the Between people. Changing innocent humans against their will broke every single treaty Elan had ever negotiated. If anyone found out about this—if they couldn't cover it up fast enough—all of his kind would pay. The shockwaves of a lone man's insanity could bring them all down.

He couldn't allow that to happen. Even if the Between wanted to have one country for themselves as a safe haven, they couldn't. The U.S. had given the Between San Amaro Island as their sovereign territory, but it simply wasn't big enough for all of them. They *needed* their treaties to hold.

An unamused smile crossed Elan's face. Kind of them to "give" the Between the island considering the Delacourt family had *owned* San Amaro outright for several generations, but the royal title was not guaranteed to stay with any one family for long. In the end, it didn't really matter, since the alternative was having everything stripped away while they carted him and all his kind away to shifter reservations or internment camps. Humans outnumbered Betweens, so they could easily force such a move. However, Elan recognized a certain psychological advantage he had in that, even though humans knew logically that they could overwhelm Betweens through sheer numbers, they still feared the power and magic they didn't possess themselves. He exercised that advantage ruthlessly when he dealt with human politicians the world over.

The standard compromise he negotiated was that every Between must be licensed and registered, both as a human and as the animal they shifted in to. He'd also signed nonaggression treaties with many nations across the globe, and his ambassadors were constantly whittling away at the rest in order to help the Between there. It wasn't an ideal situation, but it was better than being rounded up, having all worldly goods taken away, and being corralled like mindless beasts. This way, they at least kept most of their freedom.

Still, he understood the razor's edge his people danced on to keep those freedoms.

A knock sounded on his study door, and he jolted out of his reverie. Right, the Reid woman. His newest citizen. "Come in."

The door swung open, and the first sound he heard was her laughter. Her green eyes twinkled with warm flecks of gold as she glanced at his brother. When she faced him, she drew the long coat she was wearing tighter around her, and her smile faded as though it had never been. Her eyes hardened to emerald, and she offered him a silent nod.

This didn't bode well.

Kira and Max filed in with Rhiannon and flanked the door like the well-trained soldiers they were. He noted both their gazes swept the room in an automatic security check. He smothered a grin. It was interesting to see his normally smart-assed, carefree younger brother work. He'd left the Marines and taken control of the King's Guard when Elan became ruler, insisting that no one would do as thorough a job of overseeing his protection. Kira had joined him with a similar story, abandoning her position with the Los Angeles Police Department. It warmed him to know that his friends had such faith in him, in his rule. He'd never let them down. Not like his father had let them all down when he'd forced the Between out in the open.

Rhiannon moved to plant herself directly in front of Elan, lifted her eyebrows, and gave him a very leisurely once over. A grin made dimples form in her cheeks. "So you're the lion king. You're not exactly what I expected."

"And you're my new subject. You're also not what I expected." He didn't elaborate on that statement because he was too busy biting back a curse. His body reacted to her blatant perusal, his cock hardening in an insistent reminder that it had been far too long since he'd taken time away from his duties to take a lover.

He looked back at her with similar thoroughness. She was lovely, not *beautiful*, but…lovely. Her chin jutted a bit. "I am *not* your subject."

He arched his eyebrow at that blatant foolishness, but continued his inspection of her. Her dark red hair rippled down to the middle of her back, not curly and not straight, but a rich texture somewhere in between. Her eyes were an intense mixture of green and gold, the color seeming to change with her moods. She wasn't tall, but she wasn't petite. A description of her was difficult to pin down, and he had a sinking suspicion that the rest of her would be equally difficult to control. The stubborn set of her jaw and the way she folded her arms over her breasts told him she wasn't going to give over easily.

His blood heated with the challenge, which was the reaction of a man, not a king, and he tried to rein himself in. A man panting after her was the last thing this woman needed. "Legally, all Between are my subjects, but you'll keep your American citizenship as well."

"I want to *not* be a Between anymore." She gestured down at herself. "I didn't choose this, and I don't want it. You're the king, you have to know how to undo this."

He shook his head, staring at her as disbelief trickled through him. Was it possible that anyone was so ignorant of how becoming a Between worked? He bit back a pained groan. "There's no *undoing* anything. Once the magic is in your blood, you can't get it out."

He could almost see the gears spinning in her mind, trying to find a way around what he was saying. "What about a total transfusion—get the Between blood *out* and put all new blood *in?*"

"Uh...no, sorry." He folded his arms to ward off a twist of remorse at the desperation on her face. He spoke as gently as possible. "If you've shifted, and obviously you have, then it's not just in your blood. It's everywhere. It's embedded in every fiber of your being now."

She mirrored his stance and folded her arms, but offered him a glare. "No."

"I'm sorry. There's nothing I can do for you." His lifted his palms in placation. Her position was not an enviable one, but the sooner she accepted it, the better.

But the woman wasn't about to be placated. An angry flush rose to her cheeks. "This is bullshit. I grew up in a suburb. I teach yoga and Pilates at the health club I own in Portland, Oregon. I'm not some kind of *magical creature*."

"You are now."

"No, I am *not*."

He watched the rage tighten her face, her fingers fisting at her sides. Then shock flashed over her expression and her body dissolved in a quick sputter of silver light, leaving a hissing orange tabby cat at his feet. Her back arched, her claws dug into the folds of the coat she was standing on, and she snarled before silver light whipped into a slim tornado that reformed in to Rhiannon's lush body. Her very nude body. She wasn't the least bit shy, planting her fists on her hips and glaring at him. "What are you looking at? Turn around."

He clenched his teeth to keep from chuckling as he spun on his heel, but he was fairly certain she could tell he was laughing from the way his shoulders shook.

When her coat stopped rustling, he decided it was safe to face her again. Her eyes sparked with heated gold. "When the media get ahold of this story—"

Ice froze in his veins at those words, all humor in the situation evaporating. No. A thousand times, no. Such a story would be his people's undoing. He could see every political victory he'd built up the last ten years collapse like a house of cards. "This will never make the news. No one will ever know."

"Are you kidding me?" Her mouth dropped open for a moment. "*I know.* If there are crazed Between out there torturing humans, then people deserve to know about it so they can protect themselves."

"And start mass anti-Between hysteria because of one bad man?" His voice dropped to a low, dangerous hiss.

She snorted at him. "Easy for you to say when that *one bad man* never came within a hundred miles of you or any other *guy*. Instead, he preyed on defenseless *women*. And that's totally okay with you?"

"No, it's not." His words came out stiffer and more defensively than he would have liked, but her words stung. More self-reproach to add to the ever-present burden that weighed on his shoulders. How much more could he take before he broke under the strain? "I sent people to take care of him, but you'd handled that for us."

"You're welcome, O Great and Mighty Majesty." She bowed in a mocking show of subservience. The movement made her coat gape at the top, giving him an amazing view of her cleavage. He dragged his gaze away from her creamy flesh and forced himself to pay attention to what she was saying. "But what about the next guy? And the one after him? They all just get to get away with murder—*literally*—because you say so? No way in hell. If you're not going to tell people, then I will when I get back."

"You won't be leaving San Amaro for a few weeks, at least, Pollyanna." If then. She could never be allowed to tell the media about what had befallen her. It wasn't that guilt didn't crawl through his belly at the thought of what happened to her and the other women, but Arkon had been taken care of, the threat to humans had passed. The threat to Between from this woman was very much alive and real. It would have been much more convenient if she had died with the others, and though he hated himself for thinking it, it didn't make it untrue.

"Oh, awesome," Rhiannon snarled. "Another fuckwad Between who wants to hold me hostage, but I'm sure you're all really good people who shouldn't have any kind of anti-Between hysteria going against you."

His nostrils flared in annoyance and his teeth ground together. He'd never met a single soul who made him want to strangle them so quickly. Her comment about holding her hostage made bitterness flood his tongue, but it couldn't keep the irritation at bay. He spoke slowly and carefully, enunciating the way one would to a small, stupid child. "I'd like you to remain here so that medical professionals who specialize in working with Betweens can keep an eye on you until you settle on a single animal form. From all reports, you haven't done so yet."

"I don't want to settle on an animal form." She poked a finger toward his chest. "I want this to go away. I want my life back. And you're like, 'oh, it's nothing, just forget about the guy who did this to you and your friends—he's dead, so who cares if there was a rabid Between out there changing and killing people?'"

Wondering where the cold regal demeanor he was renowned for had gone, he shoved a hand through his hair. "I care about my people."

"But not the humans your people maim and murder? Nice."

"You have no idea—"

"You care about your people, and I care about mine. Consider the gym I own as my little corner of the world, my fiefdom. I've known most of those women for years. Some of them were my very first club members after I was old enough to take over the place. Those women came camping with me because they knew me and they trusted me. I couldn't protect them, and I get to live with that, but I can make sure no one else has to go through something like this ever again. So, yeah, I think I do have an idea of *exactly* how little you give a shit about humans like them, you sanctimonious asshat."

*That* made him angry, something no one had managed in the ten years he'd been king. The heat of it ripped through him and if he'd been in lion form, his mane would have stood on end. He didn't like the intensity of his reaction, but that didn't keep him from closing the distance between them in two swift strides and looming over her, his nose less than an inch from hers, their gazes locked. He heard her breath catch, saw her pupils dilate as she searched his face. The bitter words died on his tongue. Passion whipped between them so fast, it caught him off guard. Mild physical attraction was one thing, but this was something else. His cock throbbed painfully, so rigid it chafed against the fly of his slacks, and he could smell the wet heat of her desire.

She stepped even closer, deep into his personal space, and squinted up at him. "Are those contacts?"

He blinked down at her, startled. His mouth opened and then snapped shut. His gaze shot to Kira. "I thought you said on the phone that she was stable."

"I am stable." Rhiannon shoved her hands into the pockets of her coat and rocked back on her heels. "Your eyes are a very odd amber color, and I asked if they were, in fact, contact lenses. How is that not a perfectly rational question?"

He shook his head, clearing the fog of lust. "Is that truly the only thing you can think to ask right now?"

"No, but my other questions aren't as nice as that one, so I thought I'd start with a slow pitch, Simba."

Kira and Max choked on horrified laughs, and Rhiannon turned to give them an evil grin.

"I really, really hate that movie." Elan sighed, easing away from her.

She smirked. "I bet."

He lifted an eyebrow. "Though no one's ever mentioned it to me before."

"Maybe not to your face." She flashed a teasing smile, deep dimples popping into her cheeks, and he could only blink stupidly at her again.

Nothing indicated that the woman was insane. It was often a smell, an acrid stench, a rising of hackles, that warned an animal had gone rabid. Rhiannon set off none of those reactions in him even though she'd gone from flirtatious to enraged to teasing in the space of a few minutes.

No, the only reaction she set off in him had little to do with his mind and instincts sending a warning, and everything to do with a fire burning in his belly. His cock had hardened the moment he caught her sweet scent, and seeing her naked had only made him ache with want. Neither her anger nor his had made his erection subside.

This was going to be damned inconvenient.

The woman was a catastrophe on multiple levels, and the fact that she'd been turned weeks ago, had been able to fully shift on her first try, and hadn't settled on a single animal form was worrisome. Then again, her personality seemed so mercurial, he wasn't all that surprised she hadn't settled on one animal yet.

He sighed, scrubbing a hand over his hair.

Yes, she was trouble. For him. For his people.

And yet he couldn't be upset that she had survived. She had courage and determination. Those were traits he liked to see in his people. Those were traits that he admired in anyone, especially a woman who'd been through what she had.

Now he just had to figure out what to do with her.

# Chapter Three

Hours later, Rhiannon stripped and eased into the steamy, wet embrace of a Jacuzzi in the palace's private fitness area. A large room with gym equipment was separated from two smaller rooms with a sauna and a hot tub. It had been so good to be back in the familiarity of a gym, to push her body until it ached from a nice, hard workout. And the Jacuzzi was so divine, she groaned softly.

Max—who was apparently the king's younger brother—had led her past the gym on the way to the room Rhiannon was staying in tonight. A few changes of clothes had been there, including workout clothing. She hadn't been able to resist. Even though the halls in the palace twisted and switched back a million times, she hadn't gotten lost, which was odd because her sense of direction had never been great. But she had just *known* how to get where she wanted to go.

She shook her head, refusing to consider why that might be, and just enjoyed the tension easing out of her muscles. If she was stuck here for a few weeks until the shifter doctors gave her a clean bill of health, at least there were some perks. This place was a lot better than the last one she'd been trapped in, so she might as well make the best of it. She heard someone enter the room next to her—the one for the sauna—and reminded herself to leave the hot tub before they got out because she didn't have a bathing suit and had left her sweats and sports bra in a heap on the tile floor.

A sigh escaped her and she let her mind drift. Her thoughts honed in on Arkon and what he'd done to them, the memories replaying on a horrifying loop. She had to get back to Portland, had to talk to those women's families and apologize for talking them in to coming with her. Had to apologize for being the one to survive. She swallowed and squeezed her eyes shut tighter, desperately struggling to maintain some equilibrium. Just escaping wasn't enough to make it all okay. People had died, right before her eyes, and she was left wondering why. All she could do was try to hold on to the Rhiannon she'd always been and pray that somehow, someway, it *would* get better. Forcing her thoughts to stop racing and her body to relax, she sighed again and dipped deeper into the hot tub.

She wasn't certain if she'd fallen asleep, but she slowly became aware of someone standing beside the Jacuzzi. She didn't have to open her eyes to be certain it was Elan. Another thing she just *knew*.

"You're in my hot tub." His voice was like sandpaper and silk sliding lightly over her skin and her nipples tightened in that unnerving way they had when she'd been in his study earlier.

At least it was a distraction from her ugly memories, and she clung to it like the lifeline it was. The old Rhiannon would've flirted with a man this sexy, so she let a small smile curve her lips and rolled her head against the side of the tub to look up at him. "Possession is nine-tenths of the law."

His brows lifted and he sipped pale amber liquid from a tumbler. "Not on Between land."

"Thanks for sharing?" She gave him an easy grin, letting her gaze slide down his muscled body. He wore only a towel, the white terry cloth a sharp contrast to his darker skin.

He turned to close the door to the room behind him and she got a good look at his well-defined back and legs. She ran her gaze over the silver spiral that marked the side of one calf. "So that's where your Between mark is."

"Yeah." He grunted, twisting his leg to glance at it before he faced her again. He *looked* like a lion, even in human form. Tall and broad and golden. His hair was dark at the roots, but the strands turned tawny at the tips. She had a feeling if he grew it long, it would look like a true lion's mane. But his eyes were what truly mesmerized her. They were such an intense amber, they seemed unreal, which was why she'd asked him if they were contacts.

Her gaze slipped lower, taking in the hard planes of his pecs and the ridges of his abs.

She wondered what it was like to touch him, if his skin would be soft or slightly rough under her fingertips. Her leisurely perusal dropped to the edge of his towel. One of his hands clenched on the knot holding the cloth together, and she could see the outline of his rigid erection underneath. She wanted to see all of him.

"Are you naked?" His gaze sharpened as he peered beneath the shadowed surface of the water. He set his glass on a wooden bench that lined the wall.

"Mr. Arkon didn't let me bring my bikini." She gave a little shrug and knew her grin had turned wicked. She ran a fingertip along her collarbone. "I hope that doesn't bother you, Your Majesty."

Challenge flashed in his gaze and his long fingers worked at the knot in his towel. "Since this is my private gym, I didn't bother to bring swim trunks. Look away if you're shy."

She kept her gaze pinned to him, not wavering for a single moment. There was no way she was going to miss seeing the rest of his body. It had been so long since she'd felt anything but fear and anger and pain, the desire was so sweet it almost ached.

The towel dropped to the tiles, and her gaze traveled up his long legs to his groin. His cock rose in a hard arc to just under his navel, flushed and dripping with beads of pre-cum. Not a hint of embarrassment at his aroused state flashed over his handsome face as he slid into the water across from her.

"Thanks for the show." Her tone was teasing, but she had to squeeze her thighs together to contain the sudden throb of need in her sex.

He chuckled and it made his eyes dance and twinkle. The change was startling. He went from regal and forbidding to gorgeous and approachable in a split second. She liked his laugh. She had a feeling he didn't do it often enough.

It was nice to know after what happened that she could still find a man physically attractive. The thought of touching him didn't horrify her at all. In fact, it sent heat trickling through her, warming her muscles.

But could she go any further than attraction? She wasn't sure. Butterflies took wing in her belly—nerves or anticipation? She clenched her jaw. She would *not* let what Arkon did to her ruin her life. What he'd done was in the past, and she wouldn't give him that kind of power over her future. Starting right now. Determination and anger whipped through her, settling the butterflies.

Not giving herself time to reconsider, she pushed forward until she could set her hand on the edge of the tub next to Elan's shoulder. Her other hand rose so she could let one finger follow the trail of a bead of moisture down his chest. When she met his eyes, they burned with amber fire.

He swallowed, his Adam's apple bobbing, but he didn't look away. "This is…unexpected."

"The last few weeks have been all kinds of unexpected for me." She shrugged. "Sometimes you just have to roll with the punches."

He grunted. "I never do. I like to be in control at all times."

"I kind of guessed that about you, Your Majesty." She grinned, but it faded quickly. She sighed and concentrated on circling his nipple with her finger. It tightened for her instantly. "I want to pretend this whole mess never happened."

She could feel how his heart raced beneath her fingertip, though his tone remained even. "It did happen, and I'm sorry for that."

Unable to deny the truth, she nodded. Now she had to move forward from here. She met Elan's gaze again. "He took something from me. I don't feel right in my own skin anymore. I want that back. I want control of my body back. *I* decide who touches me and when."

"I understand." His eyelids had fallen to half-mast, but she could see the pleasure at her touch in his gaze. It made her feel good, powerful. Exactly how she wanted to feel.

Gathering her courage together, she said the words that would start the healing process for her. "I want you to touch me. Now."

One of his hands lifted from the water, dripping warm liquid over her shoulder and down her arm. She shivered at the sensation, her nipples tightening until they ached. He arched an eyebrow. "Where?"

"Everywhere," she breathed.

His hand moved back to push against the side of the tub, propelling him forward until his lips hovered over hers, a hairsbreadth from making contact. "Should I start here?"

"Elan." Rising up on tiptoes, she pressed her mouth against his and closed her eyes to savor the taste. Brandy and sugar, and something hotly masculine.

His tongue flicked out to run along her bottom lip. She opened for him and he licked his way inside her mouth. She moaned, his unique flavor bursting over her taste buds. His hands brushed down her back, dipping beneath the water to shape her buttocks with his broad palms.

Yes, this was what she wanted, what she needed.

Whimpering low in her throat at the heat that whipped through her, she wrapped her arms around his neck and cupped the back of his head. His hair was even softer than it looked, the texture silky against her damp hands. One of his arms slid around her waist, jerking her tight against the full length of him. They both groaned at the hot contact. Her breasts flattened against the hard wall of his chest, and she could feel the way his heart pounded. Its rapid beat matched her own.

Breaking her lips from his, she sucked a ragged breath into her starved lungs. "God, you feel good."

"Not a god, just a king." He used his grip on her ass to grind his thick erection against the juncture of her thighs. "And you feel pretty fucking amazing, too, but I think we can do better."

Her laughter tangled with the desperate moan of need that ripped from her. She snapped her legs around his waist, beads of steam and sweat rolling down their damp faces while the water sealed their bodies together. His fingers slipped inward to touch her pussy from behind. A shudder coursed through her as he stroked her slick lips. She was so hot, so wet.

When he pushed two fingers into her sex, she clenched tight around him. "Hurry, Elan."

He groaned and began moving those thick digits deep within her, widening her passage. "You're too tight, baby."

"*Please*." She arched into him, rubbing herself against his thick cock. He hissed and jerked his fingers out of her. A heartbeat later, she felt his dick probe for entrance inside her. "Yes. Oh, yes." Then her eyes flared wide when a sudden thought hit her. "Wait, *no*."

"Do you want me to stop?" His voice was a low rumble of pain, but he didn't move as he waited for her answer.

"No, I don't want you to stop. We just need a condom."

His breath escaped in a relief-tinged laugh. "No, we don't. Between can't get sick or carry diseases. And creating a Between is always a conscious choice, whether it's through conception or marking. We have to *choose* to share our magic. A female Between has to want to get pregnant, and a male Between has to want to get her pregnant." The flared crest of his cock began to slip into her throbbing pussy. "We're fine like this."

A quick knock sounded on the door before it opened a sliver. They both froze where they were, his cock still poised to thrust into her sex. Someone cleared their throat and it echoed in the room. "Your Majesty."

Rhiannon pushed back, paddled to the far side of the Jacuzzi, turned to grip the ledge, and shielded her breasts from their intruder.

Her new instincts had already told her it was Kira even before she spoke from the doorway. "Sorry to interrupt, sire."

"Don't worry about it." But Elan's voice was strained and gritty. A breeze fluttered through the room as the door opened all the way. "What do you need?"

She hesitated and Rhiannon felt the other woman's gaze burning into her back. Kira's soft response bounced off the walls, and Rhiannon tried not to flinch. "Dr. Singh has finished the autopsy on Raymond Arkon's body. His report is on your desk, sire. You said you wanted to know immediately."

Rhiannon sucked in a ragged breath at the man's name, clenching her fingers on the edge of the tub. Her life to this point had been pretty normal. She'd never imagined having to make the choice between her life and someone else's, never even pictured what it would be like to have to kill someone in order to survive, but she didn't regret what she'd done.

Maybe that's what surprised her the most. She was angry about what Arkon had put her through, sickened by what he had done to the other women he'd kidnapped, and completely unsympathetic to the fact that he was dead. Her ruthlessness stunned her. She'd never have thought herself capable of it, but she'd never have thought she'd have to live through what she had. Arkon had gotten what he deserved, which was something she'd never have said or thought about anyone before now. She was a people person. She worked with them, she cared about them. But Arkon? She felt nothing but relief that he was dead and couldn't hurt her or anyone else ever again. She just wished there was something she could have done to help the women who hadn't survived.

"I'm sorry you had to hear that." Elan's hands settled over her shoulders gently. The simple touch made her body clamor for what it had been denied. She still wanted him. Badly. "Kira could have spared you and sent me a private mental communication."

"Kira doesn't seem like the type to coddle anyone." She swallowed, working to process the many emotions flickering through her. She had never been one to question why she felt the way she did about anything. Emotions were just a part of living, and she'd always savored every moment of life, no matter how crazy. "That's why she's in charge of your Guard, isn't it?"

"She's the executive officer—second in command. My brother is the commanding officer of my Guard." His fingers drew comforting circles on her skin as he spoke and she could sense his remaining concern through the touch.

"Ah." She flicked a glance over her shoulder at him, releasing her death grip on the tub's ledge. "Don't worry. I'm fine."

It was a half-truth at best, but how she handled everything going on inside her was no one's concern but her own. The most important thing was getting home to the business that had been her parents' dream and then hers, back to the friends and employees who counted on her. She'd been gone too long, and the delay on San Amaro wasn't going to be easy, but she was alive and healthy, and she had to be grateful for that. She'd take this moment with a sexy man, enjoy it, and reclaim some vital parts of herself in the process. The hollow ache within her wasn't going to subside in one night. So, she was as fine as she could be, considering.

He frowned down at her. "It's all right if you—"

"What happened was bad, but I want to put it behind me." She gave him a wry smile. "I'm not going to cower in the corner just because you think that's how I should be dealing with this."

Shaking his head, he ran his fingertips down her biceps. "I don't want you to be afraid."

"I'm not. Let me prove it to you." She pressed herself back into his arms, dismissing Arkon from her thoughts. He had no place here—only Elan and she did. Letting her hands slide through the water, she gripped the sides of his heavy thighs. Heat wound through her body, making her heart race and her breathing speed up. Her sex throbbed, and she felt herself begin to grow slick again just having his muscled length against her. She squirmed until his cock settled into the cleft of her buttocks. Almost where she wanted him, but not quite.

He groaned. "Rhiannon, I don't think—"

"Good. Don't think. Let's try *feeling*." If he didn't give her some relief, she was going to go for regicide. It would be completely justifiable at this point. She grabbed his hand, slid it down the curves of her belly and between her thighs.

His breath stopped, and every muscle in his big body tensed. She pushed his fingers deeper inside her, guiding him to stroke over her hardened clit. He took over the movements, sliding into her wet channel. She moaned, letting her head fall back on his broad shoulder. "Can we get back to where we were about five minutes ago? *Now?*"

He urged her forward until she was leaning against the side of the Jacuzzi, slipping his knee between hers to open her. She widened her stance eagerly, the water caressing her limbs as she moved. It made the experience even more erotic, the way the heated liquid embraced them and swirled around them. His fingers pressed against her walls to stretch her and she wriggled impatiently.

"*That* was not where we were five minutes ago." She pushed her hips back until his cock slipped between her legs. "*That* is where we were."

"Are you always this demanding?" But he obligingly moved forward until his cock replaced his fingers. He rubbed his thumb over her clit and she shoved her hips back to take him deep in one hard plunge.

"Jesus. Christ. You're big." The fit was painful, and she had to clench her teeth to keep from crying out. She had been damp, but not damp enough to take him easily. It felt like a thick, hot pipe had been pushed inside her.

"I said you were too tight." He rolled his thumb over her clit, distracting her from the burn of her overstretched flesh. His breath brushed against the back of her neck. "Why didn't you let me wait?"

"I couldn't." She'd wanted to be filled, to know she could do this before her courage deserted her. Swallowing, she closed her eyes and tried to relax her muscles. Even through the pain, the sweetness of her skin gliding against his made her pant. "Don't stop."

His mouth opened over her shoulder, sucking lightly on her skin. A hum slid out of her, and she jolted a little when his fangs scraped her flesh. The pleasure caught her by surprise and her sex clenched. He groaned, but still didn't move from where he was embedded inside her. His fingers played with her clit, slipping down to stroke the lips of her pussy around his cock. A shiver rippled over her and wetness flooded her sex.

"That's perfect, sweetheart." His tongue slid up the side of her neck, leaving goose bumps in its wake. When he sucked her earlobe into his mouth, she moaned.

She writhed against him, arching her back. The pain had been lost in the tidal wave of other sensations sweeping through her body. "Move."

"No." Those maddening fingers continued to tease her while his other hand dragged curved claws up her torso until he cupped her breast in his palm. "Give me more."

He pinched her nipple, twisting it between his clawed fingertips. The dual feeling made moisture gush between her thighs. "*Please.*"

"Not quite yet." He purred, the sound supremely masculine and supremely feline. The lion had her right where he wanted her and they both knew that there was little she could do about it. That didn't mean she had to like it.

She cast an annoyed glance over her shoulder. "Okay, Simba, move your ass."

He arched into her in retribution, lodging himself even deeper inside her. "My name is *Elan.*"

Grinning, she moved her hips with his, satisfied now that she'd gotten exactly what *she* wanted. He filled her so well, and at this point, she was so wet that the slide of his flesh inside of hers made her sigh. "My mistake. Elan. I'm glad we got that straightened out."

"You are a pain in the ass." But he chuckled, scraped his fangs over her shoulder, and pinched her nipples.

A gasp escaped her and her pussy clenched around his cock. "Takes one to know one."

But any further response melted away to nothingness as his thrusts picked up speed and force. She just *felt*. Her body flamed with need, moving with his in a race to ecstasy. He rubbed her clit harder and faster, pressing her closer to him. The water swirled around them, the steam and sweat making moisture trickle down their overheating flesh. She squeezed her inner muscles tight around his cock, making them both groan. Tingles exploded down her skin and she shook with the force of the feelings thrumming through her body. His cock stretched her, teased her, maddened her as he plunged into her over and over again.

She could feel orgasm rushing to claim her, and a silver glow haloed her limbs. "*Nooo.*"

God, no. This couldn't be happening. She couldn't shift while he was...while she was...but she couldn't think, sensations rocketed through her.

"Shh," Elan murmured against her skin. "Close your eyes and concentrate for just a moment. You can hold on to control of the instinct to shift while letting go of control of everything else."

She frantically reached for the shift, that glowing magic deep inside her, and clutched it tight. She needed to come so badly, she couldn't shift *now*.

He rolled his hips and she felt her control slip a bit. She tensed and felt her orgasm fading. Frustration ripped through her, which only made the situation worse. A sob caught in the back of her throat. It took every ounce of discipline she had to utter the next words, "Maybe we should stop."

He froze behind her, his cock buried deep and throbbing inside her. "Are you sure?"

Damn, he was so big. The fit was amazing. Her sex flexed around him, and she shuddered. "I don't want to stop" —she choked when he immediately surged into her, deeper than he'd gone before— "but I don't think I can keep from shifting." A tear slid down her cheek. Something else that was being taken away from her because of Arkon.

"It becomes automatic eventually. You won't even have to think about it. We can practice while you're here." He chuckled and the sound rumbled against her back.

Her heart leapt at the idea of touching him again. And again. Getting her fill of the big lion. If she could control her shifting and not end up a little tabby cat or a bird or a bear or a—

He moved within her again, slowly, shutting down her train of thought. She shuddered, her body held on the screaming edge of unrequited need and satiated fulfillment. It was there, shimmering just beyond her reach.

"Do you have control?" Elan kissed his way up her shoulder until he could suckle her throat.

A moan slid from her. "It's hard to concentrate when you're doing that."

She felt him smile against her neck. "I like that, but we'll be here all night if you can't keep a grip on the magic inside you."

"All...all night?" Her voice was a breathless rush of sound, tripping up the playful tone she wanted. "There's no way you can stay hard that long."

"Do you want to bet?" He surged into her, slowly...so slowly. It wasn't enough, but it still felt too good. Made her whimper with the craving she couldn't stop.

"No, I want to come." Closing her eyes tight, she focused on the unfamiliar magic within her. So foreign, and yet already such an integral part of her being. She forced herself to breathe deeply, drawing in the hot scent of Elan, of steam, of sex and sweat. But she pushed down the magic that rose with her excitement. She controlled it—she wouldn't let it control her. Caging it like the beast it wanted to make her, she locked it within her.

For now.

Rocking her hips back into his, she let him know she was ready to pick up the pace. He purred his approval and sank his cock deep with each pounding thrust. Her excitement boiled over in moments, her over-stimulated senses screaming. Her blood sizzled in her veins and she gasped for air. Her pussy clenched every time he entered her and she knew she would topple over into orgasm with the next few thrusts. The magic threatened to explode out, but she held it at bay as the tension finally snapped and she cried out in release. The walls of her pussy milked his length in rhythmic waves, ecstasy ricocheting through her with every contraction. A lion's roar echoed off the tiles as Elan slammed deep one last time and pumped his come into her. Her body convulsed around his cock, white-hot pleasure obliterating everything around her. She slumped in his arms, completely spent.

A triumphant smile curled her lips. She'd done it. Pushed away the ugliness of Arkon's memory, and controlled the magic inside her.

In the end, she'd won.

# CHAPTER FOUR

The next morning, Elan stood in front of the huge Baroque mirror in his bathroom and straightened his tie. He should be going over his itinerary for the day, but his mind strayed back to Rhiannon. She'd left for her appointment with the Between royal physician an hour before, and it had taken all his willpower not to haul her luscious form back into bed with him. It was unnerving the way his body reacted to her. Perhaps it was because he'd been between lovers for quite some time. And Rhiannon was definitely not the kind of woman he usually chose. He hadn't been with someone who was so *opposite* of him in a very long time. Ever, if he was completely honest with himself. His lovers were usually carefully selected Between women who understood that his royal duties would often inconvenience and interrupt their plans.

It was the nature of the beast, and he needed a woman who wouldn't be put out by it.

But Rhiannon was something he hadn't planned, on every possible level. He hadn't expected anyone to survive Arkon. He hadn't expected her to be so attractive. He hadn't expected her defiance or to be so intrigued by it. He hadn't expected the untamable passion that had exploded between them. The feeling was too good to ignore, and while she was here, he intended to take advantage of it. If she was willing, so was he.

Waking with her in his bed, in his arms, had felt...amazing. A satiated grin curled his lips. He couldn't wait for her next "lesson" in not shifting when excited. Shrugging into his suit jacket, he turned for the door to his suite, ready to work for the day. The only way he was going to get to that lesson before midnight was if he kept his mind on business. No allowing himself to become distracted by erotic memories of scent and taste and silky curls and soft, soft skin. He cursed under his breath as his cock began to rise.

His brother's scent caught his wandering attention and he whirled with an annoyed snarl. Too bad it was himself, his own wayward body and mind, that he was annoyed with. Striding across the room, he wrenched open one of the glass doors to his private patio, and a red wolf slipped through.

*» Touchy this morning, aren't we, brother?«*

Elan rolled his shoulders as Max's thought pushed into his mind. Folding his arms, he watched his brother come in out of the light spring rain. It would be back up in the nineties tomorrow, but today the sky was gray and dismal. Max shook his lupine body, the rusty underlayer of the wolf's coat showing through as water flew in every direction.

Elan hissed and stepped back. "Really, Max. It's bad enough you're getting the floor wet, but I'm a cat. We don't like water."

*» Sorry, Majesty. «* Max's laughter floated through Elan's mind as his tongue lolled out of his mouth. The wolf almost looked like he was smiling.

Elan rolled his eyes and snorted, rubbing an affectionate hand over his brother's head. Stepping back into the bathroom, he pulled a towel off a hook and lobbed it at the wolf. It smacked him across the snout.

Shifting into human form, Max grabbed the towel and wrapped it around his waist. "Oh, that's nice. I give you loyalty and obedience, and what do I get?"

"To be spoiled rotten?" Elan arched an eyebrow and smirked, moving to prop his shoulder against the carved wood of his bedpost.

His brother growled and forked his fingers through his hair. "Shut up."

"Is that any way to speak to your king?" There was a point to this meeting, Elan knew. Max would have waited until after the workday was over if he'd just wanted some familial bonding. That he'd approached him privately was unusual, but Elan was willing to trade quips until they got to the crux of the matter. It was rare for him to have anyone he could be himself with anymore. It was why he'd surrounded himself with people he'd known before he was king, people who'd wanted nothing from him but friendship.

Max folded his arms, mimicking Elan's pose. "Fuck you, Your Majesty."

He chuckled and slid one hand into his pocket. "You sound remarkably like Rhiannon."

Any humor that lurked in Max's gaze winked out. "She's dangerous."

"Rhiannon?" Elan blinked, straightened with a snap, and the sickening twist in his gut told him *this* was the point of his brother's visit. The quiet anticipation of a few minutes before crumbled into nothingness. "She wouldn't hurt anyone."

Max's fingers made deep furrows in his dark hair, but he didn't glance away, didn't back down. "She killed a man with her bare hands."

"He was torturing her." Elan's knee-jerk defense of the woman, his anger, was abnormal and told him he was already involved deeper than he should be with a woman he'd slept with for only one night. And he wanted more nights in her arms. The quiet vulnerability in her gaze and the fierceness in her voice when she'd told him she wanted back what Arkon had taken from her flashed through his mind. He slipped his other hand in his pocket so his brother couldn't see his fists clench.

Max gave the kind of formal bow he hadn't offered since the day Elan became king. "That's not the kind of danger I was talking about, sire."

Closing his eyes, he sighed. "I know."

His brother kept talking, driving the cold, hard blade of reality into Elan's chest. "She's a danger to us all, to every Between under your rule."

"I know." The words ground out between gritted teeth. He didn't want to hear this, didn't want to think about it. But the truth wasn't pretty. One night with the woman didn't mean she'd changed her mind about telling her story to every reporter who would listen. He'd almost managed to convince himself to forget that unfortunate part of the day before. Sex had a way of muddying things, didn't it? But he was supposed to be immune to that, above it, as the king. Damn it.

"What are you going to do about it?"

"That...I'm afraid I don't know. Yet."

"Don't let your cock lead you around on this, brother." Max arched an eyebrow when Elan narrowed his gaze. "It's my job to know where you are and who you're with at all times. Even if it wasn't, this room reeks of sex and the two of you. What other conclusion could I come to?"

"I'm not discussing that with you, Max. Some things *are* private." A low lion's growl vibrated his throat, and he felt his fangs press against his lips.

The wolf met his gaze, his pale amber eyes cool and steely, showing the hardened soldier beneath the surface of his charming brother. "You know what you should do."

"Yes," Elan bit out. Rhiannon should be killed, that was what Max was saying. It wouldn't be the first death Elan had had to order during his reign. Hell, the first death that lay at his feet was his own father's. Arkon's had just been the most recent, and Elan had hoped it would be the last for a long while. Bile stung the back of his throat.

"I can see to it she doesn't suffer." Max's voice seemed distant, his tone still calm and unrelenting. "What happened to her wasn't her fault."

"And, yet, it has already cost her life once. You're suggesting we make that a permanent solution." God, he had slept with her last night and he was talking about letting his brother assassinate her. Horror fisted in his belly. A sense of unreality slid through him and he leaned against the bedpost again to keep his legs underneath him. What kind of monster was he to even be contemplating this?

"I'm sorry." His brother stepped forward, catching Elan's shoulder. "I think only of what's best for the Between."

"I know. The final decision is mine, and I will make it soon." *No.* Everything in him rebelled at even having this conversation, let alone what it would mean for Rhiannon.

"I hope, Majesty, that you can find another solution, but I don't think there's a better one."

He nodded but didn't speak. He felt Max withdraw. Closing his eyes, he sighed and rubbed a hand over the back of his neck. He'd fought so long and so hard to keep his people safe and *free*, that it seemed inconceivably unjust for one woman to be able to bring it all crumbling down around him. But it could and would if the truth got out. The tightrope he and his people walked had frayed to a mere thread long ago—one false move and it was all over.

She was a danger to them all, Max was right about that. But should she have to pay for Arkon's crimes? Hadn't she already paid enough?

In most situations, he wouldn't even need to ask the question. His people came first and foremost. It was a ruler's duty to see that his subjects were protected. But his very soul wrenched at the thought of any harm coming to even a single hair on Rhiannon's head. Pain fisted in his gut at the warring emotions. Save her or save them all?

God help him, he knew what he should do, and for the first time since he became king, he wasn't certain he could give the order to see it through. He might not know her well, but the thought of her never smiling again, laughing again, was repugnant. It meant he'd never watch her eyes sparkle with temper, fight with her, kiss her, lose himself inside her tight, wet heat. In one night, the woman had wormed her way under his defenses. He *liked* her. He wanted to know her. He wanted *more*.

It wasn't fair. But, then, when had life ever treated anyone fairly? Being a king didn't change that unavoidable fact.

*No.* He wouldn't do it. Not yet. There *had* to be another way. He had weeks to come up with something else. Until then, there was one order he could give to protect everyone. It would piss her off, but she wasn't going to be permitted to contact *anyone* off of San Amaro Island until he was certain she wasn't a threat...one way or another.

# Chapter Five

R hiannon jogged through the light patter of rain, and the grass squished under her shoes. "Third building on the left. Two stories."

Hoping she was on the right path in the first place, she swiped her wet hair out of her face and bounced up the red tiled front steps. Before she reached the top, she froze, every one of her too-keen senses lighting up.

A deep growling grunt sounded from the porch and a bear walked into view. It stood on its hind legs when it saw her, looming over her from where she stood four steps down. It was black with a cream patch on its chest, cream snout, and paws tipped with huge curved claws. A scream tangled in her throat and she scrambled to the bottom of the stairs.

»*Wait, Ms. Reid.*« A quiet masculine voice filled her mind. »*I'm Dr. Singh and you have an appointment with me. I'm sorry I startled you.*«

She sucked in a deep breath and too many scents overwhelmed her. It was like this when her new senses went on red alert—they inundated her with more than she could process at once. When she turned around, the bear was back on all fours, watching her calmly. Clenching her shaking fists, she tried for a smile. "Sorry, I'm just not used to being around shape-shifters yet."

»*Understandable. Again, I'm sorry I scared you. Will you come with me, please?*« The bear turned and pawed his way in the front door, glancing over his shoulder to see if she followed.

Forcing her feet into motion, she hurried up the steps and out of the rain. The smile she offered was much more genuine this time. "So, you're a black bear?"

»*A sloth bear, actually. The true animal species is native to the Indian subcontinent.*« He nodded a greeting to two nurses sitting in the reception area, and they each gave a little wave. He continued down a short hallway and stopped to gesture with his snout into an exam room. »*Let me change, and I'll meet you in here, but first a nurse will be in to see you. Is that all right?*«

"Sure, why not?"

After he disappeared, one of the nurses from the front bustled in and took her vitals, asked a bunch of questions, wrote everything down on a chart, and then bustled back out again.

"Hello, Ms. Reid." The human version of the telepathic voice she'd heard from the bear sounded from the doorway. The man was...beautiful. Not ruggedly handsome like Max, or commandingly charismatic like Elan, but very attractive. His eyes were dark brown, his hair was jet black, and his skin was a deep golden tan. He was at least partially South Asian, but that was about as precise or informative as someone thinking she was partially Western European.

"What's up, Doc?"

He blinked at her as though he couldn't believe she'd gone for the clichéd line. Well, he really didn't know her, did he? She could always be relied upon to swing at the slow pitches.

After a moment, he resumed that calm, unflappable persona. "Let's get started, shall we?"

Several hours and a battery of tests later, she felt like a pincushion. And some of the tests had involved Dr. Singh using his senses and magic on her by making his hands turn into silver energy that passed through her. It was the strangest visit to a medical office she'd ever had. Then again, what about the last few weeks had been normal? Would anything ever be normal again? One more thing she didn't know.

He finished taking a few notes on his chart, set the file aside, and offered a gentle smile. "We're done for now. You'll need to come back in a few days so I can check your progress."

"Sure." She forced a grin. "I've had a month of being poked and prodded. It's not like this was any worse."

His smile faded, his face sobering. "Rhiannon, I know what Arkon—"

"Can we not talk about that guy?" She tucked her hair behind her ears, hoping he didn't notice the way her fingers trembled. "If I never hear the name *Arkon* again, it'll be too soon."

"Then you haven't—" He hesitated, then shook his head and his expression cleared of any emotion. Turning away for a moment, he straightened the papers in her file. When he looked at her again, his dark eyes were warm and understanding. "If you need to talk to talk to someone about this ..."

Her eyebrows drew together. "You mean, like, a shrink?"

"A psychiatrist, yes."

She brushed invisible lint off of her long skirt, not meeting his gaze. "The Between have those?"

"We have the same things you had before you became Between. We are human, you know. It's how we passed even the most advanced medical screening before we went public. Even the Between marks on our skin can be disguised. Aside from the magic that science can't detect, there's no real difference between us and everyone else."

From what she'd seen, that was hardly the case, but she wasn't going to talk about it. Their kind was larger than life, both good and evil. She sighed. "No, I think I'll be okay."

"The offer is open, if you change your mind." He didn't press the issue and she was grateful. From moment to moment, she was barely holding on, and if she had to talk about it, she was pretty sure the calm she'd pieced together would shatter like so much glass. All she needed to do was make it through long enough to be allowed to go home to her gym and her people. Then she'd deal with the sea of change in her life. Go with the flow, the way the old Rhiannon always had.

If she could make it through Arkon, she could make it through anything.

A shaky smile curved her lips. "Thanks."

"Ah, and here's Ms. Seaton." He turned his head toward the closed exam room door and Rhiannon tilted her head, letting those instincts she'd recently acquired take over. She heard the almost-soundless pad of Kira's light step, smelled her scent, closer than the others in the mass of humanity on the island. How would she survive if she ever let her instincts expand in a metropolis like Portland?

Kira knocked once and opened the door. Her gaze landed on Dr. Singh and she asked, with a completely straight face, "What's up, Doc?"

Rhiannon cracked up and Dr. Singh rolled his eyes. "You've known me how long, Kira?

You can call me Josh."

"Save the informality for Genesee." One of Kira's eyebrows rose. "We all know you've been sniffing after her for years."

The first show of genuine emotion flashed across the doctor's face as he flushed lightly. Then he gave a thoroughly masculine grin. "She's worth the wait."

"I admire your perseverance." She nodded and held the door wide, focusing on Rhiannon. "I'm here to give you the grand tour of the island and to show you to your new digs." Her mouth curved in a tiny grin. She gave a sly wink and Rhiannon saw the fox through the woman's eyes. "And, you know, save you from the medical types."

"I really think I'm going to like you," Rhiannon quipped.

Kira sputtered on a laugh as she slid her fingers through her short hair. "Likewise, newbie."

Pushing herself to her feet, Rhiannon gave Dr. Singh a wave good-bye. "See you in a few days, Doctor."

"Josh is fine for you, too." He tucked her file under his arm and then offered his hand to shake. "I'll see you soon."

She gripped his fingers, shook, and withdrew. "Bye."

"Good-bye."

Turning to Kira, she motioned toward the front of the building. "Ready?"

"Your Majesty, I've arranged for a small house in the staff quarters for Ms. Reid for the duration of her stay. I've seen to it that she has clothing, personal items, and foodstuffs delivered to her new lodgings. Also, I've put in the paperwork to begin her registration as a Between—we'll complete that when she's settled into one animal form. Her replacement identification—driver's license, etcetera that was in her wallet—is also being expedited and will be awaiting her upon her return to Portland."

"Thank you, Genesee. Very thorough, as always." Elan sat back in his chair, taking in his assistant's tight mouth and pale cheeks. "Have you met Rhiannon yet?"

"No, sire." She fidgeted under his steady gaze, highly unusual for his dedicated right-hand woman. "I can't imagine that she'd want—I thought it best not to."

He rose from his seat and looped around his desk to lay a hand on her shoulder. "You're not responsible for what your father did, Genesee."

"She's been through enough." Genesee pinned her gaze on his chest, refusing to look at him.

He grunted. "She's a very nice woman. She wouldn't hold it against you."

The thought sparked an idea in his mind. A way out of the mess Max had pointed out to him that morning. If Rhiannon was as protective of at least a few Between as she had been of the women who'd been captured with her, if she *cared* about the Between and what might happen to them if she told her story, then he'd eliminate the problem before it started. It was something to consider. He fought a grin. If it meant he had the duty of making sure she cared about him—the Between king—then he would gladly suffer for his people. His work was never done.

Shrugging off his grip, Genesee stepped away from him with a crisp nod. "If she's that nice, then I'm sure she'll make a wonderful new Between citizen."

He sighed, but didn't press the point. The island wasn't that large and the odds were good Genesee wouldn't be able to avoid Rhiannon for long, especially if Elan had her in the palace as often as he'd like to. But what was it with him and difficult females lately? Even his driven and devoted assistant was growing stubborn. Kira had always been that way. And Rhiannon. Well, he doubted she'd ever been the pliable type.

Except when he got her in bed, and she was ready and willing to melt under his touch. His cock hardened at the mere thought. Soon, he'd have her again soon. He'd dedicate himself to the task of making her a very satisfied Between. Dragging himself back to the present, he looked at Genesee. "When is my next meeting?"

She didn't even glance at her watch. "You're running fifteen minutes ahead of schedule."

"Imagine that." He folded his arms and leaned his hip against the corner of his desk. "I don't know what to do with myself."

Genesee managed a laugh, scooped up the documents he'd just signed, and moved to exit his office. When the door opened, he heard Rhiannon's irritated voice speaking to Genesee's intern. "Fine. Do you know when he'll be done for the day?"

"Let her in," he called. His blood heated with the challenge of another verbal sparring match with Rhiannon. Not exactly what he wanted, but he'd make do until he found a way to get her alone tonight.

"Elan?" She poked her head in his doorway and he could all but hear her teeth grinding. "Sorry to interrupt, but—"

"I have fifteen minutes to spare, so you'll have to make flaying me alive quick." He slid his tongue down a long fang. "Come in and shut the door."

"Yes, *sire.*" She planted a hand on her hip.

He grinned, enjoying the fact that she didn't seem at all bothered by his status. "*Please,* come in and shut the door."

"Well, that's better. You'll have to keep practicing." Her palm smoothed down the long, floaty skirt she wore. It looked soft. He wanted to touch it, her, but he doubted that was where this conversation was going.

"All right, let me have it. You've obviously got something on your mind."

Her eyes flashed dangerously, a hint of the newly awakening animal within her. "I understand that I'm not allowed to make phone calls off the island. Or send e-mails. Or text messages. Or, hell, smoke signals."

"No, you're not." He straightened from his desk. "You'll have no contact with anyone off the island until you're cleared to leave it."

Cold, green eyes narrowed to slits. "A little autocratic, don't you think?"

"I am a king, so yes."

"Are you sure you're not a jackass-shifter? Because you're doing a great impression of one."

He couldn't remember the last time anyone had spoken to him like this. He fought the urge to chuckle, knowing it would be the stupidest thing he could do at this moment. "Sorry, no. Only the lion gets to be king. That's me, for the moment."

"Look, whatever, Simba." She sliced her hand through the air. "This isn't a joke, damn it. It may seem stupid to you, O Mighty One, but it's a big fucking deal to me. I've lost enough. I won't lose my business, too. It's all I have—my gym and my friends. That's it. That's who I am. And that means I have to get back, Between or no Between. I've been away far too long as it is."

Scrubbing his hand over his hair, he sighed. "Your assistant manager stepped up after you went missing and has done an exemplary job in your absence. You should give her a raise."

She huffed out a laugh and paced in a circle around his office before stopping in the middle of the opulent space. "Well, it's great that *you* know what's going on at *my* health club, but that doesn't do a thing for me. I haven't been there teaching my classes, keeping my books. I need to see for myself that everything is okay. I need to get in touch with my employees and let them know I'm all right and give them an estimate on when I'll be back."

"You'll be compensated for any monetary loss your absence has incurred. I can get you copies of pertinent business records since you left, but that's it. No communication. But you won't lose your gym, I promise you that. No further harm will come to you or anyone else because of what Arkon did." He met her gaze, willing her to believe him, to begin to trust him as he needed her to for his plan to work.

She hissed at him, wounded insult flickering in her gaze. "Money isn't going to shut me up, King Elan, so you can keep it. Or, better yet, shove it where the sun don't shine. I'm still going to make sure people know about this, no matter how long you keep me on this island. I will not let other people die like *my* people did."

"Between are people, too."

"Says you, the Between king." Her arms folded stubbornly across her chest, but her eyes gave her away. Her fiery words didn't hide the way her lips quivered. She was scared and she was hurt and no matter what she wanted to do to help the women who were beyond her help, she still needed comfort for herself. She needed someone to hold on to, to depend on. He would make sure that person was him for as long as he had her on his island—long enough to eliminate her as a threat and keep her alive.

Time to begin the siege on his newest citizen's defenses. Stepping toward her, he stalked her like the predator he was. He slipped around one of the couches and approached her. Her gaze flashed a bit of wariness. Too late. Backing her up until she hit a wall, he braced both hands on either side of her head. "Yes, says the Between king. Who is also just a man."

"Right. *Just* a man." Her voice came out a breathless whisper and he sensed her awareness of him deepened. He groaned when she licked her lips. She raised an eyebrow. "This doesn't mean I agree with you. About anything."

He nodded sharply, but cupped her cheek in his palm. His voice emerged a gentle purr. "Good, because it doesn't mean *I* agree with *you* about anything either."

"Fine. Then we can keep arguing about this until I win." A knowing grin spread over her face while he chuckled. Her other eyebrow arched to join its twin. "How many minutes do you have left?"

Tilting his wrist up, he checked his Rolex. "Seven and a half."

"Then we'd better hurry." She looped her arms around his neck.

A short laugh slipped out of him. "I like you so much."

She laughed with him and he caught the sound in his mouth. He wrapped his hands around her trim waist and lifted her against the wall. She struggled to twine her legs around his hips, and he fumbled to help her shove her skirt up. She arched against him, moaning into his mouth. He could smell her wetness, and he was grateful. He didn't think he'd last even the seven minutes they had. The need for her was sharp and desperate.

He wrenched open his fly, freeing his cock. Not bothering to set her down to remove her panties, he jerked the inset aside and plunged into her in one hard stroke. She tried to break free of his mouth, but he ruthlessly covered her lips with his. Screaming and moaning had its place, but his affair with Rhiannon was *not* his staff's business.

This was madness. He was in his office, with his staff of highly-sensitive Between less than twenty feet away, having a quickie with a woman who might bring his people's peace treaties to an end.

And he couldn't make himself stop.

Nails digging into his shoulders, she clung to him as he rode her hard against the wall. Her damp sheath hugged him like a glove and he slammed himself into her while gravity did amazing things to keep him deep inside of her. Her pussy clenched tight, and from the sounds she was making in her throat, he could tell she was close. Thank God. He groaned, hammering into her hot, wet channel. She moved with him, rolling her hips to take him to the hilt on every thrust.

The slick clasp of her pussy was enough to make his head feel as though it was going to explode. Burning hot pleasure ripped through him, and he ground himself against her, praying he could hold off long enough for her to come first. She arched and froze, her sex fisting around his cock in hard pulses. He gave up any attempt at control and slammed into her in hard, jamming strokes, jetting his come into her tight pussy.

He finally let her mouth loose, dropping his sweaty forehead to her shoulder as a shudder ran through him. Her pussy clenched one last time and he groaned softly.

"Well...that was exciting. Arguing and fucking really get the blood pumping." Her fingers slid through his hair, tugging his head up for a quick kiss.

"Tell me about it." He slid out of her and set her down before she could make his cock rise again. He knew from experience just how quickly she could manage it. He'd reached for her far too often throughout the night. When the lust cleared from his brain, he came to a startling realization. "You didn't even come close to shifting."

"I'm a quick study." She chuckled and straightened her clothing.

His fingers itched to shove her skirt back up and have her again. And again. "You don't need to practice then?"

A grin curved her lips and she stepped forward to wrap her arms around his waist. "I think we should make sure this wasn't a fluke, don't you?"

"Just to be certain." He kissed her swiftly, but couldn't resist coming back for more.

His tongue traced her lips, savoring the sweet-spicy taste of her. She hummed in her throat and met his tongue with hers, bunching her fingers in his shirt. The press of her breasts against his chest made heat whip through him. Reluctantly, he angled away from her and reached back to pull her hands from his body.

"God, it's never been this good for me before." Her lips were swollen and she panted lightly. "Tonight?"

"It'll be late. We're gearing up for a state dinner with the president of France. Lots of dignitaries, all my senior advisors in one room, not my favorite part of my job." He ignored the guilt that pinched his insides when she smiled and stared at his lips. She was so open, even with her anger and pain, and he'd just turned their affair into a matter of state, a game of strategy for her sympathies, whether she realized it or not. He ruthlessly suppressed the remorse at his deceit. If the other option was death, any reasonable person would choose this path. He wanted her, she wanted him, the rest was semantics.

"You know where to find me when you're done for the day." She ran her palms up his chest and then straightened his tie. "I'm just down the path behind the palace. The last house before a big ravine."

"I know the one. I'll have the business files I promised delivered there this afternoon." He smoothed his hand down her curls. "And I'll see you tonight."

"Fair enough." She gave his tie one last tweak. "I'll be waiting. Impatiently."

# Chapter Six

A knock sounded on Rhiannon's front door as she toweled off from her shower. Glancing at the clock, she frowned. She'd already received the documents Elan had sent, and it was far too early for the man himself to arrive. A frisson of heat went through her at the thought of what he'd done to her in his office, at what he might do to her tonight. If she had to be here for a few weeks, isolated from everyone and everything, this was a stellar way to pass the time. The old Rhiannon and the new Rhiannon were in complete accord for once. And whether he liked it or not, Elan was definitely going to be revisiting the phone privileges discussion with her. She shoved one leg into a pair of jeans, hopping on one foot to get the other leg in. Snagging a shirt off the stack of brand new clothing sitting on her dresser, she jogged out to the living room to see who it was.

Before she got there, her senses alerted her to the identity of her visitor. Not Elan, sadly.

"Kira." She pulled open the door to see the somber face of the other woman. "What can I do for you?"

"You teach yoga and Pilates, right?"

The non sequitur made Rhiannon blink. "Um...yeah. Why?"

"Because." The fox-shifter stepped forward, giving Rhiannon no choice but to step back or be trampled.

She shut the door behind them, lifting her eyebrows as she watched the woman sniff around and look at everything. Rhiannon hadn't done much to the place in the twelve hours she'd been there, but she doubted Kira missed even the slight changes. "So...you want me to give you a yoga lesson?"

Flicking her short platinum hair out of her eyes, Kira glanced back. "Is that a problem?"

"No." Rhiannon hadn't exercised yet today...unless she counted the workout in Elan's bed early this morning or his office this afternoon, but it wasn't a bad thing to have company. As taciturn as the other woman was, she was as close to friend as Rhiannon had here.

Since she'd been orphaned at a young age and raised by a starchy, proper, emotionally distant grandmother, she'd made up for the lack of close family by making and keeping more than her fair share of friends. She liked having people around. Even when she'd been working full-time at the health club and getting her business degree, she'd still managed to keep an active social life. She hadn't slept much, but it had been worth it to finally take over from the manager her grandmother had hired to run the gym. There'd never been a moment in her life when she considered doing anything but owning and operating the health club. It was the last tie she had to her parents, and continuing their legacy meant the world to her. Even as her memories of them had faded and blurred with time, she always had that. And she needed to get back to it, back to her work, her customers, her employees, and her friends—many of whom had joined her gym when she took over. Four of whom had died in the wilderness. Her stomach turned and she swallowed, forcing a smile for Kira—who was staring at her strangely.

She shouldn't think about Arkon now. She was supposed to be convincing everyone she was fine and ready to go home. Time to focus on something else, something less horrifying and painful. Kira was here and ready to offer a distraction. That was good. She could use a distraction. Besides, Kira knew Elan, and Rhiannon was more than a little curious about the man who'd gone from antagonist to lover in under a day. Turning away from the unpleasant memories she doubted she'd ever truly escape, she padded across the room to enter her bedroom. "Let me change into something I can stretch in."

"Fine."

Sudden suspicion made her turn back when she reached the door. "Did Elan tell you to come here?"

"No." Kira paused for a beat before a slight smile quirked the corners of her lips. "He knew he didn't have to."

"I see. I'll be right back." Rhiannon waved a hand over her shoulder and hid a grin. "Try not to snoop too much."

A soft laugh followed her out of the room, and her grin widened. It might have been a tragedy that had landed her on this island, but so far it wasn't bad being among the Between. Then again, she hadn't had to deal with *being* a Between out in the real world. Her smile died. It would be a whole different story then. The Between were treated with equal measures of fascination and fear. As far as she knew, she'd never met one before, but with what Dr. Singh had said and with seeing how normal they looked when they weren't going all silver swirls or feral beastie made her doubt she'd have been able to tell. In their place, she'd hide what she was among humans, too.

A low groan slid out of her as she caught herself and pinched her eyes closed. Shit. She *was* in their place now, wasn't she? The helpless rush of bitter anger over that fact was one she couldn't stop. It was so wrong that this had happened to her, and still, she was the lucky one. But...what if there were more Between doing this to other humans? How many cover-ups had there been? How many people had lost their lives? How many people had suffered like she was now, knowing that the oasis of San Amaro wasn't going to save them from being a social pariah when they left? *No one* deserved to have this forced on them.

That was something about Elan that she couldn't agree with, couldn't even understand. They might have great chemistry, but that was about as much as they had in common. She got that the Between came first for him, but why didn't those humans matter too? Why did they have to remain ignorant about those Between he *knew* were a danger to others? Why didn't they deserve some protection from what she faced now?

Reality was going to be one ugly bitch when she got back out into the real world. She didn't let herself flinch away from it. Even knowing how awful it could—and probably *would*—be, she still had to go as soon as she could. Her business awaited, her friends, and a talk with each of the families of the women who'd been with her. She might not like the turn her life had taken, but at least she still *had* a life. They didn't, and their loved ones deserved to know why. Then she'd cope with the rest of the shambles her existence was in.

There was never going to be a time when she'd enjoy having to deal with what she'd really become—a monster among the people who'd once been her friends—but that didn't mean she got a free pass on dealing with it. She shook her head and sighed. As much as she *wanted* to reclaim herself, life as she'd known it was over, but what was left? Who would Rhiannon Reid be now? She didn't know.

She just...didn't know.

# CHAPTER SEVEN

The woman played havoc with his sanity. Elan worked himself into the ground every day for a week, just to prove to himself that Rhiannon wasn't really a distraction. As long as the hours he normally kept were, he worked more, drove himself harder. Even when he was ready to drop from exhaustion, he found himself seeking Rhiannon out at night. And during the rare occasions he had a free lunch. He did his best to avoid her, he really did. He just...couldn't control himself when it came to her.

The worst part was, he was *supposed* to be winning her over, to be gaining her sympathies. To accomplish that goal, he couldn't allow himself to stay away from her. He wanted to push her away, he needed to draw her closer. He didn't like how she confused everything inside him, made him crave what he knew he'd never deserve.

Glancing up from the paperwork in front of him, he watched one of his young aides stumble as he walked through the office door. Elan sighed and rose to his feet. His muscles protested from having been hunched over his desk too long. As much as he thrived on his work, as fulfilling as he found it, he knew he'd pushed them all too hard lately. Scrawling his name on the last of the documents, he scooped them up, stretched, and stepped through the doorway to see the haggard determination stamped on every one of his staff member's faces. "All right, people. That's enough. Go home for the night."

Genesee swayed as she rose from her desk, a protest on her lips. "But the state dinner is—"

She stopped when Elan held up his hand. "We all need sleep before we drop. Everyone wrap up." He gave his assistant a hard look—if anyone was more of a workaholic on overdrive than he was, it was Genesee. Too much guilt hounded them both, but he forced himself not to think about it. Now wasn't the time to dwell on the past. He had too much on his plate already without dredging up old pain. "I can have security escort you out, or you can leave under your own steam. Go on. Now."

A disgruntled sigh huffed out of her, but she obediently began shutting down her computer. The rest of his staff followed suit, rushing for the exit before he changed his mind. He rolled his tight shoulders, shoved his hands in his pockets, and left the room to wander down the hallway that lead to his suite. He smiled tiredly at the Guards positioned along the hall, and they nodded back.

His eyes burned with grit, and he knew he should sleep, but doubted he'd be able to. The way his muscles felt, he'd probably do better if he spent an hour in the gym before he crawled into bed. What he should *not* do was call Rhiannon to see if she was still up. Nor should he walk down the long pathway to her house and just surprise her. So far, she'd protested neither, no matter how late he worked. She just slid her hands over his body and kissed him as greedily as he kissed her. No questions, no accusations, nothing but a quiet understanding of the momentary escape from reality they both needed.

And, God, he needed.

It was dangerous and stupid to crave her like he did. Even more dangerous was that he enjoyed talking to her as much he enjoyed fucking her. Sex was one thing, but any other kind of intimacy shouldn't even factor into this affair. *He* was supposed to be winning *her* over, not the other way around.

"Sire." The Guard stationed outside Elan's suite snapped to attention and held the door open. "You have a visitor."

The other man didn't specify who, but he didn't need to. Only a handful of people had permission to be in the king's private quarters, and when Elan stepped into his sitting room, he drew in a lungful of her sweet scent.

Rhiannon.

Tilting his head, he waited for the feel of her boundless energy to vibrate along his senses. It didn't come. Frowning, he followed the smell of her into his bedroom and over to the wide expanse of his mattress. She lay curled on her side, one palm tucked under her cheek in sleep. His chest tightened with a tenderness he didn't want and shouldn't feel. The pose made her look impossibly young and innocent, something he knew wasn't true. A smile curved his lips. The woman more than matched him in insatiable wickedness.

Reaching out to push back a flaming curl gently, he watched her eyelashes flutter. She yawned, rolled onto her back, and stretched. Those changeable eyes locked on his face, unpredictable as her moods, and she smiled. "Mmm. I tried to stay up, but the bed looked too inviting. What time is it?"

"Very late. Or very early, depending on your definition." He let his fingertip trail over her soft cheek, down her throat, and across her collarbone as he mapped his way to her cleavage.

Arching into his touch, she chuckled. "I wore myself out today. Kira has me teaching yoga to the poor, unfortunate guys on your Guard. The women on the Guard are loving the show, and I'm pretty sure Kira's just enjoying watching the men be tortured."

He knew that. Every move she made was reported back to him, but listening to her animated retelling made him smile. "How's my brother doing with it?"

"Very well." She licked her lips and stared at his mouth, desire shimmering in her gaze. "And flirting with me outrageously while he shows off."

Elan's hand froze, hovering over her silken flesh. He shoved back the totally unfamiliar jealousy, reminding himself that the more Between Rhiannon liked and cared about, the more successful his plan would be. He closed his mouth tightly, hiding the fact that his fangs had elongated to deadly points.

Sitting up, Rhiannon tugged her shirt over her head and tossed it to the floor beside the bed. "It's good that I'm keeping in practice with my teaching for when I go back to Portland. I'm going to have to hit the ground running at the gym."

His muscles tightened as the blow of her leaving hit his gut the same way his jealousy had. That she was leaving wasn't a surprise—that he hated the idea was. It was a bad sign and it worried him. Shoving his hand into her long red tresses, he pulled her head around until he could slam his mouth over hers. The possession in the gesture angered him because he knew he had no right to it.

Her lips parted under his, welcoming his kiss. He groaned and filled his hands with her breasts, desperate to touch her, to claim her. The lace of her bra maddened him, kept him from softness of her flesh, the tightness of her nipples. A quick jerk and the fabric gave under his superhuman strength. He threw the offending garment in the same direction as her shirt.

She cried out when he bent his head to suck her nipple into his mouth. Her fingers slid into his hair and he felt the bite of talons scrape against his scalp. He shuddered, letting his fangs drag lightly over her beaded flesh.

»*Elan!*« Her sob echoed in his mind, which only drove him onward.

Pushing her back against the pillows, he shredded her jeans and panties with his claws. She laughed, her eyes sparkling as she pressed herself closer to him. After retracting his claws, his fingers delved into her sweet heat, and she spread her thighs wide to give him all the access he wanted. God, he adored how unabashedly passionate she was. He would miss this when she was gone.

His eyes pinched closed at the thought, but he didn't have time to dwell on it as she writhed against his hand, seeking deeper contact. When he opened his eyes, he saw her cheeks flushed with desire, her body arched in offering. »*You are so gorgeous, baby.*«

»*Please. Don't stop, Elan. I need you.*« Her fevered thoughts reached him, and he forgot about everything but the need to take her.

Ripping at his suit and tie, he shed the trappings of civility until he was as naked and hungry as she was. It was so good to let go with someone that, for once, he refused to let himself regret the feeling. He rolled between her legs, braced himself on his arms above her, and groaned as his cock probed at her slick core. Sinking into her made his jaw lock, the feel of her tight pussy milking his dick almost enough to shove him over the edge. She sobbed, her nails biting into his shoulders.

Forcing himself not to fuck her like a man possessed the way he wanted to, he thrust into her hot depths slowly. She clamped her legs around his waist and gave a strangled little gasp every time he filled her. Sweat dampened their skin, sliding down their shaking limbs. Fire exploded in his veins when she squeezed her inner walls around him. "Faster, Elan."

"Jesus." From his position over her, he could see each time his cock stretched her sex. Glancing up, he saw that she watched their carnal movements as well. Fangs erupted from her gums, and she hissed softly before she splayed clawed fingers on his chest. Far from being a turnoff, the feral display almost made him come. »*I love that I bring out the animal in you, Rhiannon.*«

The gold flecks in her eyes flashed and frustration molded her features while she snarled up at him. »*If you don't hurry the fuck up, I'm going to scratch your eyeballs out, and then we'll talk about bringing out the animal.*«

He laughed in her face, which probably wasn't the smartest thing he could have done when the woman had sharp talons not six inches from his eyes. But everything about her kept him on his toes—from her incisive arguments to her quick wit that never failed to make him chuckle. He didn't think he'd laughed this often in years, especially not in bed with a beautiful, willing woman. He bucked his hips, driving himself as deep inside her pussy as possible. "Oh, I'll hurry...the fuck...up."

A smile curled her lips and made her eyes twinkle as she arched her hips to meet his. "The fuck is the important part there."

His strokes picked up speed until he was hammering inside her. He might worry about hurting her, but her encouraging moans and cries spurred him on. The slap of his skin against hers only added to the erotic symphony they created. His own fangs pressed against his lips, the scent of her moisture a heady aphrodisiac. A shudder wracked his body, his heart pounded so loudly he could feel its beat under his flesh, and heat boiled in his blood. His skin felt too tight, and he couldn't move fast enough to quench the fire inside him. He knew he wouldn't hold out much longer. Shifting his weight to one side, he reached between them to flick a single fingertip over her hard little clit.

A scream that was half woman, half animal, ripped from her throat. Her claws sank into his chest, scraping flesh away, but the pain was nothing to the pleasure. Her eyes went wide, lust flushed her cheeks to a deep crimson, and her body bowed hard. The muscles in her pussy flexed tight around his cock as she came.

He roared, the lion ripping loose of its fetters. Driving his dick into her hot, wet channel one last time, he let himself join her in orgasm. His muscles gave way and he sank down onto her. She wrapped her arms tight around him and stroked her fingers through his hair. He purred, the feline side of him loved her petting as much as the man did. Closing his eyes, he tumbled into sleep before he even managed to pull out of her body.

# CHAPTER EIGHT

Hours later, dawn filtered through the curtains in his room, bathing her face in warm light. He'd taken her more times than he could count, awakening again and again to possess her and brand her with his touch. His lips played lazily over hers, their tongues twining. She broke away and snuggled her nose into the crook of his neck, sighing in contentment. His cock began to rise as his body reacted to the scent of her and sex wafting through the air. She sprawled across his chest bonelessly, and when he cupped her ass, she whimpered. "Mercy."

A smile quirked his lips. "Mercy?"

"Mercy. Uncle. Whatever." Her tone was one of mild protest, but her legs moved to open herself to his touch.

Slipping his fingers inward, he pressed into her swollen channel from behind. "Mmm. You are tight."

Her hips bucked, automatically seeking deeper contact. She dampened immediately, her body readying her for more. A moan slid out of her, and she didn't pull away when he added another finger. "I'm going to be so sore today."

"If you shift between forms, the physical soreness is healed. It's the tiredness that doesn't go away." He rolled her under him, pushing her thighs wide with his. "At least you can sleep in. I'm going to be sitting in meetings all day with debating politicos."

"Poor baby." She choked on a breath and arched when he slid into her pussy in one slow stroke.

Grinning down at her, he pumped into her welcoming heat, her sex hugging his cock tightly. "Yes, now make it up to me."

Her face flushed with pleasure and her lips were swollen from his kisses. He adored seeing her like this, thoroughly loved and still responding to him. Possession swamped him. He *hated* that he was going to lose this when he let her go. Tamping down on that betraying thought, he shoved himself deeper inside her. For him, there would never be anything but fleeting pleasure with willing women while he served his people. He'd never before realized how empty the prospect was, and he felt the whiplash of guilt at wishing it wasn't so. He'd earned the life he had, and if this was *all* he had, he'd better learn to enjoy it. He'd never met a woman who made him regret it the way Rhiannon did, and he swooped forward to taste her lips and catch her low moans with his mouth.

Burying his cock in her wetness until he lost all sense of time and space, he turned himself over to the feral heat they generated together. Her nails bit into his back as she held him closer, her legs wrapped tight around his flanks, her tongue met his with eager passion. His lungs bellowed and his heart hammered in his chest, sweat sliding in beads down his flesh. Rhiannon's flavor filled his mouth, her scent flooded his nostrils, and the feel of her soft skin rubbing against his was nothing short of perfection. She moved with him, their bodies melding, grinding together in a desperate race for release.

He didn't even bother trying to hang on to his control, knowing that she was right there with him. He could sense every beat of her heart, every hitch in her breath, every ripple of muscle in her sex. Ripping her mouth away from his, she cried out. "Yes, yes, yes, Elan!"

"Rhiannon, I—"

Her pussy pulsed around his cock as he spilled his come inside of her. She held nothing back from him, and he gave her everything in return. He had to.

Perfect.

Collapsing onto his side next to her, he tried to catch his breath and reclaim what was left of his sanity. He really needed to step away from this and get some perspective. It was dangerous how much he wanted her. No good could come of it. Wrapping her arms around his neck, she hugged him close, cuddling into his side. He trailed his fingertips down to the tips of her curls. A hum of pleasure slipped loose and she looped her thigh over his. "Are you going to be working into the wee hours again tonight, Majesty?"

"I like my work." Try as he might, he couldn't keep the defensiveness out of his tone. He did like his work, liked ensuring a better future for his kind, but duty wasn't what drove him. He didn't crave the power the way his father had, or wield it with any kind of pleasure. All he had was his heavy sense of responsibility. Was that what a king should be? He honestly didn't know, but the worry had plagued him for years.

She kissed his chest. "You're a workaholic, honey. You push yourself too hard."

"I'm a lion. It's my destiny to be king, my duty." A reminder he'd given himself more than once over the years.

He felt her eyelashes flutter, brushing against his skin. "It must have been a lot of pressure to grow up knowing that."

Swallowing, he debated telling her the truth. He knew where the discussion would lead, Rhiannon was too curious not to ask more questions. Did he want to open himself up to that? His gut instinct said it was too dangerous for him personally. The ruthless strategist within him said that the truth would play to her sympathies and get him that much closer to winning the game she didn't know she was playing with him. He knew he truly was a bastard when the strategist won the internal debate. "I wasn't always a lion. There's only ever one adult lion at a time. Very rarely, it's a female, but normally a male."

She grinned, propped her chin on his chest, and stroked her fingers down the centerline of his torso. "What were you then?"

His breath hissed out when she scraped her nail over his nipple. "An eagle."

The questions he knew she'd ask spilled from her lips. "Why did that change? And when?"

"Just before my father died." His hand fisted in the sheet by his side at the mention of his father. It was so rare that he allowed himself or anyone else to speak of the man. The self-loathing threatened to crush him. "He was the last lion. It doesn't run in one line like a traditional monarchy, but it's been in my family for several generations now. Starting with my great grandfather."

Her gaze softened and she pressed her palm to his heart. "Your father died not long after he revealed the existence of the Between, didn't he?"

"Yes." A muscle flexed in his jaw and he closed his eyes for a few moments. God, he wanted her sympathy, her comfort. And he didn't deserve even an ounce of it.

"And that's when you became king?"

His teeth clenched. "No."

"No?" Her hand resumed its movement, petting him.

The muscles in his stomach contracted, and even he wasn't sure if it was the nauseous hollowing of his belly or the slow heat her touch never failed to illicit. God, he was so fucked up. "No. I was king before he died."

Confusion flickered through her expressive gaze. "Was he sick and couldn't rule anymore?"

"No, he was in perfect health." Bile rose in his throat and he wanted to stop this train wreck of a conversation. What he wouldn't give to cut and run, but he'd never allowed himself to do that before and he wouldn't now. "The Between don't get sick."

"Right. I forgot." She tilted her head and searched his face. "Tell me what happened."

He swallowed the bitter gorge that threatened to choke him. "You know that your soul decides what animal you are."

"Yeah, and mine hasn't settled on one."

"Right." He forced himself to breathe and hoped she didn't notice the sweat breaking out on his forehead or the way dread made his heart thud heavily. "Some people never do, though it's rare. More often you see poly-shifters who are children and as they age, they find one animal that suits them. Also, huge upsets and changes in one's life—regardless of age—can cause a change in animal form."

"Okay." Her gaze was so open, so caring.

He loved talking to her for just that reason, and even if he gained her sympathy with his sad tale, he wasn't sure he could bare the pity—or the censure—that might be reflected in those eyes from now on. "The day after my father forced all Between into the public, he didn't shift into a lion."

Understanding dawned on her face. "You did."

"Yes. Like I said, there's only one lion in the world at one time." He let the sheet go before he shredded it and covered her hand with his, stilling her gentle stroking. "My father became a jackal that day...and the shame of having his title stripped from him was just too much."

Her voice was soft and made his insides twist. "He committed suicide, didn't he?"

"Yes. I...was the one who found him." He didn't meet her gaze, couldn't look at her. It was worse to say it out loud than he'd ever imagined, ripping open a festering wound. "He killed himself because I became the king."

Jerking upright, he rolled to the far side of the bed. His toes curled as they touched the cool wood floor and he buried his face in his hands. The memories of that day flooded in, each horrific image seared into his mind like a brand.

"If it wasn't you, it would have been someone else." He heard her as though from a great distance, but knew she knelt just behind him. "It's not your fault he died. On every possible level, he did it to himself. Do you honestly think it was a coincidence that he stopped being king the moment he threw your whole race under the bus?"

Elan shook his head, denying her words as the carnage he'd witnessed tormented his mind. His hands covered in his father's blood, the anger and accusations in the older man's eyes, the hate. "I only know that the last words I spoke to my father were in anger. We argued about what he had done." So much blood, so much pain. And it was his youthful, self-righteous anger that had caused it all. If he hadn't challenged his father's authority, if he'd just kept his mouth shut for once in his life, maybe the throne would never have passed to him. "I thought he was wrong to reveal our existence. He thought it was inevitable as technology became more advanced, and...he wanted to be the savior who shepherded our people into the future."

Her slim palm touched his back and he flinched. Her hand fell away as she spoke. "He wanted the glory. That's not the right decision-making process for a king."

"Right." A harsh laugh choked out of him. Had the great Elan done so much better? He didn't even know if he really should be king, if he made the right choices from one day to the next. His own father hadn't thought Elan had what it took to rule. "Even after I was king and he was not, he still spewed his rage over the change."

"He could have helped you make the transition if he had wanted to." Anger laced Rhiannon's voice, a balm to his soul that he could never, ever earn. Hell, he hadn't even revealed his ugliest secrets to her without an ulterior motive.

His father's face filled his mind again, those last few moments where he drew breath and glared. Then the blank, lifeless stare of nothingness. Of death. "All he could see was the disgrace. He couldn't live with it."

"He blamed you."

The wrenching laugh this time brought tears to his eyes and he blinked them back. His father had more than blamed him, he'd hated him, his son. And he deserved it. "Yes."

"You blame yourself, too." She ignored his flinch this time and wrapped her arms around him from behind, pressing her body to his back. "Like if you hadn't argued with him and stood up to him about it in the first place, *you* wouldn't have become king. Maybe he wouldn't have been king anymore, but it wouldn't have added an extra bitch-slap of reality to have his own son replace him."

Swiping the moisture from his eyes, he released a breathy chuckle, a far more natural sound than the last. His hand rose to cover hers. "Something like that, yeah."

"It's not your fault." Her voice was fierce, her arms tightening around him.

Jesus, it felt good. If only it were as easy to absolve himself of responsibility.

Her next question was one he didn't expect. "Did Max blame you?"

"No." Shoving his free hand through his hair, he refused to let himself think of how his actions had cost his brother as much or more than it had cost him. "He never pushed our father the way I did, but he didn't agree with him either."

"I didn't think so." She sniffed.

He almost smiled at the incensed noise, then remembered how he had twisted and manipulated her. A necessary evil, another lie to protect his people. That was his job, wasn't it? Protecting everyone, and if he had even a scrap of decency left, he'd pull back and let her go before she gave too much. "What's your point?"

"My point is that the only people who blame you are the man who was really to blame *and yourself*. It's something you should think about." Resting her cheek against his back, she sighed. "You trust Max's judgment on everything else except this. Why?"

The last bit of truth spilled from him even as he locked his emotions down tight. He was honest enough to admit to himself that he had to protect *himself* from the caring he'd deliberately set out to illicit from her. For his sake and hers, he had to gain some distance and save them both from shattering when the time came for her to go back to the life she wanted so badly. "Max wasn't the one who had to look my father in the eyes when he was dying. Max wasn't the one who found him. My father wasn't gone yet. It was far too late to save him, but I saw the recrimination in his eyes. He blamed me to the end."

"Then he was wrong to the end. That isn't your fault." Her hands clutched his chest. "Stop blaming yourself, stop pushing yourself so hard that you forget to smile and laugh and enjoy your life."

Pushing himself to his feet, he moved out of her embrace. His voice was calm, cool, and collected. He should have been proud to regain some of his vaunted control. He wasn't. "What I do is important."

"I'm not saying it isn't." She planted her fists on her hips when he looked back at her. "I'm saying that taking a few minutes away from being *the king* and just being *Elan* again isn't going to hurt anyone. It would definitely help you."

"What would you know about it?" He forced himself to meet her gaze as he huffed out a laugh that he knew would hurt her. "You don't know me."

She winced, her eyes going flat. Not backing down, she lifted her chin. "You're right. I don't. I'm just a brain-dead human who ended up in the wrong place at the wrong time. Sorry I bothered you. Sorry I bothered to care."

With that, she rose from the bed, gathered her clothing, and left.

He closed his eyes and forced himself not to go after her and apologize. He needed her to get close but not too close, and the line between those two had begun to blur for him. God, he felt like complete shit. The phone beside his bed rang, reminding him that he had a full day of work ahead of him. He'd insisted a decade ago that he knew best what the king's duties should be and now those duties were his whole life.

His wished it was different, that *he* was different, but it wasn't.

# Chapter Nine

E lan stood with his broad shoulder braced against one of the mirrors that lined the wall of the studio where she was giving her yoga class. It was one of several in the huge gym that the Guard and many of the people on San Amaro used. The building was nowhere near the palace and Elan's office. She tried not to look at him as she finished up her workout, but her gaze was drawn to the big lion-shifter. It had been three days since she'd stormed out of his room and, as hurt as she'd been with him throwing her concern back in her face, she'd still missed him and wondered how he'd been doing.

Which just made her feel all kinds of pathetic.

She winced and tugged her hair out of its ponytail to let it fall forward and cover her face. The multitude of mirrors in this room reflected far more than she wanted anyone to see, let alone a man who made it clear she wasn't welcome to anything in his life but an orgasm. Not even friendship, which was really what stung the most. She'd begun to think of him as more than just a way to pass the time. She considered him a friend, and it hurt to realize he obviously didn't feel the same. Why he'd bothered to tell her about his father was beyond her.

After her class, she made a beeline for the women's locker room and hoped he'd be gone when she was done rinsing off the sweat. She didn't bother to speculate why he was here—it wasn't for her, so it didn't matter. No doubt he wanted to speak to Max or Kira, and then he'd be back to working himself into an early grave. A sad smile twisted Rhiannon's lips. Maybe if Elan killed himself in the name of duty, he could stop feeling so damn guilty about his father killing himself for *not* doing his duty.

She shook her head.

It was so sad that a man like Elan, who was worshipped by the men and women he ruled, couldn't see the good in himself or the wonderful things he'd accomplished. She wished there was something she could do to help him, but she wasn't stupid enough to believe she could save a man who didn't want saving. And she had enough problems of her own that she should focus on them instead of anyone else's.

A few minutes in the shower, a quick brush through her hair, a change of clothes, and she was ready to go. She tucked her gym clothes into her locker, stepped out of the locker room, and took a breath to see if Elan had left. Nope, he was nearby, though with the muddying of scents as sweat permeated the building, she wasn't sure where, exactly. Peeking around the corner, she saw a straight shot to the exit. "Sweet."

Her grin was more than a little triumphant as she jogged outside. And then drew up short when she saw Kira and Elan talking just beyond the door. Kira flashed a brilliant smile and put her hand on his arm. A growl sounded as pure envy stabbed at Rhiannon's soul. It took a moment to realize the noise hadn't come from her. She turned to see Max standing behind her, watching the same exchange she was. Her eyebrows arched. It was the first time she'd seen such a deadly expression on the man's face. It chilled the blood and made her understand exactly why Elan had put Max in charge of the King's Guard.

She swallowed and took a quick step away. "Are you all right, Max?"

"Yep. I'm great." In the blink of an eye, the dangerous man was gone, and the amiable Max she was used to smiled down at her. The mask didn't fool her though. She'd just seen what lay beneath it.

Opening her mouth to make an excuse to flee, she realized too late that Elan was now looking at her. The lion-shifter jerked his chin toward the path to the palace. "Come with me."

His tone was a blatant order from the king, and it made her hackles rise, but she ground her teeth and walked beside him in stony silence. Better to get this over with and have him go back to ignoring her than kick up a fuss he was sure to see as a challenge. So far, he'd yet to back down from one, and she just wasn't in the mood to play those games with him.

They entered the huge building from the side, through the kitchen door. Her eyebrows contracted when he smiled at one of the cooks and accepted a picnic basket and a small duffel bag from the older woman. "What are you doing?"

"Taking a beautiful woman's advice." He easily held both containers in one big hand. Flipping open a metal box mounted next to the door, he rifled through what looked like hundreds of key rings until he pulled out one with a bronze lion holding a turquoise fish in its mouth. A single key dangled from the ring.

She shook her head as he took her arm and tugged her back outside. "I don't understand."

"What's not to understand?" His amber gaze cut to her face before he turned away and pulled her down one of the many gravel pathways around the palace.

She sighed and pulled at her arm, but his grip didn't budge. "Every time you let me near, you just push me away again, Elan."

"I know." He kept moving, but she watched his knuckles whiten on the handles of the bag and basket.

Digging her heels into the ground, she forced him to stop or drag her. He stopped, but didn't face her. "You know? That's it?"

"I'm trying, Rhiannon." His chin dropped to his chest, his voice softening. "This isn't easy for me. I have no idea what I'm doing with you, and I hate that." His tone was wry and she could almost see the smile twisting his full lips. "I told you I like to be in control."

"And I roll with the punches. Usually." She wrapped her free hand around his wrist, tugging him around to face her fully. "Why don't you start that *trying* by talking to me? Why tell me about your father if you were just going to tell me to mind my own business when I had concerns about how it affected you?"

"Because I...wanted you to know me." He closed his eyes. "I wanted to matter, and I know you're leaving and none of it should matter anyway." He barked out a laugh and refocused that amber gaze on her. "That's even more pathetic when I say it out loud. But, the bottom line is, I know I was an ass and I pushed you away. I'd like the chance to make it up to you."

"You do matter, Elan." Her heart contracted and her emotions wrestled with each other for supremacy. Tears threatened to well in her eyes, and she rolled them at her lack of control. "That's always been one of my problems. People matter too much. You, my friends back home, the women Arkon kidnapped. It's why I've been telling you I have to get back. It's why I want to make sure no one gets hurt again. Everything matters to me. Every*one* matters."

"What about the people here on San Amaro?"

She laughed softly. "They do, too."

His gaze sharpened, and she knew this discussion had just deepened into something more. "Then why do the women who died matter more than they do? You have to know what will happen to the people here, to *all* Between, if you told anyone what happened—even just the women's families. Humans' fears and prejudice about us will feel justified. It won't stop at the incivilities and harassment we face now. Many innocent Between will be harmed and even killed. Why aren't living people more important than the dead?"

Her laughter died, and hurt lanced through her chest. She jerked at her arm again, but he still wouldn't let go. "It's not about who means *more* to me, Elan. Maybe it's really about who means more to *you*. Those women matter. Not to you, perhaps, because they weren't your citizens before they were murdered, but their lives and their deaths matter to me and their loved ones."

"I *know* they mattered, but Arkon is dead and can't hurt anyone anymore. And those women are dead, too. I can't save them." A muscle ticked in his jaw, and his gaze locked with hers. "And you can't save them either, no matter how many reporters or family members you tell."

The harsh truth of that stabbed at her, crumbling a protective wall inside of her. She snapped back, giving him a dose of his own bitter reality. "And *you* can't save your father, no matter how guilty you feel or how many hours you slave away, so spare me the pot-kettle speech."

He sucked in a sharp breath, his eyes going wide. His fingers tightened painfully on her arm, but she refused to wince. They both fell silent as they processed the wounds they'd just ripped open for each other.

She couldn't deny he was right. A part of her had held on to the idea that some part of her friends could be saved if she just told everyone who would listen the truth about what happened with Arkon. But nothing could bring them back. Not her anger or her sense of responsibility. She had to face the fact that she had lived.

She rubbed a hand over eyes that burned with unshed tears. Her internal reasoning sounded a hell of a lot like what she imagined was going on in Elan's head. A sad smile curved her lips. "We are pathetic little peas in a pod, aren't we?"

"Definitely." His small grin matched hers and he let go of her arm. His amber eyes were glassy and hollow with remorse and pain. "Look, I—"

"Was just about to tell me where we're going? Good plan." She grabbed his hand, unwilling to walk away just yet. Her emotions were spinning, but she couldn't leave him alone this way. They both might need something to hold on to just now.

"I'd planned for us to play and relax and just be Elan and Rhiannon for the day, as you suggested." She could see the struggle to regain his equilibrium on his face, watched as the king finally won out over the vulnerable man. A part of her regretted the change, but it was probably what he needed to feel in control of himself again. He tilted his head toward the marina, where she saw Kira standing beside a small yacht. Several other members of the Guard swarmed over a speedboat.

"We're having a picnic on a boat?" She smiled when he nodded. The look in his eyes was almost uncertain, the expression odd on his regal features. He was trying, she had to give him credit for that. She gestured to the duffel bag. "Bathing suits?"

"And towels, though there are more on the yacht if we need them." Something close to relief flashed in his gaze when she let him draw her to his side, leading her down to the dock. Handing her onto the deck of the yacht, he clamored up behind her. Kira tossed him the ropes that tied the boat to the dock, and within a few minutes they were on their way. He skillfully guided the boat out onto open water before he grinned at her. "Do you want to try it?"

Sliding into the circle of his arms between his chest and the wheel, she let him show her how to navigate and steer the yacht. "This is so cool."

He dropped a quick kiss to the top of her head. "I'm glad you're having fun."

Twisting in his arms, she pressed her mouth to his. He groaned, pulling back for the few moments it took to throttle down the boat and let them drift on the water. Then his hands cupped her hips, turning her until her back was to the wheel. His mouth was on hers, his teeth nipped at her lower lip, and his tongue slid forth to toy with hers, coaxing her to play.

His cell phone rattled across the wooden shelf above the wheel and he groaned into her mouth. Releasing her lips, he snagged the phone up and sighed down at it. "I don't know how long this will take." He glanced at her, his expression unreadable. "One of the pitfalls of being the lion."

"Okay, Simba." She ruffled his wind-tossed hair and he rolled his eyes at her. "I'm going to go work on my tan."

She grabbed the duffel bag and jogged down a set of steps to where she hoped there was a private area to change.

"Wow." The rest of the yacht was more spacious than she'd have guessed and beyond sumptuous. She found a bathroom and changed into the bikini that was in the bag. Grabbing a towel, she went back up to the deck of the boat, spread the terrycloth out and lay on her back.

She folded her arms behind her head and closed her eyes, determined *not* to think about their argument and just enjoy the day, as he'd suggested. Over the gentle lap of the waves hitting the sides of the yacht, she could hear Elan using his kingly voice, so she figured it was going to be awhile before he was done. By then, he'd probably have to take them back to shore. Ah, well. Being around him meant dealing with the demands of his job, and when he wasn't avoiding her or pushing her away, he was worth it.

Rolling on to her front, she pulled her hair out of the way to let the sunshine warm her back. The deep rumble of Elan's voice and the soft rocking of the boat lulled her. A sigh eased out and she rested her cheek on her folded arms.

"You're going to burn, sweetheart." His hands slid over her back, rubbing cool lotion onto her skin.

She moaned and arched into his touch, languid heat rolling through her. "I always burn around you, Elan."

"Mmm." His fingers massaged the sunblock into her flesh, and her muscles loosened in anticipation. Her nipples tightened and her pulse began to race at the erotic rasp of his callused fingertips stroking down her body. She clenched her thighs together, only to find that one of his knees was between her legs. He groaned low in his throat and nudged his knee forward until it pressed against her sex. "There's not much I can do about that when we're out in the open."

"Please," she whispered, lifting her body as subtly as possible into his muscular leg. As much as she didn't want to get caught with her pants down on the deck of a boat with the Between king, she also wanted the man with a fierceness that hadn't quit since the moment she'd met him.

His big hands curled around her ribs, rubbing his fingertip along the bottom edge of her bikini top, stroking the undersides of her breasts. Pleasure sang through her body, made her moan in rising need. "Is there anywhere below deck we can ..."

"Yes." Urging her to her feet, he pushed her in the direction of the short staircase.

Her breath came in quick, excited pants, and she tried to keep a little control. She'd gone three long days without him, and her need ran so hot and fast through her blood, she worried she might have a hard time keeping a handle on the magic again. Her legs shook beneath her as she waved a hand around to indicate the elegant interior of the yacht. "This thing is plush."

He hummed in the back of his throat, running his hands down her hips. "It's one of the job perks. Helps make up for the inconvenient phone calls."

"I'm still waiting for you to be like Mel Brooks and go 'It's good to be the king.'" She did a crappy imitation of the line from the movie *History of the World, Part I*.

"You are *such* a brat." Whipping her around, he shoved her over the edge of a table rimmed with padded bench seats. He made short work of her bathing suit bottoms and his pants.

Twining his fingers through her long curls, he draped her hair over one shoulder. It tickled her bare skin and made her shiver. Her nipples tightened to aching points, her pussy spasming, and he hadn't even done anything to her yet. She heard a creaking pop and turned her head to see a bottle of lube in his hand. "What's that for?"

»*What do you think?*« His voice purred in her mind, and excitement whipped through her. His hands disappeared from her line of sight, then she felt one of his fingers probe the recessed pucker of her anus. Her hips moved in shameless abandon as she helped him work the lube inside her.

"Please," she gasped, shudders wracking her body.

His hands came up to press hers flat to the tabletop, covering them and holding her down. He shoved his thigh between hers, forcing her legs wide as his weight rested on her back. The head of his cock slid forward to nudge her anus. Her breath locked in her throat and she choked. She rose onto tiptoe, her body poised for flight even though he had her trapped between him and the table. "Elan ..."

"Shh. You can take me, honey." Biting the back of her neck, he held her in place while the hard width of his cock stretched her ass. The lube helped ease his way, but he was *big*. Pain-soaked pleasure ricocheted through her, and she needed *more*. She screamed, but the sound wasn't entirely human. It was as much feral beast as frustrated woman. She bucked against him, but it only drove him deeper, and her shriek dissolved into a moan.

He chuckled, and the vibration made her moan again. He began driving into her ass with slow, hard thrusts. He went deep every time, filling her with exquisite perfection. Silver shimmered around her hands and left her fingers tipped with razor-sharp talons that scraped over the wooden tabletop. She didn't have to press her tongue against her teeth to know she had fangs. Holding tight to the shift, she didn't let the magic finish the process. She had no idea what animal her body was trying to turn into, and she didn't want to know. She wanted Elan.

Her hips slapped back against his, moving as much as her pinioned position would allow. It was enough to make him groan deep in his throat. She liked that. Liked that even when he went all dominant alpha male on her, she could still make him react to her.

Releasing her hands, he skimmed one palm down her torso to delve between her thighs and thrust inside her wet, empty sex. Pressing her palms against the table, she arched up as far as she could, a low keening breaking from her throat. Her position made room for his other hand to jerk the triangles of her bikini top out of the way. He plucked and twisted her nipples one at a time. Every roll of his fingers made her pussy clench around his pumping fingers. She could feel his blunt fingertips rubbing his cock through the thin membrane of flesh that separated her two channels. "Do you know how good you feel, Rhiannon?"

"Oh, my God." Tingles rippled up and down her limbs and she threw her head back against his shoulder. She flicked her tongue over the salty skin of his neck. "Please."

Her senses heightened to painful intensity, all her focus centering on him. His hands moving over her, his cock moving in her, his scent filling her lungs, his rich taste filling her mouth. Her body quivered right on the brink of orgasm—she could feel it building inside of her in dark waves that threatened to overwhelm her. She welcomed the ecstasy, willing it to drag her under.

"Elan, I'm going to come."

The lion-shifter snarled at her words and came deep inside her. She climaxed with him, her inner muscles clenching tight. Her body bowed and jerked as they rode out their orgasm together. His cock continued to work inside her, to stretch the ring of her anus, until the pleasure was more than she could bear and she collapsed in his arms, caught safe in his strong embrace—safer than she'd ever been in her entire life, even before her parents died. Too bad it couldn't last.

It was the last thought she had before unconsciousness swept over her.

# CHAPTER TEN

Rhiannon couldn't believe it had only been three weeks since she'd come to San Amaro, even though she knew it meant she'd been away from her life in Portland three weeks longer than she should have. She let her toes dig into the sand on the island's warm beach as she stared out across the Pacific Ocean. Somewhere north of here was Oregon. Home. But everything felt different. Everything *was* different. Where was home now that everything she was had changed? She shook her head and sighed, closing her eyes to savor the sunshine on her face, the salty breeze whipping through her hair.

Time had slid away from her, days of getting to know everyone on the island blurring into nights with Elan. Her senses, both human and Between, drowned in his touch, his scent, his taste. With him, she felt more alive, more aware than she ever had with any other lover. Was it because he was Between? Or because she was now? Did being king make him *more* than other Between? Either way, her reaction to him felt...right. She'd never been one to question her feelings. They were or they weren't. With most men, they weren't. She enjoyed them for a while, and then she moved on, but this was more intense, more real. She wanted to dismiss it as an overreaction to an unusual situation, but she couldn't. She just wasn't sure what to do about it. Enjoy it while it lasted, sure, but then what? What would it mean for her when it was time to go home? Would he ever want to see her again? *Should* she see him if he did?

Nothing permanent could come of this, and for someone who liked her relationships and her men light and easy, Elan was just *different* from what she usually preferred in every possible way. And, yet, they fit. It solved none of the problems outside of their relationship, but there it was. When they were together, it worked. Once they parted for more than a handful of days, maybe it wouldn't work as well. The dread that had begun to twist inside her when she thought about leaving gave an especially vicious wrench. She wanted to go, she wanted to stay. It made no sense. Things had just gotten so tangled and twisted in her mind.

Shaking her head, she shoved her hands in the pockets of her turquoise capris. The fabric was soft under her palms. She grinned. Whoever had bought her new clothes had done a good job—better than Rhiannon did on her own. Sighing, she turned away from the sea and padded through the sand to the path that lead up to the palace. It was a bustling madhouse up there today. The state dinner was supposed to be tonight, and Elan had asked—or actually, insisted—that she go with him. A rueful smile curled her lips. That was Elan, a ruler to the core. With him it was always half request and half command. It should bother her more than it did, but she rarely resisted the urge to needle him about it. Or make a "king of the urban jungle" lion joke. He tolerated it, for now, but she had a feeling if she pushed him a bit more, he might lose his cool. The thought made a tingle of heat rush through her. She wanted to see that veneer of civility stripped away to reveal the wildness he kept inside. Hints of it flashed through when they were in bed together, but she wanted all civility gone. She wanted all of him, even though she knew she shouldn't, even though feeding her fascination would probably hurt her in the end. And it didn't stop her desire. That she was setting herself up for more pain after all the pain she'd already been through lately probably meant she should see Dr. Singh about having her head examined.

Skirting the more public areas of the palace that held the arriving ambassadors and advisors, she stepped into the chaos of the main kitchen. She'd pick up the sandals she'd left in Elan's suite the night before and be on her way. As much as she'd love to see him, he'd be hip deep in too much to do, so she'd just have to wait to get her fix this evening.

Her body slammed into another woman's as she hurried out of the kitchen and into a narrow service hallway.

The woman stumbled back, dropped an armload of paperwork on the floor, and watched helplessly as it scattered. She looked like she was going to have a meltdown any moment. It was the same slender blonde who'd given her the frigid ice-bitch look the first day Rhiannon had dared to interrupt Elan's day for an argument and a quickie, so she scooped up papers, stuffed them into the woman's arms, and spun to walk back into the kitchen. She paused on the threshold, dropped her chin against her chest, and knew she couldn't just *leave* the other woman there. She was such a softy. Sighing, she turned back around.

"Um...are you..." She stopped, unable to finish the stupid question. Of course the woman *wasn't* okay. Taking a breath, Rhiannon smiled and tried again. "Can I help with anything?"

A horrified look crossed the other woman's face before she smoothed it into a cool mask. "N-no, nothing, ma'am. Everything is fine."

"That's obviously not true." Rhiannon gave her a kind smile. "Elan mentioned that you're having a party with dignitaries and such. He asked me to be his date."

"Yes, I know. I had a gown shipped over from the mainland for you and it's been delivered to your house. I hope Prada is all right."

Rhiannon arched her eyebrows at the exorbitant designer label. "For shoes?"

"And dress. They do more than shoes." The woman brushed a hand down her expensive-looking skirt and gave Rhiannon an incredulous look, like any moron should have known that fashion detail.

"Oh. Sorry, I own a health club and teach yoga." She shrugged. "I do workout pants, a sports bra, and a tank top for most days."

The shorter woman gave a tentative smile. "Ah, yes. I used to take yoga before..."

"Before what?"

An uncomfortable expression crossed her face, as though she thought she'd said too much and regretted it. "My fiancé died."

"I'm sorry for your loss." Rhiannon set a hand on her arm and squeezed gently.

"Thank you." The blonde cleared her throat and looked away. "I need to get back to work."

"How can I help?" It wasn't a question, but a command. Rhiannon had picked up that little trick from Elan, where even a request came out a royal edict. Since this woman served him, she reacted predictably, and Rhiannon had to struggle with a smile.

"Right now it's just checking a million details. The food, the flowers, the table settings, the waitstaff."

"Okay, I can make sure the flowers and table settings are nice. I do know how to set a formal table." Thank you, uptight grandmother.

"It's a little more complicated than that. Politicians from multiple countries, and all the ranks of Between advisors that will be here." For a moment, the petite woman looked like she was going to hyperventilate. "We've only done two of these since Elan assumed the throne, and this is the biggest one yet."

"Okay. I'll take the flowers, then." Shuffling through the paperwork, the other woman reluctantly handed over a few pages of notes. Rhiannon glanced at them before offering another grin. "I never thought I'd meet anyone *more* driven by their work than Elan, but I think you might have him beat."

A wan smile answered that. "I just want everything to be perfect. I'm the king's assistant and general Girl Friday. There's a fancier title for it, but that's what I am. If anything goes wrong, I'll feel responsible."

"I understand. I'm Rhiannon Reid, by the way."

She gave a little chuckle. "Everyone knows that by now. You're the new Between the king is completely infatuated with."

A flush of pleasure heated Rhiannon's cheeks and she leaned forward to study the papers in her hand so that her hair swung into her face. "Ah."

"I'm Genesee Arkon," the woman whispered.

*That* name brought Rhiannon's head up with a snap. "Arkon?"

"Yes, Arkon. And, yes, he was related to me. My father." Tears welled up in her wide eyes, melting every remaining trace of the ice princess. Rhiannon wasn't sure who'd gone paler—her or Genesee. "I'm sorry for what he did to you and all the others. I...wish there was something I could do to make up for it, but there isn't. I just get to live with the horror and shame of what he did to innocent people."

"It's not your fault." The words were automatic, a reflex of years of helping people.

A single tear slid down her porcelain cheek. "He was my *father.*"

Rhiannon looked at her for a long time, and the woman looked back. The blue eyes were the same, but other than that, nothing about Genesee even looked like her father. For the weeks of her captivity, Rhiannon had lived on the hatred of that man, and putting a name to him had only intensified it, giving her a label to spew like a vile curse. And this woman bore that name, that label, too.

She winced as she realized this was what Elan had been trying to get across to her since the first day they'd met. The only person who should have to pay for Arkon's crimes was Arkon. And he had paid, hadn't he? With his life. Rhiannon's friends had paid with their lives, too, but Elan was right that it was too late to save them now. It *wasn't* too late to save all the Between who could be hurt by this. It wasn't too late to save Genesee. It wasn't too late to save Rhiannon. She might have lost the life she had known, but at least she had the chance to start over. Still, the guilt in Arkon's daughter's eyes twisted Rhiannon's heart—so like Elan's when he'd spoken of his father.

It wasn't fair. Not to Elan, not to Rhiannon, not to Genesee, not to any of the women who had died.

Reaching out slowly, she squeezed Genesee's hand and tried for a smile. "Something else you have in common with Elan—an overdeveloped sense of responsibility. I know why he is the way he is, and if *this* is why you are the way you are, then you can stop now. I don't blame you for this. You weren't there, you couldn't have stopped him, you didn't make him do what he did. The only one to blame is him, and he's dead." She swallowed and let Genesee's hand go, let go of some of the last dredges of her bitterness. Some of it would probably always be there, but she didn't want to keep more than she had to. A wry smile stretched her lips. "You know, some people might be pissed at me for killing their dad, no matter what he'd done to me."

"It was self-defense." Genesee's voice was flat, staccato. "Who wouldn't have done the same in your position?"

"Thank you." How she would have coped if someone called her a murderer for what she'd done, Rhiannon didn't know. She was simply grateful she didn't have to deal with that, along with everything else. Lifting the papers in her hand, she shrugged. "Back to work for us, right?"

"Right." But the color had come back into the other woman's face and some of the tension seeped out of her body. Rhiannon could sense her relief. "You really don't think I'm guilty by association?"

"No, I don't." Remembering Dr. Singh's offer and his discussion with Kira, Rhiannon grinned. "But if you do, I think maybe you should talk to someone about it. I think Dr. Singh might know someone."

"J-Josh?" A deep flush sped up her cheeks and she tucked her golden hair behind her ear. Rhiannon's new senses registered the way Genesee's pulse jumped, the way her body temperature rose slightly. It was still odd to experience other people's reactions on such a visceral level, but she was getting used to it.

"Yes, Josh." So, the attraction between went them both ways. Good for them. "I'm off to check on the flowers. If you want, we could have coffee sometime, after this dinner is over and things get back to normal."

"Nothing with the Between is ever normal." A rueful grin tucked dimples into Gene-see's cheeks. "But, thank you. For everything."

# CHAPTER ELEVEN

Elan stopped for a moment in the doorway of the palace's ballroom to observe his brother dancing with Rhiannon in his arms. The flirtatious smile on Max's face made Elan's fists clench with the overwhelming urge to punch his only sibling. Jealousy speared Elan straight to his possessive feline soul. He had no right to feel the way he did and he knew it. Max was more than likely trying to assess Rhiannon's threat to Between security. It was a risk to let her out in public, to give her the opportunity to tell the story of how she'd become Between to people who would love to hear it and use it against him, but...he was stunned to find that he had faith in her not to betray him that way. When he'd gone from manipulative and suspicious to trusting, he didn't know. Max wasn't happy about the possible security breach, but Elan was the king and he'd refused to yield.

A ridiculous amount of gratitude flooded him when the music ended and Max led Rhiannon off the dance floor. They parted ways and Elan shook his fists out, flexed his fingers. He watched Rhiannon smile and begin speaking with an Italian ambassador's wife. He was staggered once more by how lovely Rhiannon was, and the double punch to heart and loins whenever he looked at her struck him. He should be used to it after the last couple of weeks, but he wasn't. Everything about her fascinated him. Tonight, her red hair was piled on top of her head with fiery tendrils left to trail down her neck. The black gown and gloves set off her creamy complexion, baring just enough flesh to make him pant with need.

Snagging a glass of champagne from a passing waiter, he worked his way across the room toward her, stopping to chat as he went. She was the only thing making this evening bearable. Of all the things involved in being a ruler, the pomp and circumstance at these kinds of parties was one of his least favorite. He preferred quieter negotiations where actual results came out of the meeting. These seemed little more than grandiose posturing, though a few words in the right ears here could do a great deal for his people in the end. He respected the party's usefulness—he didn't have to enjoy it.

The women had their backs to him as he approached. Rhiannon would be able to sense him, but the human woman would not. He watched Rhiannon reach out a proprietary hand to straighten a vase of flowers. "There. Perfect."

"This is just exquisite." The human chuckled, gesturing expansively with her champagne flute, her Italian accent musical. "As charming as the king is, his other affairs lacked a woman's touch."

Since Elan had very little to do with the arrangement of social gatherings, the woman's assertion was complete crap. Genesee handled these things, so a woman's touch had been all over the other parties held during his reign.

Rhiannon shrugged and shot a desperate glance at him over her shoulder. "Um…thank you."

"We're so glad you're enjoying yourself, ma'am." He took his cue to step forward and slip his arm around Rhiannon's waist, offering up his most charming smile.

The woman grinned back, clearly enjoying the bubbly more than a little. "You make such a beautiful couple."

"Thank you." He nodded and kept his smile firmly in place when he wanted nothing more than to end this evening so he could drag Rhiannon to his rooms and lose himself in her soft body until they were both spent.

Rhiannon stroked a soothing hand up and down his back. He arched subtly into her touch, holding back a purr. Her green-gold eyes sparkled up at him. "Fabrizia was just telling me about how much she likes horseback riding."

"Was she? Then I hope she'll take advantage of the royal stables while she's here." The response was automatic, but it sent the woman into raptures about her stable at home. Before long, her husband and several other diplomats had joined them.

Letting Rhiannon direct the conversation from horseback riding to horseracing to betting on the races to gambling laws throughout the world, he was amazed at how knowledgeable she was about seemingly obscure topics, and at the ease with which she conversed with everyone from the French president to a passing waiter. One more piece of the puzzle, something else to intrigue him. It was foolhardy to like and want her as much as he did, but the last few weeks had only sharpened his craving. He sighed and refocused on keeping up his end of the conversation, maneuvering it into a discussion of Between rights in the European Union. This kind of small talk was his forte, and one of the things he thrived on as king. The maneuvering, the verbal play that always meant more than the words they spoke. If he ignored the fancy trappings of the party, he was in his element.

After an hour of political shoptalk, Rhiannon turned to wink up at him. "Your Majesty, would you care to dance?"

"I would be delighted, Ms. Reid." He didn't manage to keep in the purr this time as the thought of having her in his arms flashed through his mind and sent pleasure shooting straight to his groin. He clenched his teeth as his cock began to harden, nodded a farewell to the gathered politicians, and guided Rhiannon out onto the dance floor.

They passed Max as they went, who was speaking to one of the royal security advisors. Rhiannon followed his gaze. "Your brother likes doing the prince thing even less than you like doing the smiling, social Simba thing."

"Yeah." It was true, though he thought his brother did an admirable job of hiding his discomfiture. Max would rather be organizing the Guard's activities for the evening than being one of the party's players. But as the son of the former king and the brother of the current one, Max was a player in Between politics whether he wanted to be or not.

Elan shook away thoughts of his brother, gathered Rhiannon close, and led her into a waltz. Her body molded itself to his and he savored the feel of her. When he caught her smile and subtle wave to a couple they twirled passed, he grimaced. "You do all of this so effortlessly. I really do hate these kinds of gatherings."

"I like entertaining, and I like people. It's easy to take an interest in them, no matter how much their clothes cost. They're still people." She grinned at him, stroking her fingers over his shoulder and down his chest to circle his nipple through his tux. His breath caught and her smile somehow became both innocent and sly at the same time. "I like people."

His cock went from semi-hard to painfully rigid in seconds. The moment he pulled away from her, his condition would be more than obvious to even the humans who couldn't sense his lust. He growled low in his throat. "Keep that up and I'm going to take you over my knee and spank you the moment we're away from this crowd."

"Promises, promises." She continued to tease him just long enough to make his breath hiss between his clenched teeth—which had lengthened into fangs in the last ten seconds.

He couldn't resist grinding himself against her on the next turn. God, the woman was a nightmare to his self-restraint. She made him want to forget his duties and let loose the fetters on the lion within. With effort, he managed to retract his fangs, but he let his claws scrape her bare back lightly.

Her breathing hitched and he watched the gold burn through the green in her eyes. "How much longer will this thing go?"

"You're having fun entertaining, aren't you? You like people." His tone was casual, but he knew she saw through it. She could shred his charm as quickly as his restraint, and she seemed to delight in doing both.

It was probably what he liked best about her. That and the obvious strength and courage he'd seen in just a few weeks as she worked through some of the nightmare Arkon had put her through. There was so much he'd come to like about her, to admire about her. But how much longer would he have to enjoy her? His chest tightened with some painful emotion he couldn't name as he stared down at her. He shook himself, tightening his hold on her. Why would it upset him to lose a woman he'd only met a short while before, a woman who had a life and business to go home to? It shouldn't bother him, but it did. She didn't belong here, didn't belong with him. But he couldn't shake the feeling that when she left, she would take something vital to him with her.

He just didn't know what, if anything, he could do about it.

# Chapter Twelve

Anticipation hummed through Rhiannon as Elan followed her through the door to his suite, so close she could feel the heat of him searing her back. She should have felt crowded, smothered as she did with other lovers. With him, she didn't. She couldn't help but question why, and the answering flood of hot, sweet emotion was more than she knew how to deal with. As wonderful and complicated as he was, she couldn't have him.

Her time with him was sliding away—she could feel it slipping through her fingers like grains of sand. The thought made her heart squeeze with sadness at the loss of something that was never hers. What she did have was a place in Portland she needed to get back to. It was time to face the music, and she was as ready as she'd ever be to handle life as a Between. All she had to do was get the good doctor to clear her medically and she'd be set. Even as she thought it, accepted it, and knew it for the truth, she still hesitated to lose this *thing* she had with Elan.

And for tonight, she didn't have to. She could hold on tight, and he'd never know that it was far, far more than just sex for her now. A small smile curved her lips as she peeled her long gloves down from her elbows and draped them over the back of a chair. Elan's breath brushed her ear as he bent forward to lick a hot path up the side of her neck. Need fisted inside her, and she was wet and aching in moments. She wanted him so much. Reaching for the zipper at the side of her dress, she paused when she heard a sound between a low groan and a purr. "I'll do that, baby."

"Then do it." She lowered her hands and let her head drop forward. A shiver ran down her skin when his fingers skimmed over her bare shoulders.

He placed a soft kiss to the back of her neck, his breath moving the tiny hairs there. Another shiver quaked through her. "I'm glad that's over."

Tilting her head, she exposed her throat for him. He ran his tongue up the side of it, sucking gently. Her mouth parted and heat whipped through her. "I had fun."

"Good." She felt him smile against her neck. One of his strong arms wrapped around her, pulling her to him. She could feel the hard arc of his cock through their clothing and her pussy clenched in anticipation. Her sex grew damper. She needed to be filled by him.

Her heart pounded and she could feel each beat under her skin. He bit her throat lightly, making her jolt. "I want you, Elan."

A rough shudder shook him and his hand curved around the side of her waist, sliding up her ribs until he reached the top of her zipper. Grasping the tab, he pulled it down slowly and cool air brushed over her bare skin. His other hand moved up to dip into her bodice, running a teasing finger between her nipple and the cloth. She gasped, arching into his touch. The backless gown meant she hadn't been able to wear a bra, and his fingers rasped against her sensitized flesh.

He finished unfastening her dress and tugged until it dropped to the floor in a rush of crinkling satin. Scooping her off her feet, he lifted her out of the circle of fabric and carried her through the sitting room and into the bedroom.

The phone jangled beside his bed and she moaned. "Ah, *crap.*"

A sigh slid past her lips as he set her on her feet. Plucking the pins out of her hair to drop on his dresser, she kissed her nightly orgasm session goodbye. Someone needed the king for more than the pleasure of his hands and mouth and cock.

Elan scooped up the receiver, looking seriously put out, which was nice. "Hello?"

He paused for a moment, listening to whoever was on the other end of the line. An impatient noise erupted from him as he checked his watch. "Offices in Japan have closed for the day, and this isn't urgent, so we're not dealing with this tonight. Unless there's an actual emergency, I don't want to be disturbed again until morning, is that clear? Good."

And then he slammed the receiver down with enough force to make it jump when it landed. She startled at the sharp noise, but continued to stare at him as if he'd sprouted three heads. It was the first time she'd ever seen him grow impatient with anyone but her, and definitely the first time His Majesty had ever demanded anything for himself.

"What?" He shoved a hand through his hair, making it the slightly disheveled mane she liked so much. Shaking her head, she just smiled at him. His amber gaze slid down her body, heating as he took in her heels, thigh-high stockings, and lacy panties. "You are so beautiful."

"You make me feel beautiful." She stepped toward him until her breasts brushed his tuxedo jacket. "And I love it when you touch me."

A wicked chuckle rumbled up from his chest, and his hands snapped around her upper arms. "I'm going to do more than touch you, sweetheart."

It took her a moment to figure out what he was talking about, and she paused for just a moment too long—long enough to give him the opportunity to sit on the edge of the bed and flip her neatly over one knee.

She froze, every muscle in her body tightening as she braced her hands on his other knee. Her shoes fell off, leaving her in nothing but her stockings and underclothes. Her heart tripped. "Elan...you were just teasing me about the spanking, right?"

"No, *you* were teasing *me*. I was serious." His broad palm slid up the back of her calf, his fingertips swirling into the bend of her knee. Her hands bunched in the cloth covering his muscular thigh.

She swallowed. "I don't know if—"

"There's no one in this room but you and me, Rhiannon." His fingers played over the lace at the top of her stockings. "I would never hurt you. Trust me."

A breath came shuddering out of her. She expected ugly memories of Arkon beating her to come flooding back, and her tension doubled as she waited for the horrifying onslaught. Nothing happened. Her heart rate sped to a racing gallop, but her body slowly softened. This wasn't the same, was it? Elan would never hurt her the way Arkon had. She *trusted* Elan. There was no room for Arkon in her sexual play with Elan. It was just the two of them here, as he'd said. And that's when the excitement rippled through her and her breath sped to little pants. "Okay."

His claws made short work of her panties, tossing aside the scrap of fabric so his hand rested on her bare flesh. The first smack made her jolt in shock. It wasn't the pain that caught her off guard, but the dark ecstasy than flashed through her body and zinged straight to her pussy. He slapped her other cheek, alternating between the two globes as he peppered her ass with hard spanks. Each one made her sex clench, and the pleasure built to a fever pitch within her. "Elan!"

He pressed his palm to her burning flesh, increasing the ache between her legs. She could hear his lungs bellowing, and his cock was a rigid arc against her side. The growl of his voice flooded her mind. *»Are you all right? Do you want me to stop?«*

Wetness coated her sex, and a whimper broke from her throat, but she shook her head. "I need... Give me more."

*»Rhiannon.«* His groan was a beautiful sound. It spoke to how much this was affecting him—as much as it was affecting her. Then he resumed spanking her, harder than before, demanding more of her.

She undulated on his lap, lifting her ass into each stinging swat. The cloth of his pants felt rough against her flesh, rasping over her nipples as she clung to him. Pain became pleasure and pleasure became pain. She loved it, she wanted it because he gave it to her. No one else but him could ever do this to her. Tears welled in her eyes and slipped down her cheeks, short cries bursting from her open mouth. Each strike drove her closer to the edge of her ragged control.

Finally, she broke, her mind and voice crying out at once. *»Stop!«* "Stop, Elan!"

He froze, jerking her upright so that he could see her face. Terrified concern reflected in his eyes, but a flush of lust still ran under his skin. "Did I hurt you, Rhiannon?" He shook her shoulders when she didn't answer immediately. "Rhiannon!"

*»No, I'm fine.«*

He sagged with relief. "Why did you stop me, then?"

"I need you inside me or I'm going to die. It's an emergency."

A chuckle rippled out of him and he scooped her up onto the bed. He stood, flashing to a silver ball of light for just a moment to let his tux drop to the floor. Then he crawled onto the bed next to her, all hot naked skin, flexing muscles, and hard, pulsing cock. He rolled her to her side so he lay behind her, his rougher flesh burning against her punished buttocks. When he nudged her leg forward with his and entered her pussy from behind, the slide of his skin against hers only increased the sting.

Her breath hissed out at the whiplash of pleasure-pain. "This gives a whole new meaning to someone being a royal pain in the ass, you know?"

"All right, enough." Pulling almost all the way out of her sex, he thrust his cock into her hard, spanking his muscled belly against her flaming buttocks. "No more Simba or Lion King or royal pain."

"Oh, come on. At least give me Simba—it's cute." She squealed when he rolled his hips against her.

"No." He thrust deep and purred low in his belly.

Her breath whooshed from her lungs. "Oh, my God. Oh, my *God*, Elan!"

"No more king jokes, Rhiannon." He wrapped his arms around her, pinning her to his chest. Her sore ass was pressed flush against his groin, his cock buried deep inside her, and then he stopped thrusting. His heavy leg covered hers and kept her from moving too. Every last hormone in her body screamed in agonizing protest.

"Please let me come. Please, please, please." She wriggled and squirmed, but there was no breaking his grip unless she *wanted* to shift while he was inside her. She wanted to come so badly she could taste it, feel it shimmering just beyond her grasp.

He moved one hand to cup her breast, the other still locking her into place so she couldn't budge. One fingertip circled her areola, teasing her nipple until it was so tight she whimpered. Silver shimmered around his hand, and then a single claw raked over her sensitive flesh. She cried out, bucking against him as her pussy flooded with hot juices, and he tightened his hold. "Promise, Rhiannon. No more."

"I promise," she sobbed. "Now move your ass, Highness."

"It's Majesty for a king. Highness is for princes."

"Do I look like I care?" She shot a glance over her shoulder at him, catching the feral gleam in his amber eyes. It matched the wildness raging inside her. "I promised what you wanted me to promise. Let me come, damn it!"

His full lips curved in a wicked grin and he moved his leg, freeing hers. He ground into her, his skin reawakening the tingling nerve endings in her stinging buttocks. She kept her gaze pinned on his, wanting to see the lust overtake him the way it did her.

Excitement rippled through her, warm silver magic flickering around her hands until she was digging talons into his forearm. It was moments like this that scared her, when he looked at her in that hot, worshipful way, when the magic was easily within her control, blending with her perfectly, when every inch of her body was alive in a way that it had never been before. She loved it, and she knew she couldn't keep it.

His hips spanked against her backside as he moved, and she faced forward against it, closing her eyes to savor the slide of his hard dick in her wet sex, the chafe of his skin against her ass, the burn of pain and need. He fit her so exquisitely, in and out of bed. She'd never let anyone push her this far, this fast before, and she loved every minute of it. *Because* it was with Elan.

She was in so much trouble with him, and she loved that, too.

"I can't get enough of you." He groaned, his breath rushing in ragged pants against her ear. His palm squeezed her breast, his cock pistoning in and out of her in short, rough jabs.

God, he was hitting her just right. The stretch bordered on divine. She clenched her hands tighter on his arm, slamming her ass back into him until she thought she'd die of pleasure. He growled low in his throat, the lion about to break free. Her pussy flexed tight around him, hot tingles spreading down her limbs. She was so close. Then he seated himself deeper than he had before, rolling his hips to change the angle of his penetration, and came in hard jets inside her. It was more than enough to send her spiraling out of control, her sex fisting in rhythmic waves that made pinpricks of light explode behind her lids.

Arching into him, she let the need sweep her under, her mind whispering the truth to both of them. *»I can't get enough of you either, Elan. Don't stop. Don't ever stop.«*

# Chapter Thirteen

Elan took a hidden path down to a rocky cove near the palace. There was no beach here, no crowds gathered to sunbathe. Here, he wouldn't have to entertain the guests remaining from the night before. Here, he could unwind and think. It was often the place he went to escape and consider decisions that fell to him as king. Guilt stabbed through him as he realized his mind was not focused on untangling the political affairs of the Between, but on his personal involvement with one particular Between.

Rhiannon.

It always came back to her. She occupied more and more of his mind as the days went by. Even when she drove him mad, he wanted her near him. It made no sense whatsoever. They agreed on nothing, they had little in common, but somehow she still *fit* him. How, he didn't know, which only fascinated him more. Every moment with her was a surprise. He never knew what to expect, what she would say or do, and perhaps that was part of it. The woman was as likely to kick a man as she was to kiss him.

The lion in him couldn't resist the challenge to make her purr.

A small smile curved his lips. He'd respected her courage and passion from the first, but the weeks he'd spent with her made him see the compassion and sweetness just as clearly. He liked that. He liked everything about her. The way she wasn't afraid to confront him when she disagreed with him, the way she met his ardor with her own, the way she made him laugh. He'd had to work to remain focused on his duties. Normally, they consumed him, consumed his entire life. Until now, he'd welcomed that, felt it was right after what he'd done to his father. He didn't deserve the kind of freedoms most people did. He was bound to serve, to make up for what his actions had cost someone he loved dearly.

But what if he could have more? Whether he *deserved* it or not, could he reach out and take it anyway?

It was a foolish thought, and one he shouldn't allow himself. Rhiannon was leaving, and his life would regain its equilibrium and a sense of normalcy in short order.

The feline grace of his lion side made it an easy thing to maneuver down the steep incline to the water below and spring from boulder to boulder until he was surrounded by swirling waves. It was so peaceful here, just salt and sea. He dragged in a deep breath and let the tension ease from his shoulders.

Rhiannon's scent carried on the breeze, filling his lungs. She was close. He swiveled around and saw her standing on top of the sheer cliff on the northern side of the cove. Her red hair whipped in the wind, dancing like living flame.

His heart thumped hard, partially because just looking at her made him react, and partially because she was standing much too close to the edge of the cliff. The outcroppings had been known to give out under the weight of a person and most of this cove had jagged rocks just below the surface of the waves. He considered shouting or shoving a mental command to her to back up, but didn't want to risk startling her.

She spread her arms wide and rose to her tiptoes, bouncing lightly before she leapt over the edge. His breath froze in his lungs and his heart seized. Terror deeper than he'd ever known pumped through him. Adrenaline screamed through him to act, to *move*, but he couldn't get to her in time. He couldn't save her. It was just like his father. Too late. Too damned late to be of any use at all.

A flash of silver lit the water just before she would have plunged into the pounding surf. A falcon skimmed the surface of the waves where she had been, its wings making ripples where the tips touched water.

»*Rhiannon!*«

The bird jerked midair at his telepathic call before looping in a lazy circle until she flew toward him. The wing beats weren't entirely even, like a fledgling unused to flying, which was appropriate for the situation. She swooped down and he lifted his arm to catch her. Landing gently on his outstretched wrist, she was careful not to dig her talons into his flesh. He repressed the urge to strangle her for her recklessness. Instead, he stroked his fingers down the silky feathers under her jaw and she cooed and leaned into his touch. His heart hammered in his chest, fear still pumping adrenaline through his veins and making his hands shake.

His voice was little more than a guttural hiss. "Rhiannon, if I ever see you do anything like that again, I will—"

»*Do what?*« Her sharp tone echoed in his head. In a twist of silver light, she stood naked on the boulder with him, her hands planted on her hips. "Do what, Elan?"

"You jumped off a cliff!" And it made him angrier that, even in his rage, he swept a greedy, needy glance over her luscious nudity. He snarled.

Her eyebrows arched even as her eyes narrowed. "So? I shifted into a bird. Birds fly."

"And what if, in that moment, you settled on a less winged animal permanently?" A clawing agony shredded his soul at the mere thought. Rhiannon hurt. Rhiannon suffering. No more Rhiannon. God help him, he didn't think he could bear such a loss.

"I saw people jumping off that cliff yesterday and landing safely in the water below. Same time of day, same tide." She huffed an impatient breath. "I thought of that. I would have been fine."

The reasonableness of her voice and argument just enraged him further. Fear made ice of the blood in his veins and she was *reasoning* with him. He shook his head, lashing out. "You are impetuous and reckless with your safety. No wonder—"

He cut himself off, but it was too late.

"What? No wonder what?" A flush of fury rose to her pale cheeks, but her eyes flattened to hard emerald green. "Finish what you were going to say, *Your Majesty.*"

Swallowing, he tried to backpedal. "Rhian—"

"No wonder I was kidnapped? No wonder I was turned against my will?" Her flush deepened, her fingers clenching into fists at her sides. "I took a camping trip, Elan. Does that mean I deserved to be made into some kind of circus freak?"

He flinched, caught between anger at her and anger at himself. "So now we're freaks?"

"Not you." She slashed a hand through the air. "Me. I'm not even one kind of Between. He made me into some kind of extra special *freak.*"

"It's not him, it's *you.*" The look of betrayed hurt on her face rocked him back on his heels, and he realized how she would take what he'd said. "I didn't mean...it's your *soul* that makes you a certain kind of Between, Rhiannon."

"So I'm a freak right down to my soul." Tears rose in her eyes, and it was the first time he'd ever seen them from her. After all she'd been through that he was the one to put them there made his gut twist. A single tear escaped and she swiped it away impatiently. "That's me. A reckless, impetuous freak who deserved what she got."

He shook his head, wondering how the situation had spun out of control so fast. Then again, when it came to her, when did he ever have control? "You're putting words in my mouth. I never called you a freak."

"It doesn't matter. I'm out of here." She turned away, silver flickering around her limbs as she prepared to shift. She glanced back for a brief moment. "And just to make it official, Dr. Singh said that we'll have to register me as a poly-shifter. Some personalities are too mercurial to settle on one animal, so I'm *never* going to be a normal Between. If there is such a thing."

Then she was gone, shifting to the falcon again and soaring beyond his reach. It sent a chill of foreboding down his spine, and he squelched the reaction.

He sighed, suddenly weary as the adrenaline overloading his system finally crashed. Watching her plummet had scared him more than anything else ever had. What terrified him more was that his bone-deep fear showed him exactly how far he'd gone. In a span of weeks, he'd gone from contemplating having her killed to the mere thought of her being injured making him break into a cold sweat.

He understood that he'd craved her from the very first, but this was more than physical, more than sex.

He needed her.

He loved her.

God, help him. He *loved* her. What was he going to do about it?

P adding on silent lion's paws, he tracked her scent through her little house until he spotted her through the back window. She sat on the rear patio in one of his discarded T-shirts, her feet propped on the short, thick stucco wall that served as a railing. The patio overlooked a wild, craggy ravine that led down to the ocean. She held a glossy blue pottery mug of coffee in her hands, and he could smell the richness of it. He knew she had to sense him, but she didn't even spare him a glance when he nudged the screen door wide with his nose and slipped his feline body through the opening and out onto the terracotta tiles.

*» That's my shirt.«*

Her shoulder jerked in a shrug, her fingers tightening on the heavy coffee cup. Still, she didn't look at him. "You left it here."

He sighed, uncertain what to say to her after his earlier revelation, so many words crowding his mind that he couldn't get any of the right ones out. *»You're still angry.«*

"Wouldn't you be, in my place?" There was a catch of hurt in her voice that made his belly cramp and her laugh was a breathy sob of air. "Wait, don't answer that. You never get angry, except with me."

*»You're right.«* He dropped to his haunches beside her chair. She sat up straighter and let her feet fall away from the railing to rest on the floor as she leaned away from him. *»No one else affects me the way you do, Rhiannon. Only you.«*

Her startled gaze finally met his, her eyebrows arching. "Elan…"

*»At a loss for words? That's a first.«* He nuzzled the flesh of her thigh just below the hem of his shirt. Her breath caught at such a simple touch and her hand rose to bury in his mane. He loved the way she responded to him, even when he'd made her angry. It humbled him and it made him feel more powerful than sitting on any throne ever could.

Resting his chin on her knee, he searched her face. *»I was scared that you might be injured, but that's no excuse for what I said. I was out of line, and I'm sorry I hurt you.«*

Her lips twisted, but she set her coffee mug aside and looked at him. "You did hurt me."

*»I know. I'm sorry.«* More sorry than he could say when he saw a flicker of the pain in her eyes.

Sighing, she stroked her fingers through his mane. He leaned into her touch, loving how she petted him. "Don't do it again."

*»I won't.«* He shifted back into his human form, his cock already so hard and erect it was dripping. He placed a gentle kiss on her knee. Grasping the leg of her chair, he let it scrape along the tile floor as he turned it to face him. A small smile curled the corners of his mouth when he saw she wore nothing under the shirt. He licked his lips. "Let me make it up to you."

*»Elan, I don't think…«* She closed her eyes and squeezed her thighs together. It didn't disguise the lush scent of her desire. He swirled his tongue in a light circle on the inside of her thigh, just above her knee. He blew a stream of air over the damp skin and heard the breath catch in her throat.

He kissed, licked, and sucked her soft skin as he worked his way up her legs. Her fingers twisted in his hair until painful tingles rippled down his scalp. He nudged the shirt up until she was bared to the waist. The desperate little whimper that slipped from her made his cock throb. "P-please. I can't wait."

While it would have been fun to tease and torment her, to make her squirm, he found he couldn't wait either. He wanted her too much, wanted to feel some kind of connection with her. All he knew was what *he* felt, and he doubted he'd ever be able to say the words to her, to give someone else who knew they owned his heart the chance to leave him anyway. She wanted to go home, and he wanted her to have everything she desired. He wouldn't manipulate her further by playing on her emotions to convince her to stay with him. He didn't want her pity. All he could offer her was this.

He jerked her to the edge of the chair, forcing her legs wide with his shoulders. Then he caught the sweetness of her juices on his tongue as he licked her wet slit. *»Mmm, you taste so good.«*

*»Oh, God.«* She lifted her legs to hook them over the arms of the chair, spreading her thighs even wider for him. When he glanced up, her face was already flushed, her eyes shut tight, and her lips parted as she panted with need.

Closing his mouth around her clit, he sucked hard, and her hips shoved toward him. "Elan!"

He loved his name on her lips, the way she gave him everything and never held back her passionate responses. He worshipped her with his tongue, savored her scent, her taste, her every sigh. His cock throbbed with the need to come, but he focused on pleasuring her. She tugged on his hair impatiently and he smiled against her. So like his Rhiannon.

Slipping his palms down her thighs, he pulled the lips of her pussy apart and slid his tongue deep into her channel, thrusting until she lifted her hips off the chair in her need to get closer. When he pulled back and blew a cool breath on her hot, wet sex, she sobbed and begged in incoherent words and thoughts.

Running his tongue up her slick lips, he pumped two fingers into her pussy. She was so damn wet. He wanted to shove his cock into her until they were both wrung dry. He purred against her clit and she screamed, the high, thin sound echoing off the canyon walls beyond her house.

Her thighs tensed, her hips lifting as her pussy squeezed his thrusting fingers. He worked her hard, dragging her orgasm out as long as possible. She was sobbing and giggling when it was finally done, and his chest locked with emotions as he looked at her. He loved her so damn much, his heart fisted tight with emotion. He wished things didn't have to be this way, that *he* didn't have to be this way, that he could be a better man, but he wasn't.

"You're forgiven," she gasped.

A laugh exploded out of his tight throat. "Took you long enough."

The incensed look didn't gel with the hazy satisfaction in her gaze. "I came in under five minutes."

"I can do better." He scooped her up in his arms and turned for the house, groaning when her soft thigh brushed against his cock.

"Elan?" Her arms curled around his neck and she snuggled her nose into his throat as he walked toward her bedroom. He purred when her fingers slipped into his hair.

Depositing her on the bed, he tilted her chin up for a quick kiss. "Yes?"

"I love you." The words were so soft, if it weren't for his feline hearing, he might have missed them. Her lashes formed crescents against her pale cheeks as she looked away.

He sucked in a shocked breath, his heart slamming hard into his ribs. Of all the unexpected things she'd ever said, this was the most stunning. "*Rhiannon.*"

"I had to say it." Her green gaze met his, vulnerable and defiant at the same time.

Closing his eyes, he swallowed. Oh, God. It was the most amazing thing he'd ever felt, this deep wondrous *joy*. She loved him. And he loved her. The future had never looked so sweet as it stretched before him. "Rhiannon—"

"Look, I know...you don't feel the same way." Her lips shook and she pressed them together for a moment. "I know you probably think of me as this flighty, reckless little accidental Between, so you don't have to say anything. Whether you believe it or not, I'm a big girl and you don't have to let me down gently."

*Say it*, he ordered his brain. *Tell her you love her too.* "Rhiannon, I—"

A hard knock sounded on Rhiannon's screen door and he heard the metal bounce against the doorframe. Max's voice called loudly, "Elan, I am so sorry to interrupt, but you're needed in your office. There's a call from Sudan. There's been a development—"

"Right. Of course." His warring needs collided. He had to take this call now, it couldn't be delayed. A Between there was begging for asylum, and with the bargaining he'd been doing, he'd known things would come to a head soon. He cursed fate that it had to be now and felt the familiar rush of self-recrimination that he could begrudge helping one of his citizens gain their freedom.

"Happens every time." Rhiannon's smile formed, broke, and fell away. The sadness on her face nearly undid him. This was the life he could offer her. Always interrupted and put off for his duties. She deserved better than he could ever give her. His belly clenched and he knew beyond a shadow of a doubt that he should let her go. He'd never hated himself more.

"Elan!" Max shouted from the door. "Get the lead out, brother!"

Urgency swept through Elan—moments counted in this case. He bracketed her chin with his fingers and kissed her hard. "I'm sorry, sweetheart. Can we finish this discussion later?"

"It's okay. I said everything I needed to say."

He sighed, turned away from the only woman he would ever love, and shifted back into his lion form.

# Chapter Fourteen

E lan didn't come back that day. He also didn't show up the next morning. Rhiannon took a deep breath as the pain hit her chest again. She'd meant what she said—she didn't expect him to feel the same way she did, and she wasn't going to have a meltdown about it, but his lack of any real response was heartbreaking. She didn't regret telling him how she felt. The truth was what it was, and she wanted him to know. It wasn't in her to hide how she felt or pretend it wasn't there.

Who knew what he might have said if they hadn't been interrupted? Maybe he would have said they should see each other even after she went home. Maybe he would have let her down gently. She had no idea. The fact that he hadn't turned up since she'd dropped her little love bomb made her think it was probably going to be that last option whenever he got around to telling her. She tried to reassure herself that he'd been called away on an emergency and there was no telling how long it could have actually lasted. She'd been here long enough to understand how hectic his job could be. The platitudes rang hollowly in her mind. She knew he was the king and his people needed him, but he was also just a man and she was a woman who needed him, too.

A woman who needed him to need her back.

Her shoes scuffed the gravel path as she walked toward the gym. She'd given up waiting for Elan to come back because she was about to burst out of her skin. Patience had never been her strong suit and, after a sleepless night with far too many cups of coffee, a workout was probably the only thing that would distract her. She longed to clear her mind and let her body flow into the positions that were as familiar to her as breathing. Having people around while she did it would help. As she'd told Elan, she liked people.

Layers of smells assaulted her sensitive nose when she pulled open the heavy door to enter the gym. Flesh and old perspiration, which were typical of any gym, plus the more distinct scents of people she knew. A few of the King's Guard, Josh, Genesee, Max, and Kira were all there, though their signatures were scattered throughout the big building.

Wandering into the studio she usually used for yoga lessons, she found Max doing a martial arts routine. His muscular body sliced through the air with knifelike precision. Sweat gleamed on his well-toned chest, back, and arms. He really was a beautiful man, but he wasn't Elan.

A soft sigh slid out of her throat, and Max froze, his amber gaze—several shades paler than his brother's—cut to her. She straightened from the doorway and smiled. "I didn't mean to interrupt. I was just coming to work out myself."

His white teeth flashed in a grin. "No worries, honey. I interrupted you at a much worse time yesterday."

"I guess that makes us even, then."

"Not even close. The look in Elan's eyes when he walked out of your house was enough to gut a man." A mock-pained expression crossed his features. "Such a rough life when you have to do the wonderful, mighty, majestic king thing."

Tilting her head, she narrowed her eyes at him. His breathing was still a bit heavy and uneven from his workout, so she was unsure which part of that had been sarcastic and which had been serious. "Do you ever wish it had been you?"

"What, that I was king instead?" He wandered over to his gym bag and pulled out a towel to wipe the beads of perspiration off of his body.

She nodded.

"No way in hell." A sharp crack of laughter burst forth and his eyes twinkled with real amusement. He sobered a bit and met her gaze. "I like my job, and Elan is welcome to all the responsibility and bullshit that goes along with being king."

"You're proud of him." She could hear it in his tone when he spoke of his brother.

Nodding, he glanced away for a moment and she could sense more than see a subtle tension in his muscles. "Taking over after our dad wasn't easy on him, but he's done better than anyone else could have."

"Yeah, it's still hard on him." Their gazes met, an unspoken acknowledgment that they both knew about what had happened to the elder Delacourt. She dragged in a deep breath and offered up a light smile. "So, you've never been jealous of all the fame and power?"

Max finished toweling off, bent to stuff the terrycloth back in his bag, and came up with an old U.S. Marines T-shirt. "There's only one thing I've ever envied Elan for."

"What's that?"

He winced, good-natured chagrin filling his amber gaze. "Kira."

"Kira?"

His chin bobbed in a decisive nod. "She's been all about Elan since we were kids. Not as much since you came along, with Elan so obviously catching feels for you." He grinned and shrugged into the shirt. "I'm just glad he didn't listen to me about executing you."

"Executing me?" Rhiannon felt every ounce of blood drain from her face until her skin was cold and tingly. She couldn't have heard that right. Elan wouldn't—

"Yeah, because when you first got here you were all about calling in the reporters because people had a right to know what was going..." His voice trailed off when he finally got a good look at her face. "Shit, you didn't know about it, did you?"

She shook her head in choppy jerks. "No."

"I assumed if he was sleeping with you he'd have told—" He broke off and swallowed, his skin growing as pasty as she imagined hers was. His hand lifted in desperate placation. "It's just that Elan has always been the honest, upstanding one. I mean, when he could be. It's why he's king, why he's a *great* king."

Her ears began to buzz, and she swayed on her feet. A little laugh spilled from her throat. "Long live the king, and fuck anyone who gets in his way."

"Rhiannon, this is my fault." Max took a step toward her and she scrambled back, wanting nothing more than to escape. "I was the one who told him he should do it. For all I know, he never even intended to. Don't blame him for my big mouth because—"

"I think your big mouth has said quite enough, little brother." Elan's hands closed over her shoulders, and he turned her to face him. She stared up at him blankly. She hadn't even sensed his approach with the waves of shock rolling through her. His gaze cut to his brother. "Why don't you let me take it from here?"

She heard Max swallow hard and his voice dropped to a tortured, remorseful groan. "Elan, I am so—"

Elan shook his head. "Go. Now. Before I forget that you're my only family."

"Shit." Self-loathing filled the single word, and Max grabbed his gym bag, silently slipping out of the room.

And then they were alone. All her doubts twisted her tender emotions, and everything she felt for him came crumbling down around her. She jerked away from his hold on her and he let his hands wilt to his sides.

"Wow...and you said you'd never hurt me. You said I should *trust* you. And I *did*."

"Rhiannon, please." Something almost desperate filled that deep amber gaze.

"You were going to have me killed?" Tears flooded her eyes and a horrible sob caught in her throat. "After all that happened, after all I'd been through, you were just going to take my life."

The pain on his face was nothing to what was tearing through her. "One person's life isn't more valuable than all my people's."

She rocked back on her heels. "What could I possibly have done that would—"

"You existed, you survived, you were living proof of what Arkon had done to innocent humans." His face went carefully and completely blank the way it had when he'd pushed her away after he'd told her about his father. Well, the man knew how to let a girl know she wasn't welcome. Her hands balled at her sides. She wanted nothing more than to hurt him the way she was hurting.

"So, I was just evidence?"

His chin dipped in a short, tight nod. "Yes."

"Why didn't you kill me then?" Her numb lips continued moving, but the chill had spread through her entire body until she had to wrap her arms around herself to keep from shivering.

A tiny crack appeared in the mask his face had become. His gaze moved over her face, looking for what, she didn't know and didn't care. "I thought...I hoped you would decide not to expose others to danger by telling the human authorities."

"So, what?" She swallowed back a sob. "You sent Kira to make friends with me so I'd be more sympathetic? Was fucking me part of the plan, Elan?"

If she thought his features had gone blank before, now they were carved of solid stone. "Yes."

Stunned shock robbed her of breath—hot, burning shame following in its wake. Tears rose in her eyes, but she fiercely blinked them back. She couldn't stop the humiliated heat from searing her cheeks. She shook her head, wishing she could clear it of this whole horrible incident. "Wow, I am...far more pathetic than I knew. I hope you enjoyed it. It must have been so satisfying to hear me tell you how I loved you. Were you and Max and Kira laughing about how easy it was?"

A rough sound burst from his throat and he took a step toward her. "Caring isn't something to scorn, baby."

"I don't ever want to see you again." She held up her hand when he started to speak. "I'm not going to tell anyone what happened with Arkon. You win. Your plan worked. I don't want to see any Between harmed because of what one bad Between did." A tear slid down her face. "You win. I lose."

Slipping past him, she was grateful he didn't try to touch her as she left. Her breath sounded ragged in her own ears, her heart a slow, hard thudding in her chest. Her steps picked up speed as she went until she burst out of the gym at a dead run. She had to escape, had to get away from this, from *him*. He'd used her, manipulated something that was sweet and precious and rare for her. And for him, it had been nothing more than business mixed with a pity fuck.

Her stomach heaving, she stumbled and fell to her knees beside the gravel walkway as her breakfast came back up. The soft grass prickled her palms and rocks bit into her shins as her stomach turned again. Her hand shook as she swiped at her mouth and climbed back to her feet. She could see the ocean at the bottom of the hill, boats sailing in and out of the marina. Her gaze fell to the yacht that she'd spent a day on with Elan. The beautiful, passionate memory mocked her.

She had to leave the island. It was time to go home.

Turning resolutely for the palace, she marched down the path and into the main kitchen. She flipped open the box of keys next to the door and plucked out the set Elan had used when he'd taken her out on his boat. Refusing to let herself think about it, to care, she walked out of the house, across the great lawn, down the gravel drive, and onto the dock. Her footsteps echoed on the wood, ringing like death knells.

God, she was such an *idiot*. It was one thing for a king to take an interest in her sexually, but anything else? Doubtful. She was, as she'd told him that first day, just a regular girl. And she was okay with that.

But she'd told him she *loved* him. The humiliation of that burned through her like acid. That was the difference between them, wasn't it? She'd cared, she'd been honest the entire time. He hadn't. He'd taken what she offered and given nothing but sex in return. She'd never expected happily ever after with him, but she'd at least thought they'd become friends over the last few weeks.

"Idiot, idiot, *idiot*."

Mimicking what she'd seen Elan do, she untied the yacht from the dock and climbed onto the familiar wooden deck. She'd loved every minute of that day with him. A tear escaped to streak down her cheek, but she wiped it away and ruthlessly refused to let herself cry. She was getting out of here while the getting was good.

She slid the key into the ignition and turned the boat on. It purred to life and she spun the wheel to take herself out into open water and toward the mainland. What she'd do once she got there, she didn't know, but her soul was sliced to ribbons and bleeding. She just couldn't stay here another moment. Not with Elan's betrayal so fresh in her mind.

When she heard feet pounding down the dock at a sprint, she kicked the boat into a higher gear. No one was going to keep her from leaving without violence and destruction—which is how this whole fiasco started, but she was hardly pleased by the cyclical nature of her life lately.

The footsteps came to an abrupt halt and she assumed whoever was following her had stopped at the edge of the dock.

She was wrong.

A huge thump rocked the boat as someone landed on the deck. She whipped around to see Kira calmly dusting herself off. Her gaze met Rhiannon's. "This time Elan *did* tell me to come see you."

She choked on something that might have been a scream and might have been a hysterical laugh. "I'm not going back."

"I know. Elan asked me to see that you made it to the mainland and on to a plane to Portland safely." She pointed to the wheel in Rhiannon's hands. "Not that you're doing a bad job, but I have more experience with open water than you do. Do you mind?"

For a split second she thought about saying no, but it was futile and she knew it. First, Kira could kick her ass with her hands tied behind her back. Second, she had no idea how to get to a dock at the mainland. Third, she had no clue how she was going to pay for a cab to get to the airport, let alone a plane ticket, without Kira's help. It wasn't as if she had her wallet with her. Arkon hadn't thought to bring it with them when he kidnapped her, and she hadn't needed it since she arrived.

She leaned to one side so that Kira could take the wheel and turned to look out over the Pacific once she'd been relieved of captaincy. She deliberately did *not* look back at San Amaro Island. There was nothing left for her there.

Kira's gaze burned into the back of Rhiannon's neck, raising the fine hairs there with superhuman awareness. "So, Max opened his fat head and now you're leaving Elan. I'm going to give both of them a beating when I get back. Though I think they're both going to be doing a good job of kicking their own asses for the next little while."

"You could shoot them, too." Rhiannon's shoulder dipped in a nonchalant shrug. "I wouldn't mind."

Kira hummed in consideration. "Assassinating the king while serving as a King's Guard is probably not a good career move."

"You don't have to *kill* them." Rhiannon's lips twitched in the ghost of a smile. "Just, you know, make them bleed a little."

"I'll look into it for you." Kira sighed. "Max always knows how to say what you least want to hear. How the hell did he get on that topic anyway?"

Rhiannon wasn't even going to ask how the arctic fox-shifter knew. Everyone knew, apparently. She was the only one who was too stupid to figure it out. "He mentioned that you were into Elan until I showed up. I'm sorry if I messed that up for you. I'm sure it was a temporary bout of duty-related insanity."

"Max is an enormous idiot." The fox clipped out the words, fury lacing her low tone. "I am not interested in Elan and I never have been."

Something in the way she spoke made the gears click into place in Rhiannon's mind. "You want Max."

"Yeah." A breathy laugh escaped the other woman. "Don't ask me why, because at the moment, I couldn't tell you."

"Men suck."

"Amen, sister."

They were silent for a long time, the mainland fast approaching by the time Kira spoke again. "Rhiannon?"

"Yeah?"

"You have every right to be pissed at Max for opening his mouth and at Elan for *not* opening his, but I've known the king his whole life, and I've never seen him act like he does when he's around you. I don't think it was all business all the time, no matter what he told himself or you." She swallowed and stared at the marina ahead of them. "I just...thought you deserved to know. I thought he was serious enough that I asked him last night to be put on your detail."

"But you're second in command of the elite King's Guard." Rhiannon shook her head, confused. "Why would you do that?"

"Because I asked to be made the head of the *Queen's* Guard." The fox-shifter finally met her gaze. "I wanted to make sure you had a qualified Guard so that some jackass doesn't do anything to you."

"The Qu—" She couldn't even make herself finish the word. A harsh laugh rasped her throat. Kira had thought Elan wanted to marry a woman he'd considered having killed. Another giggle slid out, tears welling up with the sound. She desperately tried to push the thought away, to make this something to laugh about rather than sob until she'd emptied all the pain out. Forcing a weak smile, she watched the docks grow closer, willing them to arrive faster. "I'm not sure I'm okay with a friend of mine throwing herself in front of a bullet for me or even between me and another lunatic."

"You have to know I would anyway." Kira bumped Rhiannon's shoulder with hers. "Even if I wasn't on your Guard."

She sighed. "You're a pain in the ass, you know that, right?"

"So are you. I think it's why we get along."

Rhiannon laughed, and the sound was almost natural. It would get easier once she got back to her normal life. It had to.

# CHAPTER FIFTEEN

Her business was flourishing. It was now *the* health club for Between in Portland to belong to. Elan had made a phone call to see that his people knew they'd be more than welcomed there. What he couldn't throw Delacourt family money at, he could make happen as Between king. He always got what he wanted in the end.

Except Rhiannon. Her, he couldn't have. So, he satisfied himself by making certain she had whatever she wanted. Her business, her old life, her normalcy. She seemed to be settling in well, and he was glad for her, but it didn't make the empty ache in his soul abate. He missed her. Missed her smile, her laugh, her company. Her touch.

He sighed and scrubbed a hand down his face. He stood on the dock, staring at his private yacht. Kira had taken Rhiannon to the mainland in this very vessel three weeks ago today. The huge fluorescent lights from the marina stung his tired eyes. It was well after midnight, and he'd sent his staff home hours ago, but he'd been unable to sleep. Again. Every one of his duties grated on his nerves lately, things that had never bothered him before, things he knew he'd never notice if Rhiannon was here. He was on edge and there wasn't a damn thing he could do about it.

His gut clenched again as he recalled the look on her face when she'd asked him if he was going to have her killed. She'd cried. She'd been ashamed of her love for him. Nothing had ever felt so good in his life, and he'd made her feel ashamed just by being who and what he was. It made him sick to his stomach to even think about it.

Maybe that was the real lesson he should have learned when his father died. He killed the things he loved just by being himself.

All he knew was that he would regret hurting her for the rest of his life. She was the only one who was innocent in all this, and had nothing but grief to show for it.

His brother's deep voice sounded from behind him. "You should go after her and apologize. She'd forgive you—she's nice like that."

Elan didn't bother to turn around. "Go. Away."

"I can't." Max sighed, the sound heavy with regret. "You're miserable and it's painful to watch."

"Try living it." Elan laughed, but there was no amusement in it.

"I don't want to." His brother grabbed his shoulder, spun him around, and shook him hard. "I want you to *do* something about it."

He seriously considered punching his brother, would have if he thought it would relieve even an ounce of the pain and grief and loss that had pounded through him every moment of every day since Rhiannon had run away. Instead he told the ugly, bald truth. "I don't deserve her."

Max shook him again, his fists balling in Elan's shirt. "You're wrong, brother. We both know what this is really about. Don't let Dad's inability to cope be your downfall. Don't let his selfishness ruin your life. You're ten times the king and one hundred times the man he ever dreamed of being. You had something good going with Rhiannon, and you can get it back if you just *try*."

Elan gaped at his brother. They had never, ever spoken of their father since the day he'd taken his own life. While Max had told him he didn't blame him, Elan hadn't really believed him. Not that day or any of the days that had followed in the last ten years. A part of him had been too afraid to bring it up, too afraid to have his fears confirmed. But he could see in Max's fierce expression that he meant every word he was saying. The tiny crack that Rhiannon had made in the heavy stone of guilt that had lain on Elan's shoulders for years widened until it crumbled away to nothing. He pulled in a deep breath, feeling lighter than he had in years. Perhaps it was Rhiannon's comfort or Max's conviction or something Elan had known all along, but he finally faced the fact that he had *wanted* to be king, and that desire wasn't what took his father's throne or his life. His father had been selfish, he had been hungry for glory, and he had thrown everything away because he couldn't handle the truth about himself and his actions. Elan didn't want to be that kind of man. He forced himself to admit that he'd been hiding behind his guilt to protect himself from more suffering and loss. He loved his work, even if he'd hated himself for loving it, and he loved Rhiannon, even if he'd never given voice to the feeling.

Max finished driving his point home. "Believe that you should have something that's good and *yours* in your life, man. And even if you can't do that, then ask yourself if *she* wants you, then who cares what *you* deserve? Don't you think she should have what she wants?"

"She doesn't want me." Elan closed his eyes for a moment, whatever tiny spark of hope Max's speech had ignited extinguishing under a heavy dousing of reality. "Not anymore."

"She loves you. She'll forgive you if you ask." The red wolf let him go and fished in his pocket for something. When he held out his hand, the keys to the yacht were nestled in his palm—the same keys Elan had used to give both Rhiannon and him a day he'd never forget, the same keys Rhiannon had taken to leave him. "So, go ask."

G od, she was miserable.

The worst part was, Rhiannon had gotten exactly what she'd told everyone she wanted all along. Her old life back.

Thanks to Elan, she could control the Between magic within her, so everything was back to...normal. Same job, same house, same routines. While she'd lost some club members, there were remarkably few people who cared that she was Between now. It seemed the old adage was true—those who mattered didn't mind, and those who minded didn't matter. She'd only had to deal with the avidly curious when her silver spiral mark was bared during her classes and workouts. It was uncomfortable at first, but she'd gotten used to it.

Going to see the families of her dead friends had been harder than she'd ever imagined, but she'd needed to give them closure as much as she needed to have some for herself. Their questions were painful because she'd had to lie about most of what had happened and pretend ignorance over the rest. Guilt as fierce as any she'd seen on Elan or Genesee's faces ate at Rhiannon, but the families had been grateful for whatever information she could give them. Elan's people had already fed them enough lies to satisfy them, and all she had to do was go along with the story. It was the hardest thing she'd ever done, and even though she knew it was the best thing for all concerned, she'd choked on every word.

But she'd gotten through it, and she didn't regret it. She'd needed to give them whatever scant comfort she could. Her friends deserved for her to do that much.

That was weeks ago, and now she did her best to live one day at a time and find her balance again. She focused on all the things that had defined her life before she'd ever heard the name Arkon—her friends and her business. It seemed the rumor that a Between owned a gym in Portland had gotten around, and more trickled in to join every day. They never mentioned what they were to anyone, but she sensed it, and they knew it.

Because of them, her business was more than good. Her friends were good. So, for the most part, everything was...fine.

And she hated every minute of it.

Which only made her angrier at Elan. She hated that she missed him, hated that he hadn't been there to hold her when she'd talked to the families, hated that she wanted his comfort, hated that her body craved his touch, hated that she woke up every night aching with need. All she'd been was an opportunity for him, and she couldn't get him out of her system. She considered calling up one of her old standby guys, but couldn't make herself do it. Her stomach turned and her hands shook in reaction whenever she reached for the phone.

The only bright spot in her life was regular contact with Kira and Genesee. They e-mailed, they called, they texted, they checked in as though they were concerned about her. She shook herself. No, they *were* concerned about her. She refused to believe they were as mercenary as Elan had been. Even then, she had no idea how much, if anything, they were telling him about what she told them. She had no idea if he cared enough to ask about her.

She flopped down on her couch and stared at the stacks of laundry she'd just folded on her coffee table. Then she dropped her face into her hands. Everything had fallen apart. She'd thought that picking up the pieces of her life would be enough, but none of the pieces fit together anymore. Nothing worked. Caught between who she used to be and who she'd become when she was on San Amaro, she was just...*Between*.

A sob tangled with a laugh in her throat. Just what Elan had wanted her to be, and now she was more alone than she had ever been in her life. If she took a deep enough breath, she could almost smell him on the air, *feel* him haunting her every moment. She'd given him everything, and now, there was no escaping.

What was she going to do? She was going to start crawling the walls soon. There wasn't enough meditation or yoga to relax or wear herself out so she could forget. She wasn't even sure she wanted to forget. And that was the real problem, wasn't it?

"Pathetic." She knotted her fingers in her hair.

"I know exactly what you mean."

Her head jerked up and she stared at the man standing on the other side of her screen door. "Elan."

"May I come in?"

She jerked to her feet, wavering as she stared at him. "I thought…I'd just imagined smelling you."

"I'm glad." A smile tinged with irony took shape on his beautiful face. "I almost wondered why you didn't try to run before I ever saw you."

"Just *saw* me?" She stepped around the coffee table so that there was nothing between her and the door, but she didn't move closer than that. "You weren't even going to aim for talking to me?"

He pressed his palms to the screen and sighed tiredly. Dark circles lay under his eyes and deep grooves bracketed his mouth. "I'll take what I can get."

Shoving her shaking hands in her pockets, she tried for a laugh. It was a sad attempt at best. "This from the king who can get whatever he wants, whenever he wants."

"It doesn't get *you*, does it?" His fingers shimmered with silver before his claws rasped against the metal mesh. "If I hadn't been king, I never would have been in a situation where I'd even consider hurting you."

"Killing me, you mean?" But she was honest enough with herself to admit that even despite the pain he'd caused her, if any other man had been king—if his *father* had still been king—he probably wouldn't have hesitated in having her assassinated. What was worse was that knowing the Between as she did now, she could understand why. That just didn't make it hurt less that *Elan* had considered executing *her*. It was worse because she loved him, but it also made her understand his perspective. God, it just sucked.

"Yeah, killing you." She heard him swallow, but his voice emerged a grating plea. "May I come in?"

Hunching her shoulders, she gave in to the desire to move closer to him until she stood only a few inches from the door, until she could *almost* touch him. "What are you doing here, Elan?"

"I had to see you." His amber gaze moved over her face in a worshipful caress.

"You've seen me." Her fingers fisted in her pockets as she fought with herself to open the door and scratch his eyes out or kiss him senseless. She wasn't sure which option was more appealing at the moment. "Now what?"

"Let me in."

She huffed out a little laugh. "I did that once. It didn't go well for me."

He closed his eyes, pain contorting his features. "I am...so sorry, Rhiannon." The screen groaned as he pressed his palms tighter to the weave. "That's what I came for. It wasn't enough to know that you were all right because I had people watching, or even enough to wrench reluctant updates from Kira and Genesee. I had to see that you were all right myself. I had to look you in the eyes when I apologized."

His gaze locked on hers, and she could feel his sincerity rolling toward her in waves.

"I didn't make you love me as part of some scheme. I wanted you to get to know a few Between well enough not to want to hurt all of us the way you'd been hurt by Arkon. It's true, I saw how you cared for people and I used it against you. I used it *for* my people. I'm sorry that hurt you."

Her mouth twisted in a smile. "If it didn't work, and I still wanted to tell the first reporter I found, you'd have had me killed anyway."

"That was the original plan, yeah." He sighed. "By the end? I don't think I could have given that order, I really don't. You had to know I trusted you not to do that when I let you near my guests at the state dinner." He searched her face. "I wanted you to trust me, too, but I didn't set out to make you fall in love with me. That was a gift. *You* were a gift."

Lifting her hands, she laid them against his on the screen. Moisture filled in her vision. "Elan ..."

"Rhiannon, let me in. Please." His fingertips stroked over hers. "I will regret how I hurt you forever, but let me apologize."

"Isn't that what you're doing?" She shook her head, blinking away the tears. "I don't want to be like your father, Elan. I don't want to be something you regret. I don't want your guilt or your pity."

He nodded, his hands still stroking hers through the mesh, his gaze steady and sure. "I'll always regret that my father and I parted on such awful terms, and that I was too young and headstrong to even try to have some peace between us, but I know now that there's nothing I could have done to save him. He was selfish to the end, and that is *not* my fault."

It was the most un-Elan thing he'd ever said, and it made her heart squeeze when she saw the shadows of self-loathing had dissipated from his eyes. "What brought about that revelation?"

"Max." A short laugh whooshed out of him. "He basically said I should get over it and get over myself, quit hiding behind my guilt, and hold on to the good things in my life, even if I'm not entirely convinced I deserve them. He said I should come here and tell you I love you back." Elan swallowed audibly, his gaze open and honest and more vulnerable than he'd ever let himself be with her. "Please let me in, baby. I promise it'll go better for you this time. I promise you'll never regret giving me a second chance."

A tear streaked down her cheek and her heart thumped hard against her ribs. This was everything she'd ever wanted him to say, to feel, and then some. She doubted anyone would ever see this kind of openness from him but her, and she loved him even more for giving it to her. For realizing she needed him to trust her with it, even if she hadn't yet realized it herself. She swallowed hard, struggling to keep up with the rapid-fire changes of the last few minutes. God, she needed him to hold her so much. She dropped her hands from the door and covered her mouth to smother a sob.

His claws scrabbled against the screen. "Rhiannon, please. Please open the door. I don't want to have to rip through it, but I can't just stand here and watch you cry."

Reaching one hand out, she flipped open the lock. He was inside and had her in his embrace before she could even blink. She collapsed against him, all the pain and loneliness and sorrow of the last few weeks exploding forth. Scooping her up in his arms, he walked down the hall until he found her bedroom. He laid her down on the soft comforter and crawled onto the mattress beside her, pulling her against his chest.

Still, she couldn't stop crying. The dam had burst and there was no halting the force of emotions that spilled out. He rubbed her back and crooned softly in her ear. She balled her hands in his shirt, clinging to him as the storm ripped through her. "Elan."

"Shh. Shh. I'm sorry, honey. I love you. I love you so much. Shh. I'm sorry." He kept up the quiet litany, spreading gentle kisses all over her face, stroking his fingers through her hair, sliding his palm over her shoulders and down her spine in soothing circles until her sobs slowed to harsh, hiccupping breaths.

"I love you, too." Burying her face against his chest, she breathed in the warm scent of him. It was so comforting, tears misted her eyes again. She blinked them back. "What will we do now?"

He hesitated. "I don't know. I just know I don't want to live without you."

"I don't want to live without you either." She lifted her palm and cupped his strong jaw.

"Never leave me again, Rhiannon." The words tumbled out in a rush, but he leaned into her touch, deep relief and gratitude flashing in his gaze. "Fight with me, smack me upside the head, I don't care. Just don't leave."

A giggle bubbled out and she pressed her forehead against his. "Well, don't contemplate my death again and it'll be a good place to start."

"I discussed the possibility *once* with my brother. *He* started the conversation, not me. I never even came close to giving the order." He sighed and rolled his forehead against hers as he shook his head. A little grin curled up one side of his lips. "I'm never going to live that down, am I?"

"Nope." She brushed her lips over his, not quite a kiss, but enough to make his breath catch. "Not even if we're together for another fifty years. I will be rubbing your big old lion nose in it. Just to keep you human, you know? You don't want to get *too* powerful-species rulerish."

His grin widened to something joyful and lighter than she'd ever witnessed from him. "Is 'rulerish' even a word?"

"Do you really want to make this a grammar lesson?" She poked him in the ribs and he jolted back with a startled laugh. "You're *ticklish*?"

Fiendish delight wound through her and she pounced on him, tickling every part of him she could reach. He dissolved into protesting chuckles and took advantage of the opportunity to touch her as much as she was touching him. Somehow it became a wrestling match for her clothing and his, until they were both breathless and laughing. His naked skin rubbing against hers stoked the embers of desire that always flamed out of control with him. Tears pricked at her eyes as she realized how she'd given up on ever having this again. Her body was more than ready to make up for lost time, and she could feel how wet and swollen her sex had grown as her need took over. When he'd finally managed to rip the last of their clothing away, he wrapped his arms around her, rolled her underneath him, and landed between her thighs. She gasped when he surged heavily into her pussy. He purred, nudging even deeper inside her. "Yes, I'm ticklish. It's a closely guarded royal secret."

"I can see how we wouldn't want that kind of delicate information getting out." She curled her hands over his wide shoulders and grinned up at him.

His handsome face sobered as he stared down at her. "You really forgive me?"

"Yes." She ran her foot up and down the back of his leg.

"I love you." His voice was so reverent, it was almost painful to hear.

"I know." And she did. He would never have come here, never have left behind his duties as king for even a day, if he didn't. Joy unfurled inside her, growing and spreading until it touched every part of her. "Isn't it awesome?"

Doing an absolutely perfect imitation of Mel Brooks, he gave her a cocky grin and said, "It's good to be the king."

She laughed and he kissed her. She moaned into his mouth, lifting herself into his touch. She'd missed him so much, craved him so deeply. He worked his long cock inside her in slow, shallow strokes. Her need was too sharp to wait. It had been weeks since his hands and mouth and cock had moved over her and in her. She dug her nails into his hard pecs.

"Hurry," she gasped.

"Maybe." He grinned, grinding his pelvis against her clit and rubbing his cock inside her aching pussy, but not with enough force to create the kind of hectic friction she craved. "Maybe we should savor this a little longer."

"I said *hurry*." She wrapped her legs around him, bucking hard enough to flip him over onto his back. His eyes popped wide as she sank down on his dick, filling herself with all of him in a bold stroke that left no room for teasing. She winked at him. "Yoga builds core muscles. You should try it."

He laughed and groaned as he arched into her, his hands bracketing her hips and pulling her tight against the base of his cock with each of her downward movements. Splaying her hands on his muscular chest, she flicked her nails over his nipples. She grinned when they tightened for her, and the grin widened when he hissed.

She stopped moving for a moment and he growled a protest, his claws digging into her hips. Leaning down, she swirled her tongue over one flat brown nipple and squeezed her sex around his at the same time. His body bowed in reflex and she had to clamp her knees on his flanks not to fall off. "Elan!"

"Rhiannon!" His voice echoed hers with just the right amount of surprise and censure.

Giggling, she ground her hips down, changing the angle of his penetration. He broke into a rough purr beneath her, his amber eyes gleaming with pleasure as he watched her move on his cock. Lust flushed his golden skin, and his hands helped her along.

She pushed them both to the very edge of their endurance, speeding up and slowing down when they got too close to orgasm. She didn't want to come without him, and she didn't want this to end too soon. Fast or slow, it didn't matter, it was so good that pleasure rippled through her with every single movement of his big cock inside her.

One of his palms rose to cup her breast, scraping the edge of his claws softly against her nipple before he rolled it between his fingertips.

"Elan," she breathed. Her head fell back on her neck and flames streaked through her, searing her flesh. It was too perfect—she couldn't hold out any longer.

She clenched her sex tight around his dick and he groaned, the sound a desperate plea for sanity. She could relate. This was madness—and it was so good, she wanted more. And she could have more. She could have forever with him. A sob caught in her throat as she let that beautiful revelation sink in. Her pussy pulsed with every movement of his cock within her, tingles spreading down her limbs. She was so close. "Say it again, Elan."

"I love you, sweetheart. I'll always love you—" his hand dropped from her breast, dove between her thighs, and found her clit "—always need you." He touched her sensitive flesh in quick, hard flicks. "Always treasure every moment I get to have with you." His words as much as his actions tumbled her over the edge. *I love you, Rhiannon.*

"Oh, my God. *Yes.* I love you." She gasped and rode him harder, faster. "I love you so much, Elan."

The sound he made was like a volcano erupting, and she watched him lose every shred of control the way she'd always wanted. His hands bit into her hips, claws scoring her flesh, forcing her down to the base of his cock with each unforgiving, almost-brutal thrust. The light in his eyes was feral and feverish as he slammed inside her, but the punishing rhythm only sent waves of deep contractions thrumming through her pussy.

His big body bowed between her thighs, locking tight as he reached orgasm. The rumbling lion's roar echoed in her room as he gave over to the animalistic side of his nature. His fluids pumped into her, filling her while she shuddered around him.

She laughed because it was amazing, and he grinned up at her, baring long, curved fangs. Ignoring those, she leaned forward and offered him her mouth. He took it, kissing her thoroughly, his fangs nipping lightly at her lips. He cradled the back of her head, holding her in place while he wound his other arm around her waist and rolled them until they lay on their sides facing each other. Retracting his fangs, he licked his way between her lips.

He pulled her leg over his thigh and surged deep inside her. She gasped and ripped her mouth away. "Again?"

"You can't be shocked by now that I'm completely insatiable when it comes to you." A grin that was part wicked and part chagrined crossed his handsome features. "I'll never be able to get enough, never be able to pleasure you often enough, but I see it as my duty as a king to see that my subjects are *fully* satisfied. I take my duties very seriously, you know."

A smile so wide it hurt creased her cheeks. "I've heard that about the Between king, but as wonderful as he is, it's just Elan that I want."

His eyes were suspiciously damp as he ran a finger over her bottom lip. "I don't know what I did to deserve you, but it must have been really, really good."

"I know what you mean." Her fingers threaded into his silky dark hair. "Now, stop overthinking it and kiss me."

He laughed and gave her exactly what she wanted.

# TAKEN BETWEEN

## THE BETWEEN, BOOK 2

## CRYSTAL JORDAN

CJ BOOKS

# Chapter One

I t was time to put up or shut up.

A spurt of adrenaline flooded Kira's veins, and she felt a feral smile pull at her lips. Her fangs pricked at her flesh, and she ran her tongue down one long canine to the wicked point.

The arctic fox within her easily caught the scent of the man she wanted. He was a Between, like her. A shape-shifter. Max Delacourt. The rich scent of human male edged with the animalistic scent of a red wolf. It was a smell she knew as well as her own, one she'd craved for far too long.

She was through waiting. Tonight, she would have him.

A low moan sounded through the door she stood guard beside, and she smoothed her expression into a professional mask. If anyone knew how to wear a professional mask, it was her—she'd learned from her butler father. No one could poker face like a butler born and bred in England.

Kira's replacement turned a corner in the hallway to walk toward the royal suite. The Between king and his fiancée had been closeted inside for the seven hours since Rhiannon had returned to the palace. Kira had to work to smother a smile. King Elan hadn't been able to hide his impatience to have Rhiannon back on the island nation of San Amaro.

He'd barely managed to slam the door in his Guards' faces before the carnal sounds of mating began filtering into the hall.

In many ways, it was a relief to have Rhiannon here instead of running her health club in Oregon. The stubborn woman had insisted she didn't need to be followed around by security guards if she wasn't royalty yet, so Kira had had to arrange for more covert means to assure the future queen's safety. As second-in-command of the King's Guard, Kira had been pulling double duty for months, taking care of her normal job assignment, plus handling her unspoken position as the head of the future Queen's Guard.

With all the details of her business tied up and the wedding the next day, Rhiannon was on San Amaro to stay. Finally. The only person happier about that than Elan was Kira. No more juggling jobs for her. No more pretending. She was openly in charge of Rhiannon's security detail, which would officially become the Queen's Guard after the wedding ceremony.

"Everything okay?" Her replacement for the next guard rotation stopped in front of her, his face serious.

They both froze when a pleasured female's scream echoed out of the king's suite. Using every one of the skills she'd learned at her father's knee, Kira cleared her throat. "Yes. Everything's going just fine."

"So it seems," the man quipped, a faint grin on his face.

Kira clapped him on the shoulder as she headed down the hallway. "Enjoy your evening. Or something."

He snorted, and she glanced back to see him settling into place beside the door. Good.

Pushing open a side door, she stepped out into the cool night. The sea breeze off the Pacific carried the hints of salt and open water, mixing with the deeper scents of garden blooms and the people on the island. Even as the familiar environment encouraged her to relax, she did an automatic sweep of the area to make sure the palace was as secure as it should be. They'd had several serious threats against the king's life recently—one in particular that had the entire Guard on alert—and it paid to be cautious. More than that, old habits died hard, and she'd been a cop for the LAPD before she joined Elan's Guard when he became king.

It had been a crazy time for the Between. The former king had outed their kind to the human population just before he died, which left Elan scrambling to protect the rights of Between all over the world. His family had owned San Amaro, an island off the coast of southern California, and the United States annexed the land as a sovereign nation for the half-animal shifters.

Elan had done a better job for their people than his father, Phillip, ever had. Good riddance to the old bastard.

The hot smell of Max swirled through the air, scattering her thoughts. She automatically moved in that direction. It was like a Lorelei, that scent. Calling to her, tempting her, taunting her. Her heartbeat quickened, blood throbbing in her veins as her body readied itself for what she had in mind. Yes. All she needed now was Max.

"Oh my God, Josh. Why can't you just—" The sentence ended in a frustrated feline hiss.

Kira rounded a corner of the building and winced.

Lord help her, *these* two.

# CHAPTER TWO

L ord help her, *these* two.

Genesee Arkon and Josh Singh stared back at Kira, a frozen tableau where no one knew what the hell to say.

Kira sighed, slapped her raging hormones down, and tried to figure out how to extricate herself from a situation she wanted nothing to do with.

Genesee was the king's right-hand woman, and she looked utterly mortified. She pushed her long blond hair behind her ear and fiddled with her earring. Kira didn't want to make things worse, so she focused on the man beside her.

"What's up, Doc?"

Josh was the Between doctor on San Amaro. He was probably the most beautiful man she'd ever seen—he was half-Indian, with perfectly proportioned features and soulful dark eyes, and muscular enough to have the male-attracted half of the population salivating. He couldn't come anywhere near the attractiveness of Max, but objectively, he was better looking.

The anger and sexual tension between Josh and Genesee was a palpable thing, but that was nothing new. In his quiet way, Josh had been steadfastly pursuing Genesee for years, though she insisted they were only friends.

Kira thought that was complete bullshit, but Genesee had very valid reasons for avoiding a romantic relationship with the good doctor. Few of which had anything to do with Josh himself.

"Nothing's up, Kira. Thank you for asking." The doctor's voice was as mellow as always, but a muscle twitched in his cheek.

"You all right, Gen?" While Kira wanted to get back to her plans for the evening, she wasn't about to abandon a friend if she needed help.

"Yeah, I'm fine." The blonde met Kira's gaze briefly, letting her know she was serious. Clasping and unclasping her hands in front of her, she looked anywhere but at Josh. "Um...I still have some work to do before the wedding tomorrow though."

An irritated bearlike grunt escaped Josh, revealing the ursine within him. "I'll walk you back to your office."

"No, thank you."

"We haven't finished our conversation."

Genesee's gaze flickered from human blue to feline gold, showing a brief flash of the lynx that lurked just below the surface. For a second, Kira thought she'd start hissing again, but the other woman kept a death grip on her temper. "I think we've said all we need to say for one evening, don't you?"

The doctor's tight expression eased into ruefulness. "I haven't gotten to say half of what I wanted to, sweetheart."

"Please don't." Genesee swallowed audibly.

This time, his tone was gentle. "I'll walk you back to your office."

Pressing her lips together, her chin dipped in a short nod.

"Okay, then. I'm off. I'll see you both in the morning." Kira's feet crunched on the gravel path as she made to skirt around them. If she wasn't needed here, then she didn't want to witness any more of their not-quite-lover's quarrel.

She needed to find Max.

His laughter jerked her around, and she watched him step through an open door, another man just behind him. Barrett Granger, who was taking over as second-in-command of the King's Guard. Both men were tall and broad-shouldered, with Max a dark foil to Barrett's blondness and peridot eyes. Those pale green eyes lit when he looked at Genesee, and he offered her a flirtatious grin.

A noise that was pure jealousy rent the air as Josh took in the interaction. Genesee's gaze shot between the two men, a flush highlighting her cheeks.

There was a mess with the potential to be even more tangled than hers. Kira had thought she had it bad wanting her boss, but at least she didn't have two guys playing tug-of-war. And Max wasn't her boss anymore, was he? Not as of Rhiannon's return. He was the head of the King's Guard, and she was in charge of the Queen's Guard. That feral smile twisted Kira's lips again. Now all she had to do was get rid of the love triangle and everything would be perfect.

Watching Max's long, lean body move as he prowled the pathway around the palace did nothing to cool her off. She couldn't look away, her body heating with every step he took toward her. His dark hair ruffled in the breeze, his gold eyes glinting in the light from the lampposts. His white teeth flashed when he smiled, and her heart rate bumped up a notch. Her nipples tightened and she felt her skin sensitize.

She didn't bother glancing away from Max when she spoke. "Josh, weren't you going to escort Genesee to her office?"

"Yes, I was," he replied, cupping the other woman's elbow and drawing her away.

"I'll walk with you." Barrett easily fell into step beside them. "I'm headed that direction anyway."

Barrett shot Kira a grin as he passed, the evil twinkle in his peridot eyes telling her he might just be jerking Josh's and Genesee's chains. Why, Kira didn't know, but Barrett was a cat-shifter, and they liked to mess with people for fun sometimes. She rolled her eyes at him but made no comment. The trio moved away in awkward silence.

That left Kira alone with Max, just as she'd intended.

Max arched his eyebrows, a flirtatious grin playing over his full lips. "Well, now that you have me all to yourself, what will you do with me?"

Anything she wanted.

The fox within her writhed with the need to mate, to fuck, to burn off the craving that she'd had to keep in check for so many years. But the fetters were off now. Her father would be horrified at her desire to fraternize with her betters, but she pushed the thought away.

Right now, she was about to take a big, juicy bite of forbidden fruit.

Yum.

She startled when a leonine roar shattered the quiet night, her hand going reflexively to the weapon holstered at her hip. Max crossed his arms, his smile widening with mockery. "Jumpy, aren't we? Sounds like the lion king is having a nice reunion."

As if she cared. She shrugged and fought the urge to drag him to the ground. "Your brother always enjoys himself with Rhiannon. Maybe that's why he's marrying her."

His grin fell away and his gaze sharpened, zeroing in on her face. "Are you okay with all this?"

She blinked. "Why wouldn't I be?"

Then realization hit. Oh. Right. Max thought she had a jones for Elan, and she hadn't corrected that misconception for him over the years. She might even have done a few things to encourage it. The more incentive he had had to keep his distance, the safer it had been for her.

Despite being the ranking officer in the King's Guard, Max was still a freaking *prince*, and Kira's father had been his father's butler. She might have played with Max and Elan as a child, but her father and theirs had made it very clear she would never be the equal of a Delacourt. She was a servant's kid, and her father had expected her to be a servant as well. He'd been pissed as hell that she'd gone off to be a cop. Then she'd returned to San Amaro to serve the king. She might do it with a gun instead of a serving tray, but a servant was a servant. Too bad her father hadn't lived to see his wish come true.

Max had ditched all the trappings of royalty and joined the Marines when he turned eighteen, but when he came back to command the Guard after his brother's coronation, he'd still had to deal with being a prince. Which had made him not only royalty, but her superior officer.

Off-limits on every possible level.

Until today.

An impatient growl spilled from his throat. "Damn it, Kira. You have to talk to someone about this, and who else do you have? Genesee is Elan's assistant and Rhiannon is his *fiancée*. Who does that leave?"

"Barrett? Or Josh?"

Max's growl turned into a sound of feral jealousy, and Kira fought a grin. She liked him possessive—far more than she should. He jerked a thumb at his chest. "You'll talk to *me*."

"You're not my boss anymore, Max." She folded her arms over her chest, and his gaze dropped to her breasts. Excellent. "I don't have to follow your orders."

His eyes narrowed as they refocused on her face. "I have never held that over you, and you know it."

"I know." She sighed and dropped her arms. This was definitely *not* how she'd planned for the night to go. And standing around to listen to more of his brother's sexual antics wouldn't get things back on track. Spinning on her heel, she started down the path toward her small bungalow. He'd follow her. He was far too tenacious not to.

His boots crunched on the gravel as he drew even with her and matched her stride. Years of working together and decades of being friends made the silence between them companionable. Or as companionable as it could be when the arctic fox inside her reared its animalistic head to demand she touch and take. Her breathing sped, drawing that intoxicating male scent into her lungs. Her skin prickled with the body heat he gave off.

She wanted more.

She'd wanted more since she was barely old enough to be interested in boys, but the three years between their ages had been insurmountable then. That, and the fact that her father wouldn't have stood for her consorting with a prince. But, she had to see what it was like. Just this once.

The warm glow of her porch light came into view and Max followed her up to the wide veranda. Before she reached the door, he wrapped his long fingers around her bicep and pulled her around to face him. He waved his free hand between them, his expression uncharacteristically earnest. "All bullshit aside, Kira, you can talk to me about this. We're friends, and I'm here if you need me."

"I do need you." The words were out of her mouth before she could call them back. She watched his golden eyes widen with startled confusion, but it was too late now. The relentless tension that had wound tighter and tighter for years snapped within her.

Finally.

She reached out, planted her hands on his chest, and shoved. He stumbled back until he sprawled in a big wicker chair on her porch. She came down on top of him, straddling his thighs. Stiffening beneath her, his mouth fell open in utter shock. She flashed a grin, shoved her fingers in his silky hair, and hauled his face up until there was only a hairsbreadth distance between their lips. "You have no idea how much I *need* you, Max. You. Not Elan. Never Elan. Try to keep up, okay?"

Then she kissed him.

Finally, finally. Oh, Lord. *Finally.*

He groaned, his hands clamping down on her hips. She wasn't sure if it was to hold her close or to keep her from moving closer, but she didn't care. Sliding her tongue between his lips, she let the flavor of him fill her mouth. God, he tasted good. A helpless moan wrenched up from inside her. So long. She'd waited so long to touch him, taste him. Her fingers splayed over his muscular chest, slipping down until she could circle one of his nipples through his shirt. It tightened for her, and she hummed in appreciation against his lips.

A choking sound came from him. He jerked her forward until her sex came into full, hot contact with his. A few layers of cloth separated her from exactly what she wanted. She whimpered at the steely length of him pressing against her. Her hips arched, and she twisted to get even nearer. His tongue shoved into her mouth and his claws shredded her skirt.

Time seemed to leap forward so fast it left her mind spinning and the only thing to hold onto was Max. His claws scraped up the outside of her thighs, almost painfully, but not quite. Goose bumps exploded over her skin, and her nipples hardened with the intensity of her arousal. Her tongue dueled with his, their movements rough, fangs nipping at each other's lips, each struggling for control of the kiss.

He made quick work of her panties, slicing through the cotton before flicking her clit with the tip of one deadly talon. She bit his lower lip hard, her body jolting in response. Her pussy drenched in a hot rush, her hips driving forward in a carnal rhythm that was as natural as breathing. His claws retracted, and his long fingers glided between her slick lips to tease her entrance.

But he didn't penetrate her. He just coaxed more moisture out of her until she snarled against his mouth. The tension within her twisted tighter, pushing her past bearing. Her pussy fisted on nothing, once, twice. Pulling his bottom lip between her teeth, she nipped his flesh with her fangs. Shivers raced through her, and her skin felt aflame. Even his almost-gentle touch was enough to have her teetering on the edge. She could *feel* an orgasm shimmering just beyond her grasp.

She broke the kiss and threw her head back. He used the opportunity to suck her nipple into his hot mouth, biting her through her clothing. Her hands fisted in his hair, holding him closer. "Max! Max, I need..."

» *This?*« His telepathic voice was an intimate, throaty rasp. His thumb flicked over her clit, his other fingers shoved deep inside her.

It was more than enough to send her screaming over the edge. Her body froze, every muscle within her clenching tight, and then her hips jerked frantically as wave after wave of climax exploded through her.

He released her nipple and leaned back in the chair to watch her ride out her orgasm on his thrusting fingers. The cool sea breeze on her wet flesh made her shiver. A small smile tilted up the corners of his kiss-swollen mouth. Last shudders rippled through her body before she slumped against him, gasping for breath.

Lust flushed his face, drew the flesh taut across his sharp cheekbones. "I want you."

She dropped her forehead to his, stroking her fingers down his biceps. There was no way she was stopping. She *had* to know what it was like. "Yes. Hurry."

Something hot and feral flashed in his gaze at her words. His fangs bared when he smiled. She grinned back, grabbed the bottom of his shirt, and wrenched it out of the waistband of his pants. He lifted his arms to allow her to yank the garment over his head. Then her hands were on his naked chest.

A muscle in his jaw twitched, but he let her touch him all she wanted. Claws scoring into the arms of the chair, his grip went white-knuckled the longer she petted his flesh. He choked when she pinched his small, brown nipples. His golden gaze burned into her while he panted. A quick burst of power filled her, and her heart hammered as renewed passion ratcheted up inside her.

She skimmed her fingertips down the sculpted planes of his torso. Well-defined pecs led to the ridges of his abs. His stomach sucked in when she circled his navel and a chuckle burst out of him.

"Ticklish? Really?" Devilish delight filled her and she wiggled her fingers threateningly just over his skin.

He snorted. "Really. Quit teasing, Kira. I'm dying here. I need you."

Those words from his mouth made her insides seize in shock. Her breath caught and she swallowed hard. Something sweet bloomed in her chest, and she crushed it, locked it tight into the deepest corner of her soul. No. This was *physical* need, nothing more. She didn't want more. He was way out of her league.

Letting the air out of her lungs, she reached for his belt. Jerking the leather from the buckle, she opened it and his fly in rapid succession.

He shoved his hips up to meet her touch when she reached into his pants. He groaned, his chest bellowing with each rough breath. »*Please, Kira.*«

The soft skin over his hard shaft was irresistible. She stroked her fingers down the underside of his cock, pulling him free of his pants. Wrapping her hand around his dick, she pumped him fast and leaned forward to suck his earlobe into her mouth.

The sounds he made in response to her touch sent wetness pulsing into her sex. His big body jolted when she bit down on his ear, and a snarl ripped loose from his throat. She could all but hear the last tethers on his control snapping.

He let go of the chair and grabbed her hips, yanking her forward until their sexes aligned. She pushed down as he shoved upward, and they both groaned as he filled her to the limit.

Oh, God. If she hadn't been so damp, it might have hurt. He was so large. She clamped her hands on his shoulders, her pussy flexing around his cock as she worked to accommodate his girth. She could only be grateful they were both Between—there was no need to worry about disease or unwanted pregnancy—so condoms and birth control were unnecessary. All she had to consider was the exquisite sensation. He rocked himself against her, and the angle was perfect.

Rolling her hips with each movement he made, she increased her pleasure. His rich scent was all she could smell, his bare skin on hers was all she could feel, his low groans and the creak of the chair beneath them were all she could hear. Everything within her focused on this moment. With him.

His palm pressed to the middle of her back, arching her until he could suck on her nipple again. The fabric of her clothes frustrated her, but not enough to stop in order to get rid of the offending garments. Her hips rose and fell, her pussy stretched by his long cock. This was what she wanted, what she needed. Everything else was irrelevant.

Sinking his teeth into her soft flesh made her cry out in stunned ecstasy. Their movements became less fluid, more frantic. The drive to orgasm took over and they thrust and ground their bodies together in that one unstoppable urge.

»*Kira, I—*«

Anything he said was lost in the implosion that rocked her body. Her walls clenched tight on his cock, milking the length of him as she came harder than she ever had in her life. The intensity of it shook her, and every thrust of his dick inside her sent her spinning into oblivion once more. When it was over, her mind was blank and her body limp. She collapsed against his chest, and he cradled her close, the tenderness as shattering as everything else they'd done together that night.

A sense of unreality flooded her and she closed her eyes tight. Oh, God. It had been so good. Everything she'd ever fantasized about and more.

What the hell had she *done*?

# CHAPTER THREE

What the hell had he *done*?

It had been so good. Everything he'd ever fantasized about and more.

Thank God the wedding had gone off without a hitch, and Kira was in charge of security, because Max couldn't get his head in the game to save his life, let alone anyone else's. It was perhaps the only time he'd been grateful that his position as the king's brother took him away from his duties in the King's Guard.

Guests swirled around him, laughing and dancing. A small orchestra played, and he offered a reflexive smile to a passing diplomat. She was attractive, a woman he would normally have pursued for an evening of pleasure, but tonight he didn't give her a second glance. His gaze was drawn like a magnet to Kira. He swallowed hard. He'd imagined being with her for so long, but he'd never dreamed it would actually happen. Until last night, he'd thought Kira wanted *Elan*, not him. Not Max.

Sure, he'd flirted, he'd fantasized. Kira was beautiful, intelligent, and dangerous. Irresistible temptation. But he'd thought he was the only one tempted. They'd known each other their entire lives, and their relationship was as much rivalry as friendship. Even as children, he'd loved to make her react. He'd tug on her pigtails and she'd kick his shins.

It was Elan she got along with, Elan she'd come back to the island for. Not Max.

And last night had shattered everything he thought he knew about them. It scared him more than anything had in years. Not since the last woman he'd—

No. He slammed the door on that memory. Even the thought of comparing Kira to—

Stop. He shut down all emotion the way he had to any time he worked, buried it deep where it couldn't touch him. If sickness pooled in his belly, curdling into something painful enough to bring him to his knees, he ignored it.

He dragged in a deep breath, his heightened wolf senses filtering through the explosion of scents in the room. Humans, Betweens, perfume, sweat, sex, food, flowers. Taking it all in, he let his gaze rove the crowd, looking for problems. That was what he did, what he was. His job.

»*You're not on duty, little brother. Try to relax.*« Elan's hand clapped down on his shoulder, his mental voice holding only the mildest of rebukes.

»*I'm always on duty.*«

»*That's Kira's job tonight.*«

He shrugged his brother's hand away and shook his head. »*You hate these kinds of shindigs too.*«

»*It's my wedding. I'm making an exception.*«

»*Congratulations, Elan. You deserve every good thing that comes your way. And I'm not just saying that to practice for the toast later.*«

»*Shut up, Max!*« Elan's laughter rippled over the crowd, and bone-deep contentment radiated from the older man. Max refused to acknowledge the stab of envy that ripped through him. Elan and Rhiannon deserved their happiness—they'd had a rough road getting to it. Max had had his chance at that kind of happiness a long time before, and he'd blown it. There were no second shots for people who screwed up as badly as he had.

Still, his gaze went automatically to Kira, his hand tightening on the champagne flute.

She was beautiful. That was all he could think as he watched her move around the room with that controlled efficiency of hers.

Just looking at her turned him on.

Kira moved closer to his new sister-in-law, leaning in to hear what Rhiannon had to say. After a moment, both women burst into laughter. Most people's gazes would have been drawn to Rhiannon, with her dark red curls and rippling, infectious giggle, but Max couldn't take his eyes off of Kira. She was like contained fire, her bright eyes dancing in amusement, her short, white-blond hair catching the light overhead when her head tilted back in a throaty chuckle.

He smiled and didn't look away, even when Elan nudged his arm to get his attention. His brother's gaze followed his and he snorted. "They make quite the picture, don't they?"

"Yeah, they really do." Max took a deep draw of the expensive champagne.

"You should do something about that yen you have for her, little brother."

For once in his life, Max remained silent.

Elan waited a long beat, then shook his head. "Come on. I want to ask my wife to dance."

"You don't need me for that." The protest was more pro forma than anything else, because Max followed along obediently enough. Of course. He hadn't spoken to Kira since that morning, when they'd woken up in her bed together. A new threat against the queen had come in, and last-minute wedding details had sucked them both into their duties. He'd been at a run most of the day. It hadn't stopped him from thinking about how Kira had looked tousled from sleep, lips swollen from his kisses. He swallowed a curse as his cock reacted to the crystal clear memory.

"I'm more than ready to escape for the honeymoon, but you just can't pry Rhiannon away from a party." Elan maneuvered them through the crowd with the skill of a practiced politician.

"A few more hours, some royal ceremonial fun, and you'll be free." Max pitched his voice low, knowing the crowd would drown out his voice even from the sensitive ears of a Between. "Then the sexfest can begin."

Max and Kira would be serving as security for the royal couple during said sexfest. Isolated in a cabin for two weeks with a woman who'd gone up in flames in his arms. *That* thought made his cock harden to the point of pain. He was usually more than ready to get out after a one-night stand, but it was *Kira*. She was his friend, his colleague. Someone he respected. Someone who was already under his skin, which was somewhere he never let his lovers get. He'd learned that lesson the hard way.

Shit.

This was a complete disaster. What had he been thinking? What was she going to expect from him? With most women, he wouldn't even have to wonder. With Kira, he didn't have a clue. Like him, she wasn't one to have long-lasting relationships, which was his only consolation. He hated the gut-grinding sensation that accompanied the thought that she was just using him for sex. That should have been the perfect solution. They'd had an itch to scratch—it was scratched. End of story.

But for the first time in damn near forever, that wasn't enough. He wanted more. Just a little. He could handle that, couldn't he? It wasn't as if he could take back the night before, so what could a few more nights hurt?

He rolled his eyes at the justification. He was in such deep shit.

All he could do now was damage control.

Elan whisked Rhiannon away for a waltz, leaving Max gawping at Kira in silence. The first thing that blurted out of his mouth made him wince. "This ends when the honeymoon is over."

Her chin lifted, her eyes flashing dangerously. "Everyone knows you're the love 'em and leave 'em type, Delacourt. Did you really think I assumed it'd be different for me?"

He tried to reel his tongue back in and clean up the usual mess his mouth made. "I just...I wouldn't..."

"Your Highness," she said coolly, using the princely title he hated. His hackles rose, but before he could reply, she flapped her hand to encompass the royal military uniform he wore. "You couldn't pay me to live in your pomp and ceremony world. I'll take the servants' entrance over the red carpet any day."

Well, it was good to see that some things never changed. He was still pulling her pigtails and she was still kicking his shins.

"Jesus, Max." Rhiannon peered out of the French doors off Elan's office suite. A small army of men and women readied several helicopters for flight. "Is it really necessary to bring everyone in the Guard on the honeymoon?"

"Yes." The answer shot from both Kira's and Max's mouths at the same time. Max glanced over and met her eyes, knowing she was thinking about the recent threats they'd had against his brother's and sister-in-law's lives.

"I already lost this argument." Elan's lips twitched in a wry smile, and he forked his fingers through his hair. The disheveled mane made him look the part of the lion-shifter. The only lion-shifter among all the Between people, which was why he was king.

Max could only be thankful he wasn't the lion. He'd never craved that kind of power, much to his father's disappointment. If his father had had his way, Max would have been as invested in politics as he had always been, as Elan had always been. That wasn't Max and it never would be—it had taken finding a place for himself in the Marines, a place he finally flourished, to figure that out. Kira had once mocked him that the only things he took seriously were security and sex...and maybe just security.

She hadn't been far off.

Of course, his father would say that Max was suited to a military life. It was the only useful thing a born killer could do. His mother had died giving birth to him. As a boy, he'd killed a man who tried to assassinate his father. And those were the least of his crimes. Covering up the dark side of his nature with the carefree playboy prince had always served Max well.

»*Sir, we're ready for them.*« Barrett's voice filled his mind. His new executive officer. It was discomfiting after years of having Kira as his right hand.

His senses vibrated with pure carnal awareness as she brushed past him and joined Rhiannon at the door. Flicking her short hair away from her face, she glanced back at him and jerked her chin down to indicate they were good to go with escorting the royal couple to the helos. With all the wedding guests and extra hired help still on the island, security was even tighter than usual. It would be easier than ever for some nutjob to do something homicidally stupid. The king and queen went nowhere without an escort.

"Let's get this show on the road, ladies and gents." Max grinned and swept his arm toward the exit with a formal bow.

He straightened and shrugged tight shoulders. He couldn't wait to get out of this room. He hated it. Elan had redecorated the office when he had taken the throne, but Max would always remember the years of disappointed lectures, browbeating, and angry fights that made every moment in the room a misery for him as a youth. He could still see the faded marks his claws had made on the desk during a vicious beating his father had doled out. Max couldn't even recall what he'd done to deserve that particular punishment. He pushed away the unpleasant memories as he always did and focused on the task at hand.

Kira took point in the group of Guards that surrounded the king and queen, while Max brought up the rear. Ignoring the rough *thwap* of the helos' blades slicing through the air, he scanned the crowd of curious guests who had come to watch them take off, noting no one out of place. Good. The Guards worked like the well-oiled machines they were and in moments Max and Kira were in the helicopter with Elan and Rhiannon. The rest of the Guards would fill the other helos.

Kira studiously avoided his gaze on the flight to the palatial mountain cabin the Delacourt family owned. Max's great-grandfather had amassed quite a fortune before he became the Between king, and later generations of the family had kept up the entrepreneurial bent—something else Max's father had tried to push him into. If he couldn't be useful in politics, then he could at least do his duty to his family name and excel at business. Max snorted. His father had excelled at disappointment. Elan had had it worse though. The old man had seen Elan as a competitor, and Max had always suspected some part of their father had known his eldest son would make a far better ruler than he had the ability to be.

Max caught his brother passing Rhiannon a look, and he suspected the two were speaking telepathically. When his sister-in-law's gaze flicked between him and Kira, he knew what the topic of conversation was.

He sighed.

The arctic fox-shifter had said very little to him since he'd put his foot in it at the reception, and apparently the chill had been noticed. He had his doubts that their affair would continue at all, let alone for the extent of the honeymoon, and he had no one to blame except himself and his big mouth. Give him a military operation and he did fine. Put him in a personal situation and he said the wrong thing every time. One would think he'd have learned to keep his trap shut, but not so much.

He drew in a breath, and Kira's heady feminine scent punched through him. Lust rode him with a viciousness that shouldn't have surprised him, but the night before had only sharpened his craving for her. Damn his verbal ineptitude. The frustration ripping through him did nothing to cage the feral wolf-shifter within him that wanted to claim her.

The pilot raised his voice to be heard over the helo's blades. "Sixty seconds to landing."

They banked left and took a sweeping turn over forested peaks before the massive cabin and its collection of outbuildings came into view. The Delacourts owned most of the mountain, and Max had Guards crawling all over every inch of it. He wasn't taking any chances.

"I'll never get over how beautiful it is here," Rhiannon crowed with delight as they swooped closer, and Max couldn't help but grin. Her enthusiasm for anything and everything made her a lot of fun, and he knew his uptight brother needed some of that to loosen him up. Before Rhiannon, he'd been steadily working himself into the ground in a futile attempt to make up for their father's selfish suicidal death.

Such a waste of life, both their father's and Elan's.

"You said you didn't see the lake when you came up here camping with Kira and Genesee last month. You'll love it. We can go skinny-dipping." Elan winked at his new wife and she chortled in wicked glee.

Kira groaned. "Oh, Jesus. Just make sure it's on a shift where I'm *not* working."

"What do you have against skinny-dipping?" Rhiannon turned those wide green-gold eyes on the fox-shifter.

"Not a thing as long as it's me and some hot guy swimming around in the buff." Kira flicked her hair away from her face. "I don't, however, have any desire to watch the queen boinking her husband."

Elan arched one regal eyebrow. "Did you just refer to us having sex as *boinking*? We are most seriously displeased."

"And that was the royal *We*." Max leaned forward to open the door as they bumped down on the landing pad.

"Exactly. I have to learn that one." Rhiannon stuck her nose in the air. "*We* are most *seriously* displeased, peon."

Something about that made the smile fall from Kira's face, but Elan cracked up. He reached out an arm, looped it around Rhiannon's neck, and hauled her close for a quick kiss. "You're not supposed to *say* peon."

"Yeah, it's just implied." Max winked at them, hopped out, and led the way into the cabin. He'd have to find out what was wrong with Kira later—there was work to do now.

The team of Guards he'd sent ahead to secure the cabin and put in place a few extra security measures were waiting for them. Everything appeared to be in place, and a deep drag of air revealed no unfamiliar scents. Guards, household staff, his family, nearby wildlife. Good.

They'd be on U.S. soil for the next two weeks, in human territory, and while as a race humans were much weaker than Betweens, they also vastly outnumbered the shifters on the planet. His brother's position as the Between king made him a target for people who feared the magic of their species. Their father had announced the existence of the Between to the world over a decade ago, and ever since, Elan had been scrambling to clean up the mess. Some people didn't like how successful he'd been ensuring Betweens were treated as equals, as *humans*, even though the shifter magic in their blood made them half-animal.

One recent threat, in particular, made Max's hackles rise—a human started writing hate mail soon after Elan's engagement had been announced, and the messages vacillated between accusing Elan of brainwashing an innocent "sister of humanity" into the "Between beast cult" and castigating Rhiannon for being a blood traitor to her kind. The letters had become increasingly violent as the wedding approached, and the last one had been written in blood. Max didn't know who the human was, but the scent on the paper and envelopes had been the same. They'd had Josh run tests on the blood, and assuming the blood came from the writer, they knew he was male, with a high likelihood of having northern European ancestry, and he had no health problems that could be detected by blood test.

Just that morning, a wedding "gift" had arrived for Rhiannon—white roses dipped in crimson blood.

All mail was screened by Guards and royal staff, so his sister-in-law didn't know about the delivery and never would. That was why there were security measures in place: to keep the crazies from disrupting the lives of the royal family as much as possible.

The young woman who'd delivered the roses had had no idea what was in the florist's box, and his people were still trying to backtrack the order to a specific florist.

But the flowers carried the same human's scent as the letters, and the doctor had confirmed it was blood from the same person. The acrid stench had a hint of madness to it that said this was no prank. It lit up every one of Max's instincts.

» *You're thinking about the human who sent the roses.* «

Kira loped up the stairs to do a sweep of the upper floor. Of course she knew what he was thinking. She knew him better than anyone except his brother. But she didn't so much as glance at him as she passed. He answered her anyway, shielding his telepathy from everyone else. » *Yeah. I have a bad feeling about this one. I want us to be cautious while our men track this guy down.* «

» *We will. Catch him and be cautious.* « Her words were firm, left no room for doubt. Just like the woman herself.

She was right. He'd make sure of it. His only family's lives were at stake. The problem was, the letters had been sent from all over California, and it was a big-ass state with a lot of people in it. It didn't help that San Amaro was part of the Channel Islands off the coast of California. It was much too close for Max's comfort.

And they were in an isolated mountain cabin. In California. For two weeks.

Fucking fabulous.

# CHAPTER FOUR

"**G**ranger."

"Seaton." Barrett nodded to Kira as they entered the cabin's foyer from opposite sides, both turning towards the dining room and the tantalizing scent of dinner.

Calling it a cabin was a joke. Cabins didn't have *foyers*. It was a log mansion, really. When she, Rhiannon, and Genesee had come out here for a girls' weekend, they hadn't stayed in the cabin complex. They'd chosen their campsite miles from here—which was, of course, still Delacourt land because they owned half the damn mountain—and pitched a tent like the mere commoners they were. Or had been, what with Rhiannon going over to royal side.

That trip had been a personal test for Rhiannon, since she'd been kidnapped on an all-women camping trip the year before and turned into a Between against her will. The women she was with hadn't survived the experience, and Rhiannon still wrestled with survivor's guilt and a fear of isolated wilderness. She'd wanted to spend some time out in the forest again—something she used to love doing—to prove to herself that she *could*, that her now-dead kidnapper had no hold over her life, her choices.

Kira admired Rhiannon's strength and determination. She'd need it as their queen.

But thinking of that trip with her two best friends made Kira cast Barrett a sidelong glance. "So, feline, are you truly interested in Genesee or were you just messing with her mind last night?"

"Both." An utterly unrepentant grin curved his lips as they joined the queue for the buffet in the dining room. Like the rest of this log mansion, it was opulent, with an actual chandelier dangling from the ceiling.

"Granger." She narrowed her eyes in warning.

He held up his hands. "Look, if she was available, I'd be all over her. She's got an ass you could bounce quarters off of." One of his massive shoulders dipped in a shrug. "But she's not available, whether she wants to admit it or not. And I'm getting bored watching those two fumble around."

They made it to the front of the line and quickly served themselves with heaping portions of roast beef, potatoes, and mixed veggies, with huge brownies on the side for dessert. She resumed the conversation when they sat down across from each other at one of the long trestle tables. "So, as any bored cat would, you need to fuck shit up for entertainment."

Nodding, he forked a bite of potatoes into his mouth. "Exactly. I'm so glad you understand."

She just pinched the bridge of her nose.

He heaved an exasperated sigh. "Look, I'm *trying* to help a fellow feline out. Genesee might be an uptight, overgrown housecat—"

"You mean a lynx."

"That's what I just said," he insisted. "Anyway, she may not be one of the big cats, but I'm willing to lend a hand."

"By fucking with her."

An expressive shrug answered that. "It's what cats do."

"I haven't noticed King Elan breaking shit when he's bored."

"Yeah, but he's *the king*. Don't hold the rest of us to those standards."

Shaking her head, she sighed. "Do me a favor."

"Of course."

"Never help me out with my personal life. Go knock a coffee cup off the kitchen counter if you need entertainment."

"Are you sure?" He smirked. "Because I can tell Max—"

"Don't make me shoot you."

He reared back a bit. "You would actually shoot me, wouldn't you?"

"Without hesitation," she assured him, her voice going deadly soft. She'd still had Max's scent on her when the bloody rose delivery had dragged her out of bed to investigate. People had taken note of the way she smelled, of course. A Between wouldn't be able to help it. But it was one thing to notice that she'd slept with Max; it was another thing to gossip about it. She wouldn't stand for an iota of disrespect. Not of Max and not of her.

Those peridot eyes stared at her for a moment in that unblinking way that felines had, before his lips quirked in a grin. "Max is a lucky man."

She had no response for that and turned her attention to her meal. The last thing she wanted to talk about, *think* about, was Max and his stupid deadline. She knew he had already eaten and gone to do a perimeter check on the cabin complex, so at least she didn't have to see him while she figured out how she wanted to respond. Or not respond. She stabbed a green bean viciously and shoved it in her mouth.

Fortunately, more Guards sat down at the table with Barrett and her, and the conversation quickly turned to security matters. Kira had poached a few women from the King's Guard that Rhiannon liked working with—Min-ji, a hawk-shifter, and a pair of wise-cracking coyote sisters—but Kira was going to need to start interviewing more candidates to flesh out the Queen's Guard. It would be a challenge to build her team to meet her exacting standards while not making Rhiannon feel smothered by security, but Kira was more than up to the task.

She just had to make it through the royal honeymoon.

After finishing her brownie, she nodded her farewells, dropped her dishes off with the kitchen staff, and headed to her makeshift office to finish up some paperwork and review applicants for the Queen's Guard. An hour later, annoyed with her lack of focus, she gave up on work and opened the palace's web conferencing software on her laptop. If she couldn't work, she might as well phone a friend. Predictably, Genesee answered immediately. Because, of course, the little workaholic would still be at her desk, avoiding any hint of a social life.

"Hey, Kira." Genesee's image popped up on-screen, still wearing her bridesmaid's hairstyle, makeup, and gown. "Everything okay there? Did you need anything?"

"Everything's fine. Why are you still dressed for a wedding that ended hours ago?"

"Oh." She looked down at herself. "I came back to the office after you guys left to drop off some paperwork, checked my email, and then...just didn't leave."

Kira smirked. "Plus, it's a designer gown and you like expensive threads."

"Absolutely." The other woman's expression relaxed into a grin, flashing dimples that turned her from aloof and icy to utterly adorable in an instant. "Especially when the king and future queen insist on paying for them."

"There is that. Plus—"

An earsplitting leonine roar cut her off.

Genesee's eyebrows arched nearly to her hairline. "Did I just hear—"

"Yep." Kira sighed, since this was why she hadn't been able to focus. "That was the subtle sound of the lion king getting off."

Cringing a bit, Genesee replied, "I mean, I know they can be exuberant, but—"

"Girl, my bedroom is two doors down from their suite. My office is right underneath them." As if to prove her point, what sounded like heavy furniture scraping across the floor came from above her. She'd guess they'd accidentally moved the bed during their sexual gymnastics.

Genesee's mouth pursed. "If it were an apartment building, you'd be banging on the ceiling with a broom, yelling at them to keep it down."

"Definitely." Kira snorted a laugh. "Okay, new topic, because we cannot discuss our respective bosses' honeymoon boning."

"Right, because we are *professionals*."

This statement was punctuated by an ecstatic feminine scream overhead, and both women's shoulders shook in silent laughter.

"Yep. Professionals." She cleared her throat. "*So*, I spoke to Barrett about last night."

"Oh, man. I hope you didn't yell at him for hitting on me." Genesee waved a dismissive hand. "He's not really interested—he was just messing with Josh and me. Because he could."

"Felines are weird. Seriously, *weird*."

"It's what we do."

Kira rolled her eyes. "And, in fact, he would be interested in you if you were available, but you're not."

"I'm single," her friend insisted.

"He also said he was getting bored with watching you and Josh fumble around. So, he wanted to 'help a fellow feline out.'" Kira lifted her hands to put air quotes around the words.

Now it was Genesee's turn to roll her eyes. "I'm going to leave a partially dead animal on his pillow when he gets back. As a present."

"Of course you are. Because: felines."

"And for the millionth time, Josh and I are *just friends.*"

"But he's a friend you'd like to fuck. Over and over again, until neither of you can walk a straight line."

Her mouth hung open for a moment and then snapped closed. "I never said I wasn't attracted to him."

Snagging her bottle of water off the desk, Kira opened the cap to take a swig. "Does he know why he's been relegated to the friend zone?"

Genesee looked away, giving a small shake of her head. "He assumes it's because of my dad."

Genesee's father, Raymond, was a serial killer. He'd kidnapped Rhiannon and her friends, turned them into Betweens, and then tortured and murdered them one by one. Rhiannon had killed him in self-defense before the King's Guards been able to rescue her, and it still amazed Kira that Rhiannon and Genesee had managed to become friends under those circumstances. Or maybe not, considering how resilient both women were. They'd had to be to survive what Raymond had put them through.

But even resilient people had their weak spots.

"And you let Josh *keep* assuming that avoiding him is about Raymond." Since the topic had been broached, Kira decided to ask something she'd never dared to before, given how touchy Genesee was about her private life. "But it's not about the father you hated, is it? It's about the fiancé you loved."

Tears swam in Genesee's eyes, making her blue irises shimmer. "Yeah."

"I only met him in passing when I came home to visit my dad. He seemed...kind." Kira had known Genesee for almost as long as she'd known the Delacourts—after Raymond abandoned them, her mother came to San Amaro to work for the ferry company that shuttled people to and from the mainland—but they hadn't gotten close until Kira had moved back to the island as an adult. Genesee had been a girly-girl into fashion and makeup while Kira had been a tomboy jumping off cliffs into the Pacific with Max and Elan.

"Kind, yes." Genesee's head dropped back for a moment, a breathy laugh escaping her. "Omar was the exact opposite of my father. He was everything I wanted in a partner."

"He was a doctor."

She nodded, blinking back those tears, regaining her vaunted self-control. "He was finishing his residency to specialize as a Between general practitioner. He wanted to open a practice on San Amaro."

"He wanted the job that Josh has now." That was something Kira hadn't known. Even contemplating dating Josh probably made Genesee feel like she was trying to replace her first love with a carbon copy.

"Yes and no. Philip was our king then, so Omar didn't want to be the royal physician on top of being a GP the way Josh is."

"Who could blame him?" How or why fate had let Philip Delacourt be their king, Kira would never know.

"Exactly." Shaking her head, Genesee offered a smile tinged with bitterness. "You know what's really sad? The night before Omar died, I remember thinking that my life was pretty perfect. I had just started a great job doing event planning for the palace, I was going to marry an amazing man, my fabulous mom had started dating someone new and was *finally* moving on from my dad. Everything was falling into place." Tears welled again. "And then it all fell apart. Omar and my mom both died on the job. I lost everyone I loved inside of three months."

For Genesee's mom, that meant a boating accident, but how did a doctor die on the job? Kira hadn't been on the island when it happened, and her dad had had his theories, but very few details. "What happened to Omar, Gen?"

Genesee was quiet for a long moment, and Kira thought perhaps she wouldn't answer.

"Betweens can heal themselves of any injury when they shift forms, but they need to have the energy available to make the shift. An exhausted Between can't save themself."

This was basic information for Between, but Kira remained silent and refused to rush her friend. If this preamble helped Genesee sidle her way up to the truth, then Kira would give her the time she needed.

"We turn to pure energy for a moment when we shift forms, and our doctors learn to hold that energy state to help assess patients and to transfer energy, when needed, so that patients can shift forms and heal themselves." Genesee's throat worked for a moment, grief reflecting in her eyes. "But if a doctor transfers too much of their own energy to their patient, they won't have enough left to assume a solid form again."

Oh, Jesus. Kira's mouth felt too dry to speak, but she knew she had to say something. "We have our Guards take first responder training on energy transfer, and the thing the instructors hammer home is how to assess your own energy levels during the transfer, so that doesn't happen."

"I know." Genesee's hand came up to press to her throat. "But we push our limits when it's our loved ones involved, don't we?"

"Please tell me he didn't die saving you."

"His younger brother. He...fell down one of the canyons. When we found him, he was like a ragdoll, he'd broken so many bones." Tears were now slowly streaking down her cheeks. "Omar managed to give him enough energy to shift, but then..."

Kira pushed a hand through her hair, sympathy winding through her. Poor Omar. Poor Genesee. Poor Josh.

"You might consider telling Josh the truth. He'd understand." Then again, hadn't Kira let Max assume she was interested in Elan to keep him at arm's length?

When Genesee nodded, another tear escaped. "He would understand, and then he'd try to logic me out of my fears."

"Fear's not logical."

"Nope." She swiped impatiently at her cheeks. "He'd point out that he's a lot older than Omar was, more experienced. He knows his limits."

"All true."

"I can't be with another doctor, Kira, especially one as kind and selfless as Josh." Grabbing a tissue from the box on her desk, Genesee dabbed at her eyes. "I know energy transfer's an important skill for Between doctors. I know Josh needs to use that skill in his practice, that he does it all the time. But what if he misjudges someday? He'd just...disappear right in front of my eyes."

"Like Omar." Kira's chest squeezed tighter and tighter with every word that fell from her friend's lips, at the anguish on her expression, the bleakness, the hopelessness.

"Yes, like Omar." Blowing out a hard breath, Genesee shook her head. "I can't lose another one. I just...wouldn't survive it again."

"I'm sorry, Gen. I shouldn't have brought this up." Kira sighed, not even sure why she'd pushed this topic, other than that she needed to think about something—literally *anything*—other than the fact that the scent of sex permeated this part of the house, and it was putting her on edge.

"Josh and I can only ever be friends." Genesee's voice firmed and her chin lifted. "No matter how much I might want to tear off all his clothes and use him as my personal jungle gym."

A short laugh cracked from Kira's throat. So much for not thinking about sex. "That's a visual that will stick with me."

"You're welcome." Smoothing back a lock of golden hair that had dared to come loose from its pins, Genesee's eyes narrowed. "So, that's enough about me. Let's talk about you.

I heard you finally broke the seal with Max."

"You heard, huh?" The only way she'd know that is if someone investigating the bloody roses had blabbed. Which meant Kira might need to beat some Guards' asses. "Who did you hear that from?"

"Josh."

"Figures." She couldn't beat up a doctor.

"He said he was called in because another threat had arrived from the creepy guy who writes death threats in blood." Genesee had had the dubious honor of being in the mail room when a Guard opened the first letter from this guy. "Josh needed to confirm the blood was the same but gave me no other details. Except that you and Max showed up at the same time positively reeking of each other and sex funk."

"Josh said *sex funk*?"

"I'm paraphrasing."

Kira really, truly did not want to talk about Max. Or sex. Or sex with Max. So, she kept it brief. "Yes, we broke the seal. But then he said he only wants our affair to last until the end of the honeymoon."

Righteous anger flashed across her friend's face. "Well, fuck him. Or, rather, *don't* fuck him. If he wants more than a one-night stand, then he needs to discuss that with you like an adult. How dare he just dictate?"

A part of Kira felt a little better having her friend get irate on her behalf. "Well, he *is* a prince."

"No, he *is* being an ass. That's got nothing to do with his rank. Especially since, as of today, the two of you are *exactly the same rank*: head of a royal guard."

An uncomfortable pang hit Kira's chest at anyone saying she was the same rank as Max. Whatever else he might be, he was still a prince.

Genesee folded her arms, making her breasts swell over the top of her bodice. "Did you tell him to piss off?"

Kira rubbed a hand over her brow. "We were at the reception when he said it, so I kept it civil. Mostly."

The lynx-shifter tilted her head, her gaze turning speculative. "Are you going to agree to his terms?"

"No. Yes. Maybe? Damn it." Kira dropped her face into her palms. "The fuckfest going on upstairs is *not* helping me think straight."

"The animal inside us doesn't care about human thoughts or feelings. When the beast wants to rut..." Genesee gave a delicate shrug.

"Is that how it feels with Josh?"

"Every. Single. Day."

Kira sighed. Yeah, she knew that pain, and it was worse now that she'd actually had Max in her bed. "Have you considered making him a friend with occasional benefits?"

"More often than I care to admit." Genesee shook her head. "But it wouldn't be a casual affair for him, and I'd only end up hurting him. Friends don't do that to each other."

Fortunately, neither Max nor Kira had the same romantic inclination as the doctor, but that still didn't help Kira decide what to do about Max dictating the length of their affair.

"Speak of the devil," Genesee said, just as a light tapping sounded through the computer. "Come in, Josh."

In the corner of the screen, she saw the door behind Genesee open and the doctor's head poked through.

"Looks like he's there to escort you home. Good night, Gen."

"'Night, Kira. Keep me updated."

"No." She cut off Genesee's spurt of laughter when she disconnected the call.

# CHAPTER FIVE

Kira shut down her laptop and pushed to her feet, grunting in annoyance when a deep groan echoed overhead. Exiting her office, she went to check in on the Guards monitoring the security camera video feeds. Everything was quiet around the complex, so she could call it a night. At this point, she was more than ready to escape to her own room. Unlike the rest of the security staff, she and Max were sleeping in the main house instead of one of the equally plush outbuildings. As she'd said, her room was only two doors down from the honeymooners.

Part of her wished she were out with the rest of the Guards.

The pheromones in the house were thick enough to cut with a knife, which had distracted her while she was trying to focus on paperwork. Laughter floated over the balcony from the royal suite, along with the occasional moan and scream. She had done her best to block out the sounds and smells of sex and concentrate on her job, but the animal within her writhed at the less-than-subtle call to mating.

Then Max's scent mixed with that of lust, and sweat broke out across Kira's forehead. Shit.

The security shift changed, and she barely managed to exchange a few pleasantries with the Queen's Guard rotating off-duty before she all but fled to her room and shut the door.

Her teeth ground together, her fangs elongating. Max's demand that they only get it on for the duration of the honeymoon stung. It wasn't as if she'd expected anything long-term. Hell, she didn't *do* long-term. It complicated things, and she was always going to have to put her job before anything else. Emergencies cropped up, dangerous situations happened, things that others might find morally questionable were just part of her normal day. Most men didn't understand that, but she was damn good at what she did, and she wasn't going to apologize for it.

Still, she didn't put an expiration date on her affairs. They lasted as long as they were good, and then they ended. Max's cutoff pissed her off. They'd both enjoyed themselves, and they didn't work directly with each other anymore, so what was his problem?

If she didn't know him so well, she might think it had something to do with the disparity in their social positions. But Max and Elan had never treated her the way their father had, the way her father had always warned her they would. No, with Max, it was more likely that he'd get bored before the two weeks were up. When it came to women, the man had the attention span of a gnat. He hadn't been that way when they were younger, but he'd apparently picked up the any-port-in-a-storm habit in the Marines.

So. She had to decide what to do. Tell him to kiss her ass and call it a one-night stand. Or take him up on the next two weeks. Her pride chafed at both options. She might not do long-term, but she wasn't a one-night wonder either. A fox-like growl emerged from her throat. She was honest enough to admit what stuck in her craw most was that *she* wasn't the one getting to end things. She wasn't the one calling the shots.

But one phone call to Max's room and she could have him again. For the next two weeks. Fire exploded in her belly at the mere thought, her pussy drenching. Damn the chemistry they generated. Damn him for backing her into a corner.

"Damn, damn, *damn*."

Frustration burned through her. She doubted she would sleep, but the morning would come early and she needed to try. With impatient movements, she yanked off her clothes and tossed them aside before she flung herself into the wide bed. The cool mountain breeze ruffled the curtains at her window, teasing her nose with the scent of the pine, teasing her overheating body with its chill. Her nipples tightened and she had to squeeze her legs together and clench her jaw to keep from groaning. She was dying to have a man's hands on her skin. She was dying to have *Max's* hands on her skin. Again. One night hadn't been nearly enough to quench her thirst for him.

"Fuck," she hissed. Punching her pillow into a different shape, she tried to squirm into a more comfortable position. It was no use, and she knew it. The only position she wanted included a man between her thighs. One phone call and she could have that.

The thought was potent, addictive. Max could put his hands on her. She could have him if she wanted him, even for a little while.

His hands could be sliding over her skin instead of the damp mountain air. He could warm her to a boiling point, make her arch like a fox in heat, make her writhe and scream and forget everything but the feel of him moving over her and in her.

Her frustration peaked and battered at her already-tenuous control. Bunching her fingers in the sheets beneath her just made her claws punch holes in the fabric. She squirmed, but the movement increased her agony. All she could imagine was Max and her, and nothing between them but skin.

"Fuck," she sighed again, and gave in.

Closing her eyes, she allowed the picture of him to form. It came to her so sharp and clear that her breath caught. Dark hair that ruffled in the lazy wind, pale gold eyes that gleamed with bright laughter and dark lust. Lightness and shadow. It was one of the reasons she found him so fascinating.

She ran her hand down her stomach, wishing it were his hand, his fingers that dipped into the notch of her thighs and toyed with her clit. The tight bundle of nerves hardened and bloomed, and she could imagine the light rasp of calluses on his fingertips.

A shudder rippled through her body and she let herself go to the fantasy. The dream Max drew lazy circles around her clit, teasing her until she thought she'd die, but it was too good to rush so she moaned and let him play with her. Pressing her legs flat to the mattress, she opened herself for more of his touch and lifted her hips in offering.

He chuckled, the sound floating through her mind, wisping like smoke. Moving her hand, she shoved her fingers deep inside her sex. She gasped, her hips bucking hard to meet the sensuous touch. The lips of her pussy were slick with juices, the inner walls squeezing and releasing around those plunging digits.

"Oh, God," she groaned between gritted fangs.

In her mind, Max grinned wickedly, his fangs flashing. There was a glimmer of silver to his skin, the sign of shifting for a Between. The red wolf couldn't hide his feral side when he felt passionately about something, and she loved the wildness. She wanted it for herself, in her bed, all night long.

He rubbed his thumb across her clit, and she arched into the caress. Heat burst through her and tingles rippled over her skin. His free hand reached for her nipple, plucking and twisting the tight tip. Biting her lip, she strangled a sound of utter need. She barely noticed when her fangs scraped her skin, the coppery tang of blood slipping over her tongue. All the while, his fingers built a steady, maddening rhythm in her pussy, pushing her higher and higher.

She was soaking wet, her sex tightening on his fingers. Every movement, every breath, intensified her reaction. Her muscles shook in anticipation of orgasm.

More. That was all she could think. More, more, *more*. Even then, it wasn't enough. It wasn't real. But it was all she would allow herself, so she focused on the daydream and pushed reality away for just a few more seconds, working herself with her fingers, just as the Max in her fantasy was doing.

He licked his lips, watching her react to him. His eyes burned molten gold, and his gaze moved over her body, increasing her need. Her breathing sped to rapid pants, and sweat slid in rivulets down her skin. A gust of cold wind brushed over her damp flesh, raising goose bumps and making her shiver. He chuckled, and his fingers curled upward until he rubbed her G-spot. A low snarl broke from her and the sensations catapulted her past the point of no return. Her pussy fisted and she undulated on the sheets, the smooth fabric rough against her skin.

"I want you inside me." The words seemed to echo in the empty room around her, the desire so deep it couldn't be kept in.

He shook his head, his smile full of sin as he stroked her just right and sent her spinning into oblivion once more. Her sex gripped the fingers thrusting within her, shudders wracking her.

"*Max.*" The fantasy exploded into a million pieces, and her dream man dissipated, leaving her gasping and alone.

Until she opened her eyes and saw the real Max standing at the foot of her bed.

M ax had never been so hot in his life. Seeing Kira writhe and gasp his name, knowing the sexiest woman alive was fantasizing about him, made his cock harder than titanium. He wanted to join her in that wide bed and make her fantasies real, but he'd been frozen in place watching her.

"Kira…" His voice was little more than a rasp.

"What are you doing here?" She removed her hand from her sex and closed her legs, hiding those sleek lips from him, but not a hint of embarrassment or anger showed on her face.

He swallowed, barely able to pull his gaze away from her pale curves. His hands shook with the need to touch her, so he fisted his fingers to stop himself. "I picked the lock. I could smell your arousal. I had to come to you."

"And what will you do now that you're here?" Her tongue flicked out to lick her lower lip, but her gaze didn't waver from his face.

He choked on the need to claim every inch of her over and over again until he burned out this clawing lust. He'd wanted her before he'd had her, but now? God, it ripped into his insides. "I want to take you. Hard."

Her eyes closed and her head fell back. Dragging in a deep breath lifted her pert breasts. She sighed and shook her head, but her muscles relaxed as if a decision had been made. "Fine. If all you want is a couple of weeks...let's not waste a single second of it."

Was that all he wanted? Hell, no. But that was all he could allow himself. With her, he was on shaky ground. Too much more, and he'd find himself hip-deep in pain he'd sworn he'd never feel again. Light and easy was all he was good for when it came to women. It was better for all concerned. But Kira wasn't a light woman, and she'd never be easy. She was hard-nosed, stubborn, and ferociously protective of those she cared for. She was complex, with depths he'd never be able to fully explore.

Holding out her hand, she crooked a single finger. "Come here, Max."

And that was all it took.

Two weeks. He'd revel in it for every moment they had together, just as she'd said. A few steps and he was beside her, sliding across the sheets, and dragging her into his arms. The feel of her silky skin gliding against his made him snarl in need. His cock throbbed painfully, the wolf within him insisting on what it had wanted the moment he'd come into the room and seen her.

She jerked at his clothes, growling in frustration when they didn't come off fast enough to suit her. He wanted her hands on his skin. "Use your claws."

"You won't be able to wear them out of here."

"So?" That was enough talking. He slammed his mouth over hers, shoving his tongue between her lips. She bit him, and he jolted. Heat flooded his gut, boiling beneath his flesh. He pushed his fingers into her short, satiny hair, holding her in place for his possession.

A shudder passed through him when he felt the tips of her claws run down his torso and she sliced through his shirt. He skated his palms down her back and cupped her ass, pulling her in to grind himself into the juncture of her thighs. She spread her legs for him, wrapping them tight around his flanks and lifting herself into the thrust of his hips. He groaned, feeling the heat of her through his slacks. So fucking good. It was all he could think, and he wasn't even inside her yet. This was the most amazing thing he'd ever experienced. Even more amazing than...he quelled the thought, withdrawing from it and from Kira.

He shouldn't be doing this. Alarms sounded in his head, warning him that he was far too close to an edge he didn't want to fall over.

Kira let him pull back and used the distance between them to wrestle his pants open. One of her hands slid inside and caught him. His brain malfunctioned when she began to pump him in the tight ring of her fingers.

"God, Kira." He groaned, arching himself into her touch. The pad of her thumb rubbed the underside of his cock and he sucked in a breath. "That feels fucking incredible."

She hummed, her eyes glinting with laughter as she bent forward to suck his dick into her mouth. *»And how does this feel, Max?«*

"Holy shit," he choked.

She hummed again, and he damn near came. His fingers fisted in her hair, pressing her closer, bucking his hips to drive deeper between her lips. She flicked her tongue over his shaft and her fangs scraped oh-so-lightly against the head.

It was more than his control could take. If he didn't stop her now, the party would be over before it started.

He jackknifed upward, toppling her onto her back. Husky laughter spilled from her before he shoved her thighs wide and flat to the mattress. Bending forward, he suckled hard on her clit, nipping at it with his teeth. Her low moan rose into a thin scream. The muscles in her legs jerked, but he held her down, dipping forward to thrust his tongue into her soaking channel.

"Max!" She squirmed, scrabbling for a grip on his shoulders. Her claws dug in sharply, and he growled against her clit at the pain. *"Max!"*

Her moisture flooded his tongue, and he drank her musky flavor. His cock ached as it chafed against the soft sheets. He needed inside her. Now. He couldn't wait.

Drawing away from her sex, he blew a cool stream of air over her slick, swollen lips. She shuddered, a sound of pure need mewling from her. "Inside me, Max. *Now.*"

She didn't have to tell him twice. Crawling up the bed, he settled between her thighs and probed her entrance with his cock. Her wetness made him grit his teeth, and his fangs scraped his lips. God, it felt good. Everything with Kira was good. Fighting with her, fucking her. He groaned and slid deep into her pussy.

Her knees came up to clasp his hips, her hands dragging him down for a demanding, greedy kiss. They bit at each other, as much animal as they were human, hungry for more. Her taste was sweet and tart at once, so like the woman herself. He couldn't get enough of it, of her.

Their bodies moved together, skin slapping, sweat gathering and slipping down their overheating flesh. The mattress squeaked beneath them, and the scent of hot sex floated around them. The carnality of it called to the wolf within him, and both man and beast relished the moment.

He buried his dick deep inside her, over and over until he thought he might die, and he'd go out a contented man if he did. Grinding his pelvis against her hard little clit, he pushed her as fast as possible toward orgasm. He didn't know how much longer he could hold out, and he wanted her with him, wanted to feel that clench of inner flesh around his cock, wanted to taste the satisfaction in her kiss.

*»Max!«* Her telepathic voice held the sharp edge of pending ecstasy, and her channel clamped down on his shaft. She clawed at his back, bit at his lips. Her urgency only drove him onward.

Faster, harder, deeper. He pushed them both beyond their limits, beyond anything he'd known before. And she was right there with him, the fox in her as feral as the wolf in him.

He released her mouth from the kiss, licked a path down to the base of her throat and sank his fangs into the sensitive tendon there.

"Oh, yes...yes, Max!" Her pussy tightened around his thrusting cock, her body shaking as orgasm took her under.

He unleashed the fetters on his control and pounded into her sex. The need to come was all that mattered, and he took her like a man possessed. Satisfaction loomed, and he threw himself toward it. His body bowed, and shudders wracked him as he jetted into her pussy. The intensity of it was just as good as the night before. Better, drawing everything from him in waves of blinding ecstasy. The heat of it should have set his skin on fire.

He collapsed on top of her, and her arms wrapped tight around his neck, holding him close while their bodies cooled and their heart rates slowed to normal. "Jesus, this is the most perfect thing I've ever felt, Kira."

Her laugh was a soft sound. "Let's not make this more than it is. This is two weeks of a good time, Your Highness. I'm a servant, you're a prince."

He didn't like the way that sounded at all, though some of it was his own fault. But not all of it. "I've never thought of you that way."

"Your father did." She yawned, settling more comfortably beneath him.

He snorted. "My father was a bastard, which every Between is well aware of."

"Yep."

"So why would you listen to him?" He frowned down at her and she arched her eyebrows at him.

She stretched her arms over her head, and her response was flippant. "Because he was my king, and I was living on his island?"

"Well, he's not anymore. And you're not even living on the Delacourt island anymore—it's just the Between island, and you're a Between. It's your island." Some of this came from his father, but some of it came from hers. That was a can of worms he'd rather not open, though. Or reopen, rather. They'd argued about this before. Then again, there wasn't much they hadn't debated over the years. The woman was fiercely protective of those she loved, and that included her dead parent. He admired that about her, but he thought she brushed over some of the more archaic notions of social class the elder Seaton had clung to.

"I'm still a servant to the king." Her words slowed, slurred as her eyes fluttered closed for a moment.

"So am I, prince or not."

Her mouth opened, then closed, but nothing came out.

"Look at that. Kira Seaton rendered speechless."

She sputtered a laugh. "Shut up, Max!"

"Sure, I'll shut up." Grinning down at her, he dropped a kiss on her soft mouth. She sighed and her lips moved under his, her tongue playing with his. It felt good to kiss her, to tease her into laughter, to just be with her like this. He left her mouth and buried his face in the crook of her neck, drinking in her scent. They lay there for a long time, wrapped together in silence. His muscles loosened and he could feel sleep beckoning. This was perfect. He couldn't hold the thought back, though he knew he should.

»*Max...*« Her mind breathed his name before she relaxed, utterly spent.

He sensed the moment she dropped into slumber, a soft sigh on her lips that belied the tough exterior.

"Kira." He said it even though he knew she wouldn't hear him. Kira. That was the last thought he had before unconsciousness dragged him into oblivion. Just her name, and a wish that this could go on forever.

Those alarms pulsed to life again in the back of his mind, but he was too content to pay heed. Sleep took him, and his dreams were sweet.

And filled with Kira.

# CHAPTER SIX

"Oh, my God!" The horror in Rhiannon's voice brought Kira to full alertness. She bolted up and out of bed, jerking on a set of workout clothes from on top of her dresser before she careened out of the room.

Her nose twitched—she could smell the stench of blood in the air. That alone was enough to send her pelting down the stairs. Max was right behind her in wolf form, taking steps two at a time, his nails scrabbling against the wood floor. He leaped over the banister, passing her as they both skidded down the hallway toward the kitchen.

Elan had Rhiannon in his arms, shielding her from something or someone, and Kira could scent the ripeness of the other woman's fear. A chill rippled down her spine as the iron stink of blood intensified.

"What happened?" She swept the room with a glance, and one of the cooks met her gaze for a moment before bursting into tears.

"I'm sorry! It looked the same. I'm so sorry!" The woman covered her face and sobbed.

Max moved around the knot of people, froze, and his telepathic voice hit everyone's mind as he swore ripely.

Stepping over to stand next to him, Kira had to fight to control her gag reflex. She squatted beside him, one hand burying in the fur at the ruff of his neck.

Someone had cut off a lion's head and put it in a meat delivery box—the same company that delivered all foodstuffs to the cabin. From the outside, the container looked normal, so that explained the cook's reaction.

»*I smell him.*« Max's mental voice was rough, his fur bristling with his anger. This dangerous side of him only came out when he worked, when his people were threatened. It sent a chill down the spine to see him this way, his rage a palpable, killing force. A few Guards took a step back. »*He wants to prove he can get to the king and queen.*«

Message received. Loud and clear.

Kira forced herself to get a grip on her own anger, to retract her fangs. She wanted to track down and destroy anyone who'd dare threaten her people. »*There can't be that may ways to get hold of a lion's head. That's one way to trace him.*«

»*Yes.*« The predatory craving for the hunt rang in his telepathic tone.

Pulling in a deep breath that only reeked of death and decay, she swallowed her rising gorge, and pivoted on her haunches to look at Elan. "Why don't you and Rhiannon retire to your room? The Guards will take care of this."

She nodded to a few of the security staff, who came forward to escort the couple out. Elan's amber gaze glittered dangerously, and his fangs flashed when he spoke. "No one is supposed to be able to come near us here. What if there'd been a bomb in that container?"

"We'll find out what happened." She straightened slowly, something in his tone reminding her of his father at his most wrathful. "You'll get a full report."

"You bet your ass I will," he snarled. "This should *never* have happened. I expect you to keep my wife safe. If you can't do that, I'll find someone who can."

Kira felt her expression freeze in place. An echo of her dad's voice sounded in her head, telling her never to let any emotion show on her face. They can't take what they don't know you have, so never give anything away. He'd warned her this moment would come—that her friendship with the Delacourts lasted only as far and as long as she was useful to them.

She offered Elan a formal curtsy—the kind she would have given his father. Servant to monarch. "I understand, Your Majesty."

Her stomach churned as Elan led Rhiannon away. The drawn paleness of the woman's face and her silence spoke volumes.

»*He's just worried for Rhiannon, Kira.*« Max's voice was a quiet rumble in her head, his anger banked for the moment, and she snapped her chin down in a sharp nod, refusing to meet his eyes.

"I'll speak to the delivery company and the cook, see how the boxes got switched."

*» I'll speak to the Guard who was supposed to check all deliveries before they were brought to the house. This was not the cook's job. «* Max's molten anger had frozen to an ice-cold rage, and any smart person would understand that was where the true danger lay. That Guard's slip was likely to cost him his job today, and he'd be lucky if he got off that easily.

"Great. Let's get to work, then." Kira turned to walk out of the room, and she could feel his gaze boring into her back. The hulking form of Barrett filled the kitchen door, a large handgun cradled in his palm. He stepped aside to let her by, and she didn't meet his piercing gaze, either. "Granger, take the cook to the sitting room and calm her down. I'll meet you there in fifteen minutes."

"Of course."

The need to vomit didn't dissipate when she got away from the stink of congealed blood. Never in all the years that she'd known him had Elan treated her that way—she'd thought he never would. Max and Elan were different from their despicable father, King Phillip.

But maybe she was wrong. Maybe her dad had been right. It was in the worst times that you saw the real person under the masks they showed the world.

# CHAPTER SEVEN

The on-duty manager for their food distributor wasn't thrilled when Kira and a team of Guards showed up unannounced, locked down the warehouse, and started asking very uncomfortable questions. But the guy had taken one look at Kira's face, blanched a sickly shade of white, and decided to cooperate.

A pity. She would have liked an excuse to unleash her claws on someone.

Which was probably the reason why, after commandeering the manager's office, the Lopez sisters had insisted on being the ones to grill every employee who'd come into contact with the cabin's delivery order. The coyote-shifters had eyed her warily, and the eldest, Xiomara, had quipped, "Boss, if you're going to kill someone, at least make sure they're guilty first."

"Xio, everyone is guilty of something." The younger Lopez, Iggy, flashed a grin. Her real name was Ignacia, but only her mother called her that. "I'm sure boss lady would make sure she didn't get any blood on your nice shoes."

The black suede Jimmy Choo pumps were undeniably nice. Not that Kira could tell the brand by looking, but this wasn't the first time the sisters had bickered over these shoes. Xio propped her hands on her hips. "Look, just because you're jealous that Mom got me a nicer Christmas gift than you—"

Iggy cut in. "She threw you a nicer quinceañera too, but I'm not mad."

Sucking her teeth in disgust, Xio rolled her eyes. "Still bringing up my quinces fifteen years later, but *noooo*, you're not mad."

The two got serious the moment the first employee came into the office, working in seamless tandem to cajole or threaten information out of people. Kira leaned her shoulder against the wall, folded her arms, and let her simmering rage make people very nervous and extremely eager to answer questions and get the hell out of the room.

In the end, it wasn't hard to figure out what happened. The guilty warehouse worker was sweat-soaked and wide-eyed with terror before he even got into the office. It was Kira's turn to suck her teeth in disgust when he started crying and admitted that the lion head had been on his porch the night before, already packaged in one of their company boxes. A sizeable bribe had been in an attached envelope with instructions on what to do with the box.

And he'd just...gone along with it, told no one, and pocketed the money.

Because: greed.

Fucking idiot.

The man dropped his forehead onto his folded arms and sobbed in earnest, and the two coyote-shifters eyed him like weak, easy prey. Before they could fully dismantle him, Kira held up her hand. "I'm heading back to the cabin to debrief the king and queen. You two stay here with the rest of the team, finish questioning him and his colleagues, check out his house, the envelope, the note, money, anything that might give us a clue." She rubbed her forehead. "Just...make sure there aren't any other surprises waiting for us. If our stalker can pay off one employee, he can pay off more. See if you can find out how he knew this was the food distributor we use—*used*, because we never will again—how he got hold of one of their boxes in the first place, and how he figured out which employee would be moronic enough to obey an anonymous note left on his goddamn doorstep."

The fucking idiot in question just sobbed harder, and Kira exited the room before she throttled him. Nodding a farewell to the Guard stationed outside the warehouse, she climbed inside one of their two SUVs. She called Max and filled him in, but he had no news to share with her. Damn it. She threw her cell phone down on the seat beside her and started the vehicle. Taking a circuitous route back to the cabin let her make sure she wasn't followed and also gave her some time to stop wringing the steering wheel like it was that idiot's neck.

She parked out front, tossed the keys to another Guard, and went into the same sitting room where they'd questioned the cook hours before. Barrett was there with Min-ji, conferring over the petite hawk-shifter's laptop.

Kira strode into the middle of the room, feeling frustration crawling over her skin like fire ants. "Where's Max?"

"Debriefing the king and queen," Barrett answered.

Better him than her, was all she could think.

"He's not just telling them what you learned about the food distributor." Min-ji glanced up from her computer screen. "I gave him an update on the bloody roses."

"We found the florist?"

"Yeah, I'm running background checks on her and everyone she's ever met." Not a joke. Min-ji was their resident hacker and could crawl through someone's digital life in ways that were downright disturbing. "So far, she seems clean. She said the order came in online, and she packaged the roses into a box. All standard practice. The only unusual thing that happened that day was someone slashed the tires and smashed the windows on her car. So, she left her shop when her car alarm went off and she was outside for over an hour, getting it towed and filing the insurance claim. I'm guessing that's when our stalker added his special sauce to the roses, resealed the package, and our florist sent them out with the rest of her orders as normal."

Another dead end.

Kira laced her fingers behind her neck and let her head fall back. "Let me guess. No security cameras?"

"No. This guy was very careful in selecting his florist." Min-ji's normally mellow voice reflected the impotent fury every Guard was feeling. "She had no cameras, no one saw anything suspicious, and none of the other businesses in the neighborhood caught anyone on camera who could be our stalker going toward her shop in the hours before or after the car alarm went off." She blew out a breath. "I'll go over the footage again to see if I missed anything, but..."

But Min-ji rarely missed anything.

The hawk-shifter set her laptop aside and stood. "I'm getting some water before I dive back into this. Do either of you want anything?"

Kira and Barrett both shook their heads, and the other woman left without another word.

Anger sizzled in her veins—at this asshole human stalker, at the other asshole human who took a bribe, at Elan's behavior, at herself for not having any real answers, at the whole damn world. She wanted to put her fist through something until these ugly feelings burned away.

"I hate this," Barrett hissed. Silver glimmered at the corners of his eyes for a moment, the feral feline in him fighting for control.

"I hear you."

"I should be out hunting this guy." He snorted. "I'd need a single clue other than *human male* to do that."

"But the fact that he's left so few clues behind tells me he's no ordinary human. He's smart and obsessive."

"And getting more unhinged by the second. His letters started arriving after the engagement announcement, but we've seen a significant escalation since the wedding."

"Agreed." Her chin dipped in a sharp nod. "I have nothing to prove it, but my gut says he's had some kind of training—military, law enforcement—to be able to pull all of this off."

"Which would mean he has some kind of record in the federal database." The big cat-shifter paced in a tight circle. "That's better than off-grid cult leader who's never even been fingerprinted."

"Dear God, don't say cult leader." Kira threw up her hands. "I want this guy to be a complete loner, so once he's caught, he doesn't have four wives and thirteen kids out for revenge."

He paused in his pacing. "Okay, that's a fair point."

Pressing her fingers into her temples, she tried to ease the building pressure. "We're chasing our damn tails while this guy taunts us with dead lions."

"I had the head sent to Dr. Singh for analysis. Maybe he'll find something we can use." Barrett dropped his large form onto the sofa. "He was thrilled to hear from me, especially when I asked him to pass my regards on to Genesee."

Kira sputtered a laugh, the first since she'd bolted out of bed that morning. "Quit messing with her, Granger. She's my friend."

And a friend her father would approve of, one who was her equal, who wouldn't turn on her because she was beneath her. She'd always thought her dad overly paranoid because Phillip Delacourt was an especially heinous asshole. She'd also suspected his distrust of others had something to do with her mother leaving. Kira had vague memories of her mom as a child, but her dad had refused to speak of her after she was gone. All Kira knew about her was that she was from a wealthy American family and had met her father when she was vacationing in London. She'd also died penniless four years after she'd left them. Anything else was a mystery, and Kira only knew that much because she'd done a background check after she joined the LAPD.

Kira had assumed her father's classist attitude stemmed from whatever had happened with his marriage and that attitude had only been exaggerated by being Phillip's servant. After today, she wasn't so sure, and the uncertainty hurt so much it burned.

"I know Genesee's your friend. I get that she must have reasons for rebuffing the doc, even if I don't know what they are. Just like I know you've had your reasons for avoiding our dear princeling. Until now. Though that doesn't seem to be going very smoothly either." He shook his head, his gaze rueful when it met hers. "What a goddamn mess. You, her, this whole day. I need a drink, and I don't mean Min-ji's water."

"Yeah." What else could she say? He'd smelled Max on her this morning. Of course he had. And then he'd heard Max's brother threaten to fire her.

This entire situation was a clusterfuck. Elan going off on her, her affair with Max, Josh's yen for Genesee, Genesee's fear of losing Josh, and on top of all that, some crazed human after the Between king and queen. A headache bloomed behind Kira's eyes.

"I'm just a spectator for most of this, despite my enjoyment of poking the bear." Barrett snorted at his own bad pun, and Kira shook her head at him. "The bottom line is, Genesee has to sort out her own mess, and we're already doing everything we can about the human." Barrett's pale green eyes pinned her in place with the unwavering stare only a cat could manage. "So, what are you going to do about your mess with Max?"

She didn't know. Everything had started spinning out of whack the moment she gave in to the urge to touch the wolf, and she didn't know if it would ever go back to normal.

She didn't know anything anymore, and she *hated* that.

M ax found Kira in the gym, her face set in concentration as she kicked the shit out of a punching bag. He leaned his shoulder against the doorjamb and watched her in silence. The anger and frustration came off of her in waves even a human could sense. Underneath that, he felt the hurt.

He winced, uncertain how to deal with Elan saying the wrong thing. Normally, that was Max's area of expertise. He took a breath and tried to smile. "Think we can talk Rhiannon into a yoga lesson? You look like you could use some relaxation."

"I'm not interested in bending myself into a pretzel, thanks." Kira took a hard swing at the punching bag and her knuckles popped on impact. She grunted and hit it again. "This is very relaxing."

"Right." He pushed away from the door and sauntered into the room. The woman looked like she was going to explode. She was pissed at a king and there wasn't a damn thing she could do about it. It was the story of his childhood. He drew even with her, planting himself well within her reach. If she needed someone to take out her fury on, he'd take whatever she could dish out. He'd unleashed his own ire on the irresponsible Guard that let an unexamined package enter the cabin, so it was only fair she got to do the same. "You do look relaxed, sweet cheeks. Yep, cool as a cucumber. I'm sure Elan would be really impressed."

Wordlessly, she pivoted and caught him hard in the jaw with an uppercut.

His head snapped back and he staggered a few steps, pain shooting straight to his brain. He shook it off, rolled his shoulders, and settled into a fighting stance. Offering her a grin he knew showed his wolfish side, he gestured her forward with a mocking flick of his fingers. "Okay, let's play. C'mon, foxy. Give it to me."

"I'll give it to you, all right," she muttered and advanced on him.

He moved to keep her in front of him as she circled him. Her lithe body was displayed to perfection in her tight pants and sports bra. Her creamy skin was sheened with sweat, just as it had been the night before when he'd sunk his cock deep inside her.

Bad thoughts to be having when he'd taunted a dangerous woman into lashing out at him. She swung for him, and his hand snapped out to deflect in pure reflex, saving him from a broken nose. A quick shift to wolf form would heal him, but it would hurt like a bitch until he did. And he doubted she'd pause the fight to give him the opportunity to shift.

"Damn it." She snarled at him, her fangs baring, and she slashed at him with her claws.

"I thought you were going to give it to me, foxy. Don't be shy now." It was the wrong thing to say. Or the right thing, if he was hoping to piss her off more. He blocked her again, his movement making her stumble into him, her curves plastered to his front. Sweat beaded on his forehead, but not from the physical exertion.

They hit and kicked each other, landing glancing blows, neither able to gain the advantage. His heart rate skyrocketed, his breathing beginning to bellow in and out, both from having his hands on her bare skin and from the grappling that brought them into full-body contact. God, but he wanted her. He spun her, shoving her away from him so she tripped and hit her knees.

A nimble leap brought her back to her feet. She whipped back around. Her dark eyes blazed with the challenge, her fangs showing when she licked her lips.

He damn near groaned at the sight.

This was a bad idea.

His cock was rock-hard and uncomfortable as hell under the circumstances. She charged him, her fist catching him in the belly while he blocked her other hand.

"All right, enough." He wrapped an arm around her waist and dragged her to the ground. Kicking out, she managed to flip them both until she was on top, her legs straddling his waist.

It was then that she finally noticed his erection because she froze above him, her fist half-cocked to punch him.

"Shit." She snapped her fingers around his wrists and pinned them on either side of his head.

Then she kissed him.

The sweet taste of her only made him burn. He shoved his tongue into her mouth the way he wanted to shove his dick into the depths of her pussy. Hard and hot and fast. He angled his head, lifting it to deepen the kiss. Any contact he could get, he'd take.

She rode him, working herself on him through their clothing. He groaned and bucked his hips beneath her, grinding his cock into the juncture of her thighs. A moan bubbled out of her and she pressed herself into him with swift urgency. The sting of her claws digging into his wrists did nothing to quell his lust—the slight pain only added to the pleasure. Every sensation ripped through him. The female scent of her dampness, the feel of her softness rubbing against his harder body, the mewling sounds she made as they moved together.

Their tongues twined, and the kiss was an animalistic mating of lips and tongues and fangs. They bit at each other, each wanting a feral claiming of the other.

He dropped his head back to the mat. "I want you naked, Kira. I want my cock inside your tight little pussy."

"Yes. God, yes." She released her grip on his arms and he wasted no time reaching out to jerk her top over her head. Her small breasts spilled free, the light brown nipples already tightening. She lay flat against him, raising her ass slightly so they could both work her pants off. His fingers curved over her buttocks, prying them apart so he could dip between them.

She shuddered when he probed at the tiny rosette of her anus. The aroma of her wetness increased, a heady aphrodisiac that made his brain short-circuit. He slipped his fingers down into her pussy, working them deep. Her hips undulated, following his lead with a whimper that drove him wild.

"Nooo," she moaned when he dragged his fingers out of her sex. Using her own juices to ease his way, he pressed two digits into the tight ring of her anus. She jolted as he twisted his hand and scissored his fingers to widen her for entry.

"I want to fuck you here." His voice was so guttural, he barely recognized the sound.

» *Yes.* « Her mental voice was soft, and her claws dug into his shoulders, but she gave a decisive nod.

"Damn it." He growled. "We need lube."

» *I'll just shift later and heal myself. Do it.* «

Pushing her, he rolled her off of him and onto her hands and knees. Dampness gleamed on the lips of her pussy. An irresistible temptation, just as everything had been with her since the moment she'd kissed him two days ago. He bent forward, flicked his tongue over her swollen clit, and suckled those sleek lips.

She moaned, her moisture flowing into his mouth. He lapped up the cream, hoping he was making her as crazy as she made him. Leaning back, he abandoned her pussy for the darker pleasures that awaited him. He ripped open his pants with one hand while he used the fingers of his other hand to press for entrance into her ass. Trailing wetness from her sex to her anus, he made slow circles on her flesh until he could slide three digits easily in and out of her rear passage.

"Now, Max."

"Don't say I never do anything for you." He withdrew his hand and patted her buttock. "Such a pretty little ass."

She snorted out a laugh. "Shut your mouth for once and *hurry up.*"

Taking his cock in his fist, he rubbed the head up and down her slit. "Shut my mouth before I put my foot in it, is that right?"

"Yep." She glanced over her shoulder, her eyes sparkling with repressed laughter.

"Well, that's fair." They both cracked up, but their amusement cut short when he pressed his dick into her anus. The initial resistance of her muscles made him grit his teeth as he bore down on her. She snarled, silver shimmering on her skin as she wrestled with her fox for control. He knew the feeling.

Small thrusts of his hips pushed his cock inch by inch into her ass. God, she was tight. He wasn't sure she could take all of him. He shuddered, and beads of sweat slid down his face and chest. "Do you want more, Kira?"

"Yes, more," she groaned.

She dropped lower, her cheek pressing to the mat and her back arching to allow him deeper. He took all the access she gave him, driving his cock into her until his balls pressed against her slick flesh.

The animal noises she made pushed him past the edge of madness, calling to the most feral part of the wolf within. Shoving her hips back, she urged him onward. He thrust slowly at first, but quickly picked up speed and force. Their skin slapped together, the sound echoing through the gym. The smell of sex permeated the air, and he loved that it was his scent layering with hers. Possession dug its claws into his soul, but he was too far gone to notice or care. All he wanted was her. His hands slid up and down her back and he could feel the way goose bumps broke over her skin. His strokes grew rougher, less controlled. Faster. Wilder. He battled the need to come and reached around her slim body to toy with her clit.

"I'm coming, Max. I'm coming!"

He could feel it. The deep contractions made her inner muscles clench and release on his cock, the tight passage squeezing him almost past bearing. The fetters on his restraint snapped abruptly and he hammered into her ass until their cries of completion mingled in the room. His come spurted into her, heat rippling over his limbs with each wave of orgasm that slammed into him.

"Are you okay?" he croaked. His heart still pounded so loudly, he could barely hear anything else.

"Um. I think so. Yeah." She collapsed beneath him and they both groaned as he slid out of her. Shivering and sighing, a slight grin curled her lips. The sight made something sweet and warm squeeze his chest, and it felt far too amazing. Far too much like something he could never deserve. She hummed softly. "I'm good."

Well, that made one of them. Heaving himself to the side, he managed not to crash down on top of her. He flung an arm over his eyes. Shit. As he had every other time he'd given in to the need to touch her, he asked himself what the hell he was doing. Sex was one thing, but this was already too deep for his liking. Most women never saw all of him. They never saw the rougher edges. The man who'd killed and the guilt and emotional fallout that often came with that. They saw the mask—the easy charmer. Kira knew the darker sides of him, the secrets. Most of them, anyway. What had he been thinking to even dream that he could have a simple affair with her? She was his friend, and now she was his lover.

This wasn't a quick fuck. It was more.

And that thought alone was enough to freeze the blood in his veins.

# CHAPTER EIGHT

"Kira."

She froze in the hallway outside Elan and Rhiannon's suite. It had been two days since the kitchen incident, and she'd buried herself in the stalker investigation, allowing other Guards to protect the king and queen. Cowardice, she knew, but she just didn't want to face it. There was a lot she didn't want to face lately. Everything had gotten so mixed up, and she wasn't sure what to do about it.

Pulling in a deep breath, she smoothed her expression, turned to look at Elan, and straightened to soldierly attention. "Yes, sire?"

A pained look crossed his leonine features. "Don't do that."

"Sire?" She arched her brows, her posture not relaxing for a moment. Her dad would have been proud, and she didn't know if that was a good thing or not.

"Don't treat me like my father."

Her mouth worked for a moment before she could get words out. "I'm not sure what to say."

"Come in, please." He stepped back and held the door open for her to pass through. Rhiannon perched on a chair in the sitting room. The woman practically vibrated in place, but she seemed determined to let Elan have his say without interference.

He gestured eloquently with his hands, drawing her attention away from his wife. "I was a jackass and I'm sorry. You know I don't think it's right to treat people the way my father did. I was completely in the wrong and I have no excuses. I'm sorry."

Her lips twisted and her eyes dropped to the carpet. She shouldn't say anything, just accept his apology at face value and walk away. Her dad would have told her to reveal nothing, to give the king nothing, to deny that she had any feelings at all. Her job was to serve, and that was all. If a powerful person knew you cared, they could use that against you. They could take what you weren't willing to give. When her dad had worked for King Phillip, she would have agreed. Now, she had to take a chance that her friendship wasn't misplaced. If it was, she'd rather know now so she could decide what to do from here. Her palms felt slick with cold sweat and her belly knotted tight. She swallowed hard, the words squeezing past a throat that didn't want to work. "It hurt. What you said."

She felt Elan flinch. "I know. I make no excuses for myself. I was wrong. I hope you know how much I value you, how much Rhiannon and I value your friendship."

"Thank you." The air deflated in her lungs. Elan wasn't like his father, she *knew* that, but...God, everything was spinning out of whack lately.

His gaze cut to his wife and softened. Rhiannon shot to her feet and moved forward to slip her hand into his. "I'm the one who should thank you for everything you've done for me."

Kira nodded, but said nothing more.

"I hope you can forgive me." His amber eyes, only a shade or two darker than Max's, reflected his remorse.

"And me." Rhiannon lined herself up beside the king. "I should have kicked him on the spot. I was still pretty shaken up."

Kira tried to form her face into a tight smile and knew she failed. "You both were. I understand."

"But we were still jerks. Elan for what he said, and me for what I didn't. What happened wasn't your fault, and we know that you and Max are doing the best you can to keep us safe. You're the best at what you do, and we know that too."

She pulled in a shaky breath. "Thank you."

"You're welcome." Rhiannon's gaze was frank when she looked at Kira. "Now tell me why you've gotten distant lately. And don't say it was Elan having his dorkfest. It started before that. I thought we were friends."

Kira folded her hands behind her back and tried not to appear uncomfortable. "We were."

"We *are*."

But, in the end, she now worked for Rhiannon. They weren't on equal footing anymore.

"It started in little ways, at first," the queen continued. "But now, all you talk to me about is Guard stuff. I talked about being in Portland and being Between and planning the wedding, and you put everything in terms of safety and security. You let Genesee be my maid of honor without so much as a protest. In fact, you bowed out completely."

"Max was already the best man. Someone had to be in charge of the Guard."

"And Barrett couldn't do it?" Rhiannon shook her head. "No, you've backed off and I want to know why."

"She's trying to get some professional distance." Elan sighed. "You'd have to have met Seaton to understand."

He was right. It was a slap in the face to realize it. God, she hadn't even *seen* it until they pointed it out. How much had she taken her consummate servant parent's words and actions to heart? Was that what she really believed, that she had to have distance with the royal family in order to serve them? That didn't seem to be the case with Max or she wouldn't be sleeping with him, and it would mean losing Rhiannon as a close friend.

"I have met Seaton. Kira Seaton." Rhiannon's gesture encompassed Kira from head to toe.

"He means my dad." She shrugged the tension out of her shoulders and forced herself to relax her stiff pose. "He was the butler at the palace."

"Why didn't I know that?"

"You never asked."

Rhiannon's green eyes narrowed. "You wouldn't have answered if I had."

"True." An unapologetic grin curved Kira's lips, and she let it widen when Rhiannon's eyes narrowed further.

She huffed and jammed her fists down on her hips. "Well, knock it off. You're one of my best friends and I don't give a damn if I'm queen or not. That doesn't change a thing. There are going to be enough people acting weirdly because I married the lion king, without adding my friends to the list. None of that professional distance crap."

"Yes, Your Majesty."

"Kira!"

"Sorry, you were spewing orders like a queen." Kira tilted her head. "I call it like I see it."

Rhiannon opened her mouth for a moment, then snapped it shut. Her expression went from annoyed to speculative in under a second, which Kira knew from experience meant the other woman was about to do something unpredictable. "Well, fine. If we're calling it like we see it, then we should talk about how you're finally getting busy with Max. About damn time."

"It's temporary."

Her mouth opened and Kira could tell she was going to say something sarcastic, but then their eyes met and the queen's face sobered. "That's too bad."

Discomfort wound through Kira, and her shoulders twitched in a shrug. "It's fine. I'm fine. We're fine."

Rhiannon pushed back her long red hair. "Yeah, that's really convincing."

"I think the lady protests too much." Elan slung an arm around his wife's waist and drew her close, but he pinned Kira in place with his gaze.

Kira pulled a sour face. "Hasn't anyone ever told you to mind your own business?"

"You have, many times." He grinned, and for a moment, he looked so much like Max, it startled her. "I just didn't listen."

She snorted. "Jerk."

He lifted his hands to concede the point, still smiling. "I'm a king, Kira, I'm automatically concerned with all my citizens, especially those I count as friends or family. Or both."

"You consider me family?" Her world took another spin. This rollercoaster of emotions was going to give her motion sickness. He considered her *family*? The king? Yes, he wasn't Phillip, but this was way beyond not being a snobby ass.

"Yes. Though I'd prefer if you put Max out of his misery and made it more official than that."

"Ha. Max doesn't want to marry me." For some inexplicable reason, tears pricked at her eyes even as she said the words. What the hell was wrong with her?

Elan's tone was careful and tinged with an edge of what might have been sadness. "Max has his reasons for being...cautious about commitment, but I'd hoped he'd move past them with you."

A short knock sounded on the door, and Max's scent reached her. He opened the door and strode through without waiting for an acknowledgement. "Sorry to interrupt, but I need Kira."

"Of course." Rhiannon's hands made graceful arcs in the air. "Don't let us keep you."

"Thanks, sweetheart." Max winked at her, wrapped his fingers around Kira's bicep, and drew her out of the room. He led her across the hall to his room, and shut the door firmly behind them.

Kira sighed and sagged against the wall, pulling away from him. "Thanks for the rescue."

A wry grin curled his full lips. "I heard them talking to you, and I guessed you could use a hand."

"Yeah. That was…rough."

"Weird to have a king apologize to you, huh? I hope you got it in writing." He chuckled. "Make big brother twist for a few days before you forgive him. He deserves it."

She strangled a laugh. "You're bad."

"So my father told me. And since I have you in my room and we're both off duty…"

She stepped into his embrace easily, willingly. For once she didn't have the energy to fight her craving for him. She didn't even want to. She was tired of fighting, of questioning herself, of doubting everything she knew about everyone she knew.

His arms locked tight around her, pulling her close until her face was buried in his chest and she could inhale the rich, masculine scent that was uniquely Max. "There's something I don't understand."

"Mmm?" She flattened her palms against his strong back.

"I always thought you came back because you wanted Elan—"

"Haven't we been over this?" A spurt of irritation threatened to quash her mellow mood.

His big hand moved up and down her back, rubbing the tautness out of her muscles. "Okay, but you didn't come back for me because you returned first. Not for Seaton, because he was already dead. So, why did you come back? What was in it for you?"

"There are a lot of reasons." The response was automatic, but she paused and made herself give the questions more thought than normal. She blinked for a moment, her conversation with Elan and Rhiannon meshing with this one. Why *had* she come back? She'd had a good life in L.A. Her career with the police department had been on a fast track. Was it just because she felt as if she should fulfill her father's wishes? Was she born to be a servant? Was that who and what she thought she was? Did she think it was beneath her to serve? As Max had pointed out, he served the king too, prince or not.

He jostled her a little. "And those reasons are?"

"Elan was my…friend." Her father would balk at calling the king her friend, but she shoved that away. Elan said he considered her family. "He was going to need help. I could help."

"Other people could have helped."

She worked her hands under the bottom of his shirt, pressing her fingertips to his warm, resilient flesh. "People like you?"

"Yeah, like me." He huffed out a breath.

Shaking her head, she smiled a little. "We are so alike. We both had to leave to feel...worthy." God, it made her ache to say that. As much as she'd loved her father, and as much as he'd loved her, his worldview meant she was never as good as her friends. The Seatons were always less than the Delacourts, no exceptions. Everyone had their place and their purpose. And Max's upbringing had been worse. She seriously doubted Phillip was capable of loving anyone.

"Yeah. I know what you mean." Max's tone turned contemplative, which was a side of him he allowed few to see. "The Marines gave me a sense of self and worth that I'd never have gotten if I'd stayed on the island."

Burying her face deeper into Max's chest, she sighed. "But there's no place like home. Living among humans meant lying about what you were. Even now, there's enough prejudice against Between that it's safer to lie."

"San Amaro is home, more than it ever was when Father was king. It's good not to have his judgment hanging over my head every day."

It was good not to have her own father's judgments hanging over her head, too, and the thought made her feel disloyal. She tensed, but Max's arms tightened around her, offering her nothing but comfort and understanding. Everything else fell away, and there was only him, only her, and only this moment. Yes. That was perfect, that was exactly what she needed.

Somehow, he had known before she had.

Her body loosened, warmed. It was going to be so hard to walk away from this. Max understood parts of her that she didn't even want to acknowledge in herself. He made her smile, he made her think, he made her *feel*.

His body against hers was divine and began to have predictable effects on her hormones. Even as she felt her arousal build in slow increments, her skin tingling, her nipples tightening, her sex dampening, she let herself lean into him, reveling in the feel of his hands stroking up and down her back in slow, soothing circles. Soon, it wouldn't be enough for her. Soon, she'd need more and more until they were naked and all but feral in each other's arms. She wanted that, but not yet. Not now. Now, she needed just *this*.

Curling his fingers around the nape of her neck, he massaged any lingering tension away. He nuzzled his nose into her temple, and she sighed.

His low voice rumbled in her ear. "Wanna do it?"

Snorting out a laugh, she drew back to give him an incredulous look. "You really never say the right thing—you know that, don't you?"

"It's part of my charm." His hands slid down to bracket her hips, pulling her close so she couldn't miss the evidence of his arousal. "Women find it irresistible."

"Uh-huh." She ran taloned fingertips up his chest until the deadly points rested against his jugular. "Is that what you tell yourself?"

He froze when her claws scored his flesh. He didn't breathe, didn't swallow, his golden gaze locked on her face. *»I think we're good together. That's what I tell myself, all joking aside.«*

*»Okay, so every now and then, you say the right thing.«* She rolled her eyes, trailing her talons down to flick open the buttons on his shirt.

He unfastened her pants and slipped his hand in to rub his knuckles over the sensitive skin of her belly. "Don't worry. I promise not to make a habit of it."

A chuckle bubbled out of her, and he grinned down at her.

"I like the sound of your laughter. You do it more when we're alone together now."

She blinked up at him, replaying the last few days in her mind. He was right. He'd always been the first to get her to laugh...and to make her temper flare, but the effect had been exaggerated since they'd begun sleeping together. They'd had nights where they'd spent hours just...playing. Laughing and teasing.

He really was perfect for her.

The thought shocked her more than even Elan's suggestion that they should marry. That was his opinion, but this was *hers*.

And there wasn't a damn thing she could do about it. Because unlike Elan, she knew Max didn't want anything past the two-week honeymoon. But Elan knew something she didn't...he'd said Max had his reasons, and sheer gut instinct told her it had to do with the years he was in the Marines. He'd come back different, but she'd always assumed it was just cutting loose of his father's influence. Now she wasn't so sure. She'd have to think about it more, consider what Elan had meant. Her brows drew together and she bit her lip, stepping back from the situation to look at it objectively.

Max's fingers dipped below the edge of her panties, making her breath catch. "Do I have your attention, Ms. Seaton?"

His other hand came up to palm her breast, tweaking the tip. The air whooshed out of her lungs at the strength of feeling. He used one claw to circle her areola, and her nipple puckered tight. She shuddered and licked her lips. "Yeah, you have my attention."

"God, you're beautiful." He leaned in and ran his tongue over her lips, just as she had done. "And you taste like sugar."

"Mmm." She hummed in her throat and opened her mouth to invite him in. The arctic fox in her was too curious not to wonder what he'd do next, and she wanted more. All of him. Everything. She just couldn't have it. Her heart twisted, but she tucked the pain away and enjoyed what she could have. This. Here. Now.

He flicked his tongue over her teeth before slipping it in to twine with hers. The taste of him was just right, hot and male and all Max.

Dropping her hands to his waist, she slid them down to cup his erection, stroking him through his pants. He jerked and then arched into her grip. "God, Kira. This is amazing. You're amazing."

"Why, thank you." She offered up a wicked little smile, and his eyes gleamed with amusement. She laughed, and it felt good. Light and free. So unlike her. But she liked it. She liked how she was when she was with him. The prince. Her Max. She shook her head and smiled.

She stroked his cock through his pants, and he pushed his hips into her, working himself against her fingers. Harsh groans spilled from his mouth, and her body reacted to his passion. Her sex grew unbearably damp, and she squeezed her thighs together to savor the ache. It was so good with him. Her breathing sped and her heart hammered in her chest, her blood coursing lava-hot through her veins.

Excitement shivered over her skin while he continued to toy with her nipple. He favored the other breast with the same treatment and she moaned. "This is so good."

"It's only going to get better."

Until it ended, he meant.

She shoved that thought away brutally.

She wouldn't let that ruin the time she had left. If this was all she'd ever get from a man who fit her so seamlessly, then she wasn't going to waste it whining about what she couldn't have.

Tightening her fingers around his dick, she pumped him harder. She watched his lids drop to half-mast and a little grin curl his lips. It made her heart stop, and an answering smile formed on her lips of its own volition.

She loved him. God, how she loved him. She'd run away from it for so long, but that hadn't stopped it. Giving in to the physical craving for him had unlocked everything else, sent it spilling out until she could no longer deny any of it. She wanted him, she loved him, she loved who she was when she was with him. Lighter, more optimistic. And he understood her enough to handle the darker sides of her too. He understood because he was just like her in so many ways.

Rising on tiptoe, she brushed his lips with hers, but continued to caress his thick sex. He drove his hand into her hair, holding her in place while he ravaged her mouth. She kissed him back, needing more of him. All of him. Everything she could get. Squirming, she worked her fingers around to unbuckle his belt and unfasten his pants. Then he was in her hands, his cock hard and pulsing.

A growl rumbled out of him, the sound of a volcano erupting. Silver flickered around his arms, the sign of incipient change telling her just how close he was from losing control. She grinned, loving how she could push him over the edge. He set her away from him, his hands urgent as he yanked off both of their clothing. He had them both naked in moments. Spinning her around, he pressed her face against the wall.

She braced her palms on the hard surface and moaned when his muscular form came into full contact with her back. His hands slipped up her ribs to cup her breasts, his claws flicking her nipples. A broken cry jerked from her, the sound edged in need. "Max, I want you inside me. Now, now, *now!*"

The lupine growl that rumbled from him reverberated against her back. His hands abandoned her breasts and dropped to grip her hips tight. His talons bit deep into her flesh as he jerked her ass toward him. Yes. God, yes. She spread her feet, supporting herself for the impact of his entry.

Arching her back to open herself further, she glanced over her shoulder to meet his eyes and demand he give her what she craved. They both groaned when he slid home within her. She could *feel* every inch of him, he filled her so perfectly. The rhythm he set for them was swift and almost rough, calling to the feral fox inside of her. Yes. Yes, it was just what she needed.

Wrapping his arms around her again, he moved one hand up to continue fondling her breasts, teasing her nipples until she knew she'd come just from that if he didn't stop. Then his other hand moved down to cover her mound, slipping into damp folds to rub the stretched lips of her pussy. It only emphasized how full she was, how deep and hard his strokes were. Tingles broke over her skin, and she bit back a scream. *»Yes, Max. Just like that. More, please, more!«*

"I'll give you more, sweetheart." He used the hot juices to trail a slippery path up to her clit. He pressed down on that sensitive spot and let his thrusts drive her forward for increased stimulation.

"Oh, God." Her face pressed to the wall, their frantic movements scraping her cheek against the rough surface. The discomfort wasn't enough to stop her. She needed this, needed him. Love squeezed her insides so tight, she ached with it. Rocking her hips into his thrusts, she took everything he could give her.

Orgasm exploded through her, gripping her deep inside and spreading outward until her entire body shook. He groaned, his hips faltering in their rhythm before he slammed deep and came with her. His fluids pumped into her pussy, and each spurt made her inner muscles clench around him. It was so right, the way they moved together, the way they fit.

Shudders wracked them both, sweat sliding down their skin, sticking their bodies together. His breath cooled the moisture on her flesh when he dropped his forehead to her shoulder. He didn't loosen his hold on her, didn't pull out of her.

He seemed as reluctant as she to end the interlude, and she knew it was a figment of her imagination, but she clung to it because she had nothing else. Time was running out and there wasn't a damn thing she could do about it. She laid her arms over his and wrapped her fingers around his wrists, holding on for dear life.

The physical was all she had to cling to, and it was bitterly ironic that a week ago she'd told herself that was all she really wanted from him.

She was such a fool.

M ax had already had her three times that night and he already wanted her again. They curled together naked on the couch in his room, her back to his front, as they laughed over some ridiculous old black-and-white comedy on TV. He'd never have imagined that Kira would be so open in a sexual relationship, and he was fiercely jealous of any man who'd ever seen this side of her. It was ludicrous, but that didn't change a thing. He wanted all of this for himself. He just couldn't have it. He couldn't even *want* to have it.

She snagged the remote off the coffee table and snapped off the television when the movie ended. Rolling onto her back beside him, she smiled slowly, lifting her hand to trace a fingertip over his eyebrow, down the bridge of his nose, and across his bottom lip. "You're quiet."

Shaking his head, he forced himself to grin and keep his tone light. "Just thinking. You know how dangerous that can be."

He expected her to laugh, but she didn't. Instead, her expression intensified. She opened her mouth to speak, but didn't. She glanced away and glanced back, meeting his gaze squarely. "There was a woman while you were in the Marines, wasn't there?"

Every muscle in his body went rigid. He couldn't help it. It was as if she'd prodded a fatal, slow-leaking wound and ripped it wide open. It was all he could do not to leap off the couch and run. "Are we really talking about my other women while we're naked together?"

That steady gaze didn't waver. "I'm not talking about all the man-whoring you've done, Max. I'm talking about serious relationships."

"I don't do those." Pain spread through him, the sickness and guilt enough to drop him if he weren't lying down.

"But you did once, didn't you?" Her hand cupped his jaw, refusing to let him look away. "There was a woman, and she was important to you. You loved her."

He flinched from her stare. "It was a long time ago. It doesn't matter. What even made you ask about this?"

"Something Elan said got me thinking." Her breasts rose and fell as she drew in a deep breath. He let himself be distracted by the sight. Any excuse to not think about what she was asking him. But the next questions hit him like a fist to the solar plexus. "What happened? Did she cheat on you or dump you for another guy?"

"*No*." His gaze flew to her face and he knew horror shone in his expression. Clenching his fingers, he tried to hide that his hands were shaking. "Athena would never have done that. Not to anyone."

"Athena, like the Greek goddess?"

"Yeah. Athena Papadopoulos. As she liked to say, she couldn't get more Greek if she tried."

"So...this Athena was loyal, and you loved her. Why aren't you still with her?" Kira's voice was low, and nothing about her tone accused or demanded an answer, which made it harder to deny her.

He blew out a breath and gritted his teeth. "Because she died, damn it."

"I'm sorry." Her thumb glided over his cheekbone, the simple gesture gutting him. He didn't deserve her sympathy.

"It was a long time ago. It—"

"Don't say it doesn't matter." Her fingers tightened on his jaw. "It does matter."

"Yeah. It does matter. She mattered. A lot." He closed his eyes and turned his head away. Kira was the last person in the world he wanted to talk to about this.

Or was she?

Perhaps she deserved to know. Perhaps it would push her away and keep him from doing something stupid, like asking her to stay with him, to keep this amazing thing they had going for as long as possible. Forever.

But forever hadn't lasted long before, had it? He swallowed and told the bald truth. "I loved her, and she died."

"How?"

His stomach heaved and he pinched his eyes closed, unable to look at Kira while he told her about the other woman who'd meant the world to him. So long ago. He'd been so young, so cocksure, so damn foolish. He shook his head and snorted. "It was stupid. We had some leave time and we went up to Yosemite to climb Half Dome. She was a Marine, too, and she knew what she was doing, so it was just us, cutting loose and doing something fun. It wasn't supposed to be dangerous. She was right behind me and she just...slipped. She was there one second, and then she was gone." He pressed his fingers to his burning eyelids. "It was just...stupid. She shouldn't have died. If she'd been Between, she *wouldn't* have died. The fall would have hurt her, but it wouldn't have killed her."

"You wish you had made her Between."

"Yes. No." He dropped his hand to meet her gaze. "Hell, I don't know. I've gone over it in my mind a million times, and I wish she'd been Between so she'd have lived, but...we weren't in a place yet where I could tell her the truth, where I could even consider turning her."

Her fingers stroked down his jaw, his neck, and his shoulder. Her touch was soothing, her expression understanding. She should be pushing him away, instead she cuddled closer. "The potential was there, though."

"Yeah. The potential was there." He sighed, and the sound was weary. He should have known the truth wouldn't scare her. Not Kira. They had that in common, the two women he'd loved. The thought should have terrified him, but it didn't. He ached from the inside out. "I'll always wonder what might have happened if she'd survived."

"I'm sorry."

"Me, too."

"It wasn't your fault, you know." She pressed a kiss to his jaw.

He shook his head, unwilling to absolve himself so easily. "I should have been watching her. I should have taken better care of her."

An impatient noise escaped from his little fox. "She was a Marine and knew what she was doing while rock climbing, you said. You couldn't have known what would happen."

"We were goofing off. I was being irresponsible. She died."

Irresponsible. The word his father had used to describe him more times than he could ever count. Irresponsible, the disappointment, the son who would never behave like a real prince, who didn't want to take a hand in ruling his people. Useless. Except when it came to making sure people ended up dead.

As much as his father had always been at loggerheads with Elan, at least they'd understood each other. They hadn't agreed on how affairs should be run, but they both wanted to have their fingers in the pie, they both wanted to be running the show. Not Max. Max was an enforcer, a thug, a weapon.

"You're not irresponsible."

He shrugged, letting his hand drift in circles over her flat belly. "I'm good at my job."

"That's not all you're good at."

A snort erupted from him. "Yeah, sex. I'm good at that. I've had a lot of practice." Favoring her with a slow smile, he moved his hand down to slip into the soft hair between her legs. "But one can never be too skilled, right?"

She gave him a look that said she wasn't going to let him off the hook. "You're a great friend, Max. You're an amazing brother. You're a good boss. You're not a great prince, but you don't need to be. That doesn't make you irresponsible."

Bending over her, he licked each of her nipples in turn. "I never say the right thing."

The shiver that passed through her made him grunt in pleasure. He loved her reactions. She began to writhe as he pressed his fingers into her sex. "But you *do* the right thing, and you make up for it when you realize you've put your foot in your mouth again."

"Again."

"Yeah, again. So what?" She parted her legs and lifted her hips for him to tease her sex. He rubbed his thumb over her clit, and her legs jolted, her knees rising to clasp around his forearm. She licked her lips, her pale brows drawing together as she struggled to focus. "How long are you going to let your dad's bullshit color your view of yourself? You told

Elan to knock that off, so why can't you take your own advice?"

He paused in his movements. "Because…"

"Because you don't think he was wrong about you." She nudged his arm with her upraised knee.

His finger began stroking up and down her slit, drawing her moisture from her core to her clitoris. "No, I don't." He spoke slowly, unable to deny that his father's view of him had helped cement his own. "I was fourteen the first time I killed a man."

"I remember. You saved your father from being assassinated." Knees clamping on his arm, she stopped him again. Her hand bracketed his chin so he had to look at her. Whatever she saw in his gaze made her shake her head and snort in disgust. "Only King Phillip could make having two strong, capable sons a *bad* thing. You know what his problem was? He was jealous of you both. You're better men than he could ever be, and deep down, he knew it."

A wry grin touched his lips. Hardly. "Elan maybe, not me."

"Yes, Max. *You.*" She poked his chest, scowling up at him. "You have the strength to do what needs doing, no matter what it costs you personally, in order to *protect* what matters most to you. You're not a murderer. You don't kill indiscriminately."

"A tool to be used. A thug."

The fox growled. "Those are your father's words. Not mine. Not Elan's. Not anyone who knows you."

"I killed my mother." God, that hurt to say. He didn't think he'd ever voiced it out loud. His father had, many times. After he'd stopped the assassin in his teens and especially after he'd joined the Marines.

"*What?*" The utter shock on Kira's face made him wince. "Oh, my God. That is such bullshit. She died in childbirth. It was a tragic accident. And your girlfriend's death was a tragic accident. There is nothing you could have done to save either woman. Don't let Phillip's endless crap twist you up so much that you can't separate *his* issues from *your* job or from your mom's and Athena's *accidental* deaths."

He stared at her silently for long moments as he let that sink in. He swallowed, but still said nothing.

She was right.

He'd let Athena's death justify everything his father had ever said about him while he was growing up. But his father thrived on controlling everything and everyone around him—Max had seen how his father's selfishness had hurt Elan and had, in fact, led to his father's suicide. Only a lion got to be king, and when Phillip had forced the Between into human awareness, he'd stopped shifting into a lion. Elan had become the lion, the king. His father couldn't handle it, and the shame had made him take his own life. What an ass. And Max had based his understanding of his own worth on that. But how could his father's opinion not matter to a young boy?

None of that brought Athena back or assuaged his guilt at her death. Had there been anything he could have done? He didn't know. He'd never know. Even then, he couldn't change it.

"You're a good man, Max. Better than your father ever managed to be. Work and sex aren't the only things you excel at, and anyone who knows you would agree with me." She stroked a fingertip over his lower lip. "I get that we all have masks we show the world, but you're not a carefree princeling and you're not a stone-cold killer. The truth isn't that simple, but it's there, if people bother to look." She pulled his head down and brushed her lips over his. "I see you."

Wrapping one arm around her, he jerked her under him and stopped the painful conversation in the most enjoyable way he knew. She opened her lips for his tongue, kissing him just as fiercely as he kissed her. Her passion always rose to match his, and when it came to her, he was insatiable.

Forcing his thigh between hers, he shoved her legs wide and mounted her. Hands clutching at his back, he felt the bite of her talons into his skin. He growled, the wolf ripping loose the way he rarely allowed with other women. But this was Kira. Kira, who knew all his secrets. Kira, who understood every part of him, good and bad. Kira, who'd never turn away from the darkness that lived inside him because of all the things his profession made him do. She had the same relentless need to defend and protect.

It was no wonder he loved her.

His chest tightened with emotion until he could barely breathe, and still he kissed her. He couldn't stop—he needed her now. He'd never get his fill of her, and he didn't want to. He poured everything he could never say into the kiss, mating his mouth to hers. She whimpered against his lips, her claws raking down his sides and her legs cinching around his waist to urge him onward.

Not yet. Not yet. He needed more. He needed this to last for as long as possible.

Slipping his fingers into the short silken strands of her hair, he pulled her head back so he could lick and suck his way down her long neck. His fangs nipped at the spot at the base of her throat that he knew made her squirm.

"I want you, Max." She moaned when he dug his fangs in deeper. "Max!"

Her cry of his name echoed in his head, her demand as much mental as verbal. He couldn't resist her. Reaching between them, he grasped his cock and guided himself to the slick opening of her pussy. She rubbed herself against him in shameless abandon, her nipples sliding against his chest and her sex dampening the head of his cock.

Driving partway into her, he withdrew and she moaned a protest. He pushed back in, deeper this time, and pulled back, thrusting still deeper every time until he was hilted inside her. She clung to him, and he reveled in the feel of her. Her satin skin, her inner moisture that welcomed him. He sealed himself against her, grinding his pelvis into her clit.

"Yes! Oh, my God!" Her back bowed and her claws raked down his flesh. He winced at the sting, a growl soughing from his throat. Her heels dug into the backs of his thighs. "Harder. *Faster*. I need...I'm going to..."

Damn, but the woman got to him. He laughed and gave her exactly what she wanted. Bracing his hands on either side of her, he used the extra leverage to fuck her hard. Ecstasy rocketed through his system as he let loose. Ramming deep into her pussy with every thrust, he took them both to the very edge in moments.

"This is so fucking good." Sweat slipped down his back, and he moved faster and faster, anything to keep this sensation going. Gazing down at her, he could see her eyes losing focus, a faint silver light glowing beneath her skin as her cries grew louder. He pounded into her, knowing he wouldn't last, knowing nothing this perfect could ever last. The scent of her passion was one he'd never forget, locked into his memory for all the days of his life. Seeing her like this was as close to heaven as a man like him would ever get. Her sex pulsed around his dick once, and he could sense how close she was. "Come for me, Kira."

Her muscles locked tight on him, her pussy flexing in waves around his cock as she climaxed. The feral side of his nature wanted to take, to claim. The wolf wanted to be in command. Silver swirled around the arms he had bracketing her body, and he felt change riding him as he rode her. He fought it, raced it, and flung himself toward orgasm.

He threw his head back, a howl ripping free as he jetted hard inside her. He hadn't come that close to shifting during sex since he was a teen. It would have been embarrassing, but he was too spent to care. She'd wrung everything from him, and he collapsed on top of her. He felt her arms come around him, and something deep within him loosened and gave way.

"Kira, I..." He paused, not certain how to say what he wanted to say, not even certain *what* he wanted to say.

"Yeah?" Her voice was smoky with sleep, her limbs falling open and away from him as her breathing deepened into that of slumber.

He'd never know now what he would have said. An affectionate smile formed on his mouth as he stroked her pale hair away from her face. For a long while, he just watched her sleep. His chest squeezed tight, and it was the most amazing moment of his life. Unlike the last time he'd fallen in love, this time, he didn't take it for granted. Nothing lasted forever, and now he was old enough and mature enough to appreciate it.

He'd just never thought he'd fall again. He hadn't wanted it, had run from any inkling of it since Athena had died, but with Kira, it had built so gradually that he hadn't noticed until it was too late. The woman owned his soul now.

Whether he ever got up the courage to tell her was another matter entirely.

Saying it somehow made it more real.

He could lose Kira as easily as he had lost Athena. But there had been sides of him Athena had never seen because she'd been human. For better or for worse, part of his relationship with her had always been a lie. Not with Kira. As she'd said, she saw him. She saw through the masks he wore for the world. She knew him for what he really was, just the way he knew her. The prospect of having her, *really* having her and admitting that to lose her was to lose a part of himself, was more than he could handle.

Maybe someday he could get to a place where he believed it could last, where love was something safe to feel. Maybe. Someday.

But not yet.

# Chapter Nine

The night before they were supposed to leave for San Amaro, someone rapped loudly on Max's bedroom door, jerking both him and Kira out of a sound sleep.

"Sorry to wake you, sir, but there's a situation," Barrett's deep voice sounded through the wood.

Max's heart slammed against his rib cage. He sucked in a steadying breath, trying to shake the sleep from his mind. If it was a dire emergency, there would have been no knock, just someone barging in to wake him. He could hear movement in the cabin, but no running or yelling.

"Is it another dead lion's head?" Kira groggily pushed her hair out of her face, glancing around at the floor beside the bed. "Where the hell are my clothes?"

He grabbed for a pair of slacks, shoving his feet in and yanking them up as he stood. While she scrabbled for her discarded pants, he strode across the room and opened the door a crack. "What's going on?"

His second-in-command looked shaken, which made Max's stomach lurch. "The queen is unwell. We've called for Dr. Singh, and he's about ten minutes out."

Kira reached over Max's shoulder and pulled the door wider. "If he's ten minutes out, you called him *fifty minutes ago*. Why weren't we told sooner?"

"Technically, I'm not telling you anything, ma'am." Barrett forked a hand through his already furrowed hair, moving his gaze so that he looked directly at Max. "Iggy's on duty for the Queen's Guard right now, and Her Majesty ordered her not to wake Kira, but after a while Iggy sent me the private thought that the queen hadn't ordered *me* not to wake *Max*." A nice bit of trickery. If Kira happened to be in the same room as Max and happened to be woken at the same time, then no one had defied the queen's orders, strictly speaking.

Kira charged around Max and across the hall, seemingly oblivious to the fact that she wore her slacks but his undershirt. He followed a step behind, while Barrett trailed after them.

"What do you mean by unwell?" Max asked, though he was no more than three feet away from the royal suite and would soon see for himself.

"Vomiting. Profusely. She's able to shift forms, but she keeps throwing up, so our medic doesn't know what it might be. He called Josh before she could tell him not to. Thank God." The last two words were muttered, but Max still heard them. Rhiannon was two handfuls when she was well—he could only imagine how unpredictable she was when sick.

But once they shifted forms, Betweens healed of all diseases and wounds. Was there a new kind of poison that could do this? And how? Panic gripped his gut as Kira shoved her way into the suite.

She shot a look over her shoulder at Barrett. "I want a report of everything she's had to eat or drink in the last twelve hours."

Xio stood by the door connecting the sitting room and the bedroom. "That's just it, boss. She hasn't had anything but bottled water, and she shared the bottle with the king. He's fine, so it wasn't the water. She skipped dinner because she was feeling a bit queasy. Min-ji is downstairs talking to the kitchen staff."

"Where's Elan?" Max asked. He couldn't imagine that his brother would agree not to call for the doctor or pretend that this wasn't a serious problem. He told himself to breathe through the welling alarm, not to make assumptions until he'd assessed the situation for himself, but he knew of nothing that would cause this kind of health issue for a Between, and that scared him half to death. He didn't even want to imagine what his brother must be feeling right now.

Barrett responded, "He just got out of an emergency conference call to Kiev. Because some things can only be handled by the king, even on his honeymoon."

Max was actually surprised they'd made it this long without Elan having to be pulled into an emergency meeting. It spoke to Genesee's exceptional abilities that she'd managed to keep all the Between irons in the fire for nearly two weeks by herself.

Lowering his voice as they moved towards the bedroom, Barrett finished, "He's with the queen now, pissed that she ordered us not to interrupt his call, and trying not to show how badly he's freaking out that she's sick."

Not waiting for Xio to open the bedroom door for them, Kira twisted the knob and pushed her way in. One of the housekeepers was on her knees, scrubbing vomit out of the carpet, Iggy stood off to the side with a watchful eye on everything, his sister-in-law reclined on a couch at the end of the bed with her arm thrown over her eyes, and his brother was pacing in a tight circle by the window.

Max made a beeline for Elan, clamping a comforting hand on his shoulder. The older man's fists bunched helplessly at his sides, and utter hell lived in his eyes. Max squeezed tighter, because there really were no words he could offer in a moment like this. Anything positive he said would be an empty platitude, and he wouldn't—couldn't—do that to his brother.

While the men were busy offering silent solace, the women had a different approach to the health crisis.

Kira loomed over Rhiannon and planted her fists on her hips. "You told Iggy not to wake me while you're puking your guts up? *Really*?"

The queen lowered her arm enough to glare up at the fox-shifter. "It's no big deal. I can't believe you guys called Josh all the way from the island."

Both women snarled at each other, a bit of fangs baring.

Sweet Jesus, this night had gone epically sideways. He was two seconds away from stepping between them—a potentially suicidal move—when Kira threw her hands in the air.

"He's the royal physician! It's literally his job to see to your well-being. Just like it's my job to see to your safety. And you are not safe if you've shifted forms and still feel sick."

Opening her mouth to protest further, Rhiannon's eyes went wide, and she bolted for the housekeeper's bucket as she retched.

Still glaring at the back of her friend's head, Kira reached down and held the queen's long hair back. "I'm off duty, so this is me speaking as your friend right now. Shut the hell up because you're going to let Josh check you out. This is not normal for a Between."

"It's probably just the flu." Rhiannon sat back and scrubbed the back of her hand over her mouth.

Elan spoke quietly, though his voice sounded rusty. "Baby, shifting would have killed the flu."

The housekeeper set aside her scrub brush and blew a loose gray curl out of her eyes. "It may not be my place to say this, but... Your Majesty, when you shifted, did it feel weird? Like, heavy, or like you were dragging something along with you?"

Rhiannon pulled her knees up to her chest, wrapping her arms around her legs. "Yeah, why? Is that bad?"

"You're pregnant," every woman in the room said at once.

"Thank fuck." Kira dropped onto the floor beside the queen. "God, you scared me, Rhiannon."

Elan seemed to go weak in the knees, and Max grabbed him before he went down, pushing him onto the couch his wife had recently occupied. While Max had no idea what it meant to have a "heavy" shift, if four Between women said that meant pregnancy, he believed them. As Kira had said, *thank fuck*. He blew out an unsteady breath, closing his eyes for a moment.

Xio pointed a finger at the housekeeper. "Yep, that's how it felt with my kid. Shifting was a little harder, because I was taking another soul along with me."

Even Iggy was nodding, though Max was pretty sure she had no children. "Yeah, our mom complained about that when she was pregnant with our little brother."

The thwap of helicopter blades overhead alerted them to the doctor's imminent arrival. Max nodded to Barrett, who stood mutely in the doorway watching the tableau play out, signaling him to escort Josh. The big cat-shifter padded out silently.

Rhiannon gawped, her eyes darting between the other women. "But...but...wait, what? Pregnant?"

"That doesn't make sense." Elan shook his head. "You have to deliberately create a Between, you have to *choose* to share your magic when you turn a human or get pregnant. There's no such thing as accidental pregnancy for us."

Xio and the housekeeper exchanged a knowing look. Xio said, "Were you talking about having children lately?"

"Yeah, but in the future. Not *now*." The king braced his hands on his knees.

The way the women bobbed their heads at each other told Max they spoke telepathically. The housekeeper sighed and cast Elan a glance out of the corner of her eye. "Okay, so when things get, you know, *feral* and magic is wanting to break loose, it's easier than you think. Like, if you know you really want to have kids with the other person. Especially if they're also Between and feel the same way. It's maybe not as conscious a decision as when you turn a human."

Xio pursed her lips like she was trying to bite back a smile, dimples tucking into her cheeks. "There wasn't a moment where you were in the middle of it and thought, 'God, I can't wait to have a family with her,' or, 'I hope our daughters are as beautiful as she is,' or, 'women are even hornier pregnant, can it really get *better* than this'?"

It was interesting to watch a king flush bright red, his expression wavering between bemusement and chagrin. "Maybe I thought something like that."

Rhiannon scratched her forehead with her thumbnail. "Uh, me too."

"Well, then." The housekeeper shrugged expressively, then pushed to her feet. "You can keep the bucket, Your Majesty. I'll go prepare a room for the doctor."

Max spoke up for the first time since entering the room. "He'll be here in a minute and can confirm if you're pregnant."

"Again, this seems like overkill." The queen released a sigh and settled her back against the couch, which pressed her shoulder to Elan's knee. He stroked a hand down her hair, and she leaned into his touch. "Shouldn't we just go out and buy a test?"

Arching an eyebrow, Max answered, "He's far more accurate than peeing on a stick."

"Is that my cue?" Josh strode into the room carrying a quintessential black doctor's bag, exuding calm assurance, as if he hadn't been dragged out of his bed and onto a helicopter in the middle of the night. Only the fact that he was wearing ratty sweatpants and a tank top revealed that this was anything other than a normal day at the office for him.

"What's up, Doc?" Rhiannon offered a tired smile, turned green, and puked into the bucket again.

The doctor shook his head, set his bag down and knelt beside the queen. Silver light shimmered around his hands, and they dissolved into pure energy, which he passed through Rhiannon's body as he examined her.

In that moment, it finally hit Max that he was going to be an uncle, and joy mingled with terror at the thought of a tiny new person to love and protect. He only hoped the little bugger wasn't as wild as Elan, Kira, and Max had been as kids, jumping off cliffs into the ocean and hoping not to hit any submerged boulders.

Somehow, Kira noticed. Of course she did. Her eyes met his and she gave him a little smile. *» Congratulations, Uncle Max. If this kid gets Elan's gift for strategy and is as* *mercurial as Rhiannon, they're going to give* all *of us a run for our money.«*

Max winked at her in return. *»Let's put Barrett in charge of the kid's security detail.«*

While Kira's shoulders shook with silent mirth, Max turned to his brother. "Congrats, man. You're going to be a great dad."

"This was not the plan." There was still the faintest hint of panic to Elan's voice, though it was clear he was trying to conceal it. "We were going to wait a couple of *years* before we tried for children."

"Apparently, deep down, you both wanted them right away." Max resisted pointing out that pregnancy was the best possible option for what might be ailing his sister-in-law. If this was a new poison or illness that could survive a shift, what the fuck could they do? It was a nightmare he refused to let himself dwell on. Such a thing didn't exist, thank God.

A pent-up breath whooshed out of Elan when Josh turned to him with a nod. "Yes, congratulations are definitely in order. Rhiannon is about a week pregnant."

Tears welling, Rhiannon reached for Elan's hand. The big lion-shifter pulled her into his lap, pressing his forehead to hers.

"Is this okay?" she whispered.

"This is amazing." Elan wrapped his arms around her. "Sooner than we discussed, but I cannot wait to meet our child."

She let out a watery laugh. "I'm really glad I'm not dying of some exotic disease."

"I think we can all agree on that." Max patted her shoulder, then motioned for everyone to give his brother and sister-in-law some privacy.

Iggy nodded to her elder sister. "I'll take over here. You go grab a couple hours of sleep. You've got an early start tomorrow."

What none of the Guards mentioned in front of the royal couple was that Xio would be heading back to the food distributor in the morning to question a couple of employees who went on vacation on or around the day that the lion's head had been delivered. Maybe leaving town at that time was a coincidence, maybe it wasn't. The Guards needed to make sure they spoke to everyone, no exceptions.

"Thanks, sis." Xio headed for the exit. "Your Majesty, I'll have the kitchen staff send up some crackers. Eat them before you get out of bed in the morning. It helps."

"Good idea." Josh nodded in agreement, reaching into his bag to pull out a vial of clear liquid and a syringe. "I can give you something now that will help with the nausea."

When he was done administering a dose, Kira pushed to her feet and waved the doctor toward the door. "One of the housekeepers prepared a room for you. Get some rest and you can head back to the island with us after breakfast."

"I'll be glad to get home." He hefted his bag and motioned her to lead the way.

"Right. Yes. I'm sure we'll all be glad." Something in Kira's expression tightened as she departed, and Max couldn't help but think that once they got home, that was it for them. Back to being colleagues, back to being off-limits, back to how things had always been. He'd done his level best to avoid thinking about it and relish every single second he had with Kira in his bed, but those seconds were quickly running out.

How he'd live with the woman he loved within arm's reach but forever untouchable, he honestly didn't know.

# Chapter Ten

I t was over, just as they'd promised.

This morning has been the last time she'd wake up in his bed.

Kira's insides churned as she escorted Rhiannon and Elan out to the waiting helicopter. Josh trailed behind her while Max kept pace beside her, close enough she could feel the heat of his skin, but the distance between them was painful. They didn't look at each other, didn't speak, didn't share thoughts.

The pain of it shredded her, and there wasn't a thing she could do about it. Except put on that professional mask her father had valued so highly and get on with her life.

But, God, it hurt. She didn't know if it would ever stop hurting.

Her phone buzzed on her belt, and she tapped the button on her earpiece to answer the call. "Seaton."

"Kira, it's Xio." The normally unflappable coyote-shifter's voice was tight with anxiety. "He bribed another employee, a logistics manager, into giving him the delivery location and the schedule for how long we'd need food delivered. He knows exactly where the cabin is *and that we're leaving today!*"

Movement flickered at the corner of Kira's vision. It was just a subtle flash of light from a distant hillside, but every instinct inside her screamed.

She didn't stop, didn't think. She simply reacted, launching herself forward to knock Rhiannon to the ground and shield the other woman with her body. The breath rushed out of her lungs when they hit the ground, and pain exploded from her side and shot straight to her brain. The sound of gunfire roared. Max howled in lupine rage, and in a twist of silver light, the huge red wolf was in pursuit of the gunman.

"Move, Rhiannon!" Hauling them both into a crouch, Kira hustled Rhiannon toward the helo.

More shots rang out, and huge holes ripped into the side of the helicopter. It looked like .50 caliber bullets and someone who knew how to use a long-range rifle.

Fuck.

One look was all it took to know that bird wasn't getting off the ground any time soon, despite the spinning propellers. Pushing Rhiannon around to the front, she scuttled under the nose of the helo to take cover on the far side. Elan and Josh, thankfully, were one step behind them.

The pilot bailed out of the helo and hit the pavement beside them just as the huge window exploded and rained glass down on them.

"Oh, my God. You're bleeding, Kira. You're bleeding." Wildness flashed in Rhiannon's eyes, and she panted for breath.

Kira ignored her, barking at the pilot. "How fast can you get one of the other helos off the ground? The king and queen need to be evacuated *now!*"

The man pointed. "That one's prepped and ready, I just need to get to it."

A bullet slammed into the propeller above them and the sound of rending metal sent chills down Kira's spine. A quick upward glance confirmed that the thing was going to snap any second. "We're going to have to make a run for it."

Elan and Rhiannon both made sounds of protest. Rhiannon shook her head, her hair whipping into her face. "No, Kira. You're—"

"No time to argue, Majesties. Let's move out!" Wrapping her hand around Rhiannon's bicep, Kira dragged her into a run. A whistling crash told her the propeller had given way.

*»Keep your heads down!«*

She sent the telepathic thought as widely as possible, hoping all her Guards remained safe. Bullets slammed into the pavement as they sprinted forward, spraying debris that sliced into her flesh. Her heart hammered, and pain ricocheted through her with every pounding footstep. Three yards to go, two, one. Their pilot clamored into the cockpit with another pilot who was already there. Kira ducked below the spinning propeller and stuffed Rhiannon into the back. Elan and Josh crawled inside with them, and the king shoved the door closed.

"Take off, now!" Kira followed the order with a mental command, hitting the pilots on every possible level. They jerked in their seats, but obeyed her as all Guards had been trained to do. In moments, they were in the air, winging away from the cabin.

Rhiannon knelt on the floor in front of her, tugging at her clothes.

"What the hell are you doing?" Kira grabbed for the other woman's hands, trying to direct her into a seat. Her grip didn't seem to be as tight as it should, and her voice sounded weak, but she pushed that away. It didn't matter. "Get up here and put your seatbelt on."

"You're bleeding," Rhiannon snarled. She wrenched the bottom of Kira's wet shirt up.

It was only then that the agony hit her, a cry jerking out of her at Rhiannon's rough treatment. Kira gritted her teeth and rode out the pain. "Shit."

"Sorry." There wasn't a shred of remorse in Rhiannon's voice. Josh knelt beside her, and Elan was just behind him with a first aid kit in his hands. Kira blinked. When had the men moved? She hadn't noticed anything.

"Get us to a hospital!" Desperation and terror made Rhiannon's voice a brittle slice of noise.

One of the pilots responded, but Kira couldn't focus on what he said. Time became fluid, slipping past her. The pain was a living, writhing thing, branding her side, radiating up to her skull. Her thoughts hazed around the edges, and part of her recognized that there was a lot of blood pooling on the floor of the helicopter. Too much blood.

Josh glanced up and met her gaze. "Can you shift?"

"No." Her lips were numb, stiff as she slurred the word. Her heart thudded slowly in her chest, every beat weakening her as blood pumped from her body.

"Would shifting help? Can it actually get a bullet out of someone?" Rhiannon's voice cracked as she pressed a thick white bandage to Kira's side. It soaked through with crimson in moments.

"Keep putting pressure on that, Rhiannon. That's good." Josh's hands shimmered with silver light, and he laid them against Kira's chest, transferring energy to her with swift efficiency. She felt her flagging strength rebound, and she tried to gather herself for a shift, but the helo banked left, throwing them all to the side, and a ragged cry tore from her throat, the anguish like an ice pick straight to her brain, scattering her concentration.

"Not too much energy," she told Josh, Genesee's tear-streaked face flashing through her mind.

"You let me decide what's too much," the doctor insisted, somehow still calm and assuring. "Just *focus*, Kira."

It was far too late for that.

She didn't even have time to be afraid. She had only a single moment for regret. She wished she'd told Max she loved him. It was a foolish, asinine, pointless wish. Max wasn't even here. She was going to die without ever seeing him again. It made her angry, so enraged to have lost any chance at real happiness, but the tiny spurt of emotion exhausted her. Tears burned her lids, hopelessness crashing down around her.

"Max." Looking at Elan, she tried to will her lips to move, her mind to send the telepathic thought. His big hand closed over hers, and the heat seared her cold flesh. "Tell Max..."

Her voice failed, the last of her strength deserting her no matter how she fought against it.

Elan shook his head fiercely, his amber eyes locked with hers, and as her vision blurred, he almost seemed to glow with his ferocity. "You can tell him yourself, damn it. I refuse to let you die."

Too late. Too late for any more foolish wishes.

Then there was nothing. The agony stopped, the shudder of the helo going at top speed, the pressure of Josh leaning his weight down on her wound, the sound of Rhiannon's sobbing, the rumble of Elan's voice. It drifted away like mist on the San Amaro coast.

And all she knew was...nothing.

>> *Be advised: the royal helicopter is safely away. The king and queen are unharmed. They're en route to the nearest hospital for Seaton. Only minor injuries here otherwise.* « The telepathic words of one of his Guards echoed distantly in Max's head, and he shook it to clear away the words, the memory of Kira's body jerking as she took a bullet, the sight and smell of her blood splattering across the tarmac.

Rage roared through him, so white-hot it was blinding.

He embraced the feeling and pushed down the terror, the guilt, the worry for Kira, to focus on the mission ahead of him: eliminating the threat to his loved ones. His nose told him where to go, where his target was fleeing. His paws stretch before him, churning up dirt as he pelted toward the mountainside.

Other Guards followed in his wake, some as humans, some as animals. Good. The more they had to hunt this bastard down, the better.

Min-ji circled overhead in hawk form, and her cool voice filled his mind as she spoke to the Guards telepathically. *»I have eyes on him. He's in full camo, heading east up the mountain. Delacourt and Granger are about two klicks behind him.«*

Knowing their target had been spotted sent another surge of adrenaline through Max. *»Monitor him, but do not engage until you have backup. I don't want anyone else shot today.«*

*»Understood, sir.«*

Pivoting on his haunches, Max swung northeast. *»I'm circling around to cut him off. Inform me if he changes direction.«*

"He won't." Barrett's boots hammered against the ground, his great height allowing him to *almost* keep up with Max. "We'll fan out and come at him from multiple angles, so he has nowhere to go but up, flush him toward you."

*»Good.«* Decision made, Max poured on more speed, leaving the others behind as he powered over terrain he knew better than anyone else. He'd roamed these woods every summer as a child, knew the fastest routes up the mountain.

Now he used that knowledge to ruthless advantage.

Staying just north of the path the stalker would likely take, he leaped over rocks and roots, ducked under a fallen tree branch, every sense electrified as he took in the sounds of the forest, the feel of dirt churning under his paws, the scent of his prey. It was moments like this when the man receded, and the wolf within him took over completely.

The beast lived for the thrill of the hunt.

He was getting close. He could hear the man's breath, his movement through the underbrush as he skirted around the edge of a clearing. The human was good, quiet. But then his movements stopped, and the hair stood up on Max's nape.

A shot rang out, the percussive boom hurting his wolf ears. A bird shriek echoed overhead.

Shaking his head sharply to clear the ringing, Max shoved a thought to the hawk-shifter. *»Min-ji, are you hit?«*

*»Grazed, damn it.«* Disgust and pain rang in her mental tones. *»Landing to shift and heal. I'll lose sight of the fucker. Get him for me. For Kira.«*

*»Yes.«* A low growl issued from Max's throat as he finally caught sight of his prey.

"Don't come any closer, you freaks!" The man's voice was harsh with fury. "I know you're there. I'll do you like I did the bird. And your queen."

The reminder that his shot at Rhiannon had taken out Kira might have provoked Max into doing something rash, but his molten rage had burned away into cold, chilling wrath.

He would end this man with no further causalities.

Max sent a telepathic thought to the other Guards. *»I see him sheltering behind a couple of boulders at the north end of a clearing. I'm above him, but need to work my way down to where he's hiding.«*

Barrett's mental voice responded. *»I'm coming up to the other side of the clearing. I'll keep him distracted.«*

*»Just don't get yourself shot.«*

*»Yes, sir.«*

From his vantage point, Max could see Barrett poke his head out from behind a large tree. The cat-shifter's movements were a bit exaggerated to Max's eyes, obviously intended to give the human a target. But the human didn't know Granger, didn't know the cat had a knack for going unseen when he wanted.

"Freaks? That's just rude." Granger called out with mocking derision. "Then again, so is taking potshots at an unarmed woman. Some might even call that cowardly."

A bullet hitting Barrett's tree was the only response to that.

"I mean, how spineless do you have to be to send nasty notes and a rotten old lion head to a woman who's never hurt anybody?" The type of disdain that only a feline could manage dripped from Barrett's tone. "Are you scared to get up close and personal with those threats, you pathetic little human?"

The human twitched at the words *spineless* and *pathetic,* but gave no other outward indication that he was listening to the cat-shifter. Padding on silent paws as close as he dared, Max dropped to his belly and eased forward toward the top of the largest boulder, where he could drop down on the human from behind.

"But it gets even more pitiful than that!" A crack of loud laughter echoed across the meadow. "How fucking incompetent do you have to be with that rifle not to hit what you're aiming at?"

Another bullet splintered the tree's bark. "I hit her! There was blood everywhere."

"You hit the queen's bodyguard."

"*No.* I hit her." Hysteria edged the human's words. "She had to die. I hit her."

"Why did she have to die, weakling? What's it to you?"

"She's my sister!" The human's voice cracked on the last word. "The king seduced her away from her family to his island of depravity, fed her lies, made her abandon us, made her *want* to be a fucking freak like the rest of you monsters. She had to pay! They both had to pay."

"Queen Rhiannon is an only child, crazy boy."

"She's. My. Sister." The human bit off each word, not a hint of doubt in his tone. "And she's dead now."

Max froze as his movements dislodged a pebble that went tumbling down the boulder. Would the human notice?

Barrett clearly noticed, because he chose that moment to step out from behind the tree, shaking his head sadly. "Sorry, no. You failed. The king and queen are safe. Far safer than you. You'll never leave Delacourt land alive."

"*Safe?*" Now it was the human's turn to laugh, standing with his rifle braced against his shoulder as he took aim at the big cat-shifter. "I've never been safe since the day I was born."

"So...what?" Barrett tilted his head. "Your sad family life means we should ignore that you're a stalker and wannabe murderer?"

The human snorted. "I'm sorry you're going to be the one I take with me."

"I'm sorry you think we don't have someone sneaking up behind you."

The man whipped around towards Max, his finger tightening on the trigger.

Too late.

# CHAPTER ELEVEN

He'd ripped the man's throat out, left him gawping like a landed fish as the life drained out of him. Max doubted the man had ever heard him coming, doubted he'd had any idea that death was so close.

Max had shown no mercy and no remorse.

He had, without a doubt, lived up to his father's low expectations for him. He was nothing but a killer. And he hadn't even managed to use that to protect the people he loved.

God, he loved her. Even now, hours later, all he could see when he closed his eyes was the blood splattering across the landing pad. All he could smell was the coppery scent of it. Her blood. Kira.

A shudder rippled through him and he buried his face in one palm.

Elan and Josh had managed to give her enough energy to get her to this hospital alive. Max didn't know what that had cost them, but he was grateful for even the hope of seeing her smile again.

Josh was in with the human doctors operating on her, pulling the bullet fragments out, pumping fresh blood into her veins, feeding her more energy. Max and the Guards had arrived at the same time as Genesee, though how she'd gotten there, he hadn't a clue.

But now they waited to see if a miracle could happen.

Rhiannon huddled in Elan's arms in the chairs across from Max. His brother watched him, concern in his eyes, but Max was glad no one tried to talk to him. Genesee sat beside him, holding tight to his hand, the only thing keeping him grounded. A few Guards paced back and forth down the sterile hallway, something that he would normally be doing, but he couldn't move, couldn't think, couldn't breathe.

Fear twisted like a coiling snake within him, a living evil that was ready to strike. Ready to kill what was left of his soul.

His stomach heaved, and he swallowed the acrid bile that burned the back of his throat. "Josh."

Max's head came up at the single word from Genesee. She released his hand as he rose to his feet, his gaze locking on the doctor coming down the hall toward them. The man looked haggard, his face ashen, his eyes bloodshot. He looked like someone who'd fought a war. And lost.

No. Please, God, no. He couldn't survive this again. Not again. Not Kira. Ice froze the blood in Max's veins and he swayed on his feet. The world tilted in front of him and a roaring filled his ears even though he *needed* to hear what the doctor had to say. His life depended on it.

He caught his hands on his knees before he slammed face-first into the linoleum. The next thing he knew, Elan was on one side and Genesee on the other, each pushing him back into the chair and shoving his head between his knees.

"Are you all right?" Josh's quiet voice sounded right in front of him, and Max looked up to meet the man's dark eyes.

"I don't know. Am I?" Because God knew, he'd never be all right again if Kira hadn't survived. And he'd been too gutless to tell her he loved her. His heart stopped as he waited for the other man to speak.

The doctor crouched in front of him, his serious expression breaking into a smile of pure triumph. "It was rough, but she pulled through."

A joyful cry spilled from Rhiannon and echoed through the small cluster of Guards. Max just dropped his head back between his knees and laced his fingers through his hair. *»Thank you.«*

He sent the telepathic thought out, and he wasn't even sure to whom. His brother for helping to get Kira here in time, Josh for doing what the human doctors couldn't, God for not taking her away. Gratitude flooded him, making his heart thud painfully in his chest. Moisture burned his lids, and he sucked in a deep, calming breath.

Elan's hand squeezed his shoulder in support. "When can we see her?"

"She's sleeping right now, but give her an hour or so, and she should be just fine."

"And we can take her back to San Amaro then?" Rhiannon flopped onto the floor next to Josh in a very unqueenly manner. "She's fine, just like that?"

"Just like that. It took a lot of energy transfer to get her to shift forms, but she did and now she's fine. Exhausted, but fine."

"*You're* exhausted." Genesee's fingers dug into Max's shoulder while she spoke to the doctor.

Josh met the blond woman's gaze for long moments, and Max could almost sense the telepathy flowing back and forth between them. Finally, Josh simply nodded. "Yes. I'm exhausted."

"Let's get some coffee. The crap they have in the cafeteria shouldn't kill you, and it's caffeinated." Genesee stood and offered her hand.

Josh gripped her fingers and allowed himself to be drawn to his feet. He glanced back at Max. "Give her an hour, and she's all yours."

The words snapped something inside Max's head. She wasn't all his, and she never would be. For all the reasons that hadn't changed and never would.

Guilt went crashing through him, and along with it, a sense of inadequacy unlike anything he'd ever known. Not even his father had brought him so low. He had done nothing to save her. Elan had. Josh had.

Max had been good for nothing.

Except killing the shooter.

"Energy transfer." Rhiannon refolded her legs, wiggling around as though she could find a comfortable position on the cold tile floor. "Maybe it's because I haven't even had a whole year being Between, but the idea of transferring your energy to someone else is just so...weird to me. Still. Maybe it always will be." She met Max's eyes. "That's what Elan and Josh did to keep her alive until we could land here."

"Don't try it yourself, sweetheart." Elan's voice deepened to a low growl. "It takes training and skill you don't have. You could drain yourself of energy until *you* couldn't shift to a solid form."

She shivered. "I don't want to try it. But I would if I had to. If there was no one who knew how and you or Max or Kira or Genesee were dying...you can bet your ass I'd try."

He opened his mouth as if he were going to argue, but then sighed. "I know you would."

The sparkle of good humor in Rhiannon's gaze made Elan grin and shake his head. She rose gracefully to her feet and dusted her pants off. "While we're waiting, I'm going to run down to get some of that battery acid coffee. You guys want me to bring you back some?"

"Yeah, bring some for both of us." Elan's hand squeezed the back of Max's neck, and he nodded to two of the Queen's Guards who had already moved forward to escort his wife. "Thanks."

She bent forward and pressed a quick kiss to his lips. "No problem, babe. Back soon."

The moment she'd gone, Elan's fingers tightened on Max's nape. "What are you thinking? It's not like you to be silent."

Max snorted and pulled away from his brother's grip. "I'm not always a loudmouth."

"I never said you were." The older man's words were quiet and measured. "I know you, Max. I know all your secrets and you know mine. So, I have to wonder why you're getting defensive when all I asked was what's on your mind."

The truth burst out of him, a dam rupturing deep within. "I'm not good enough for her."

"What? What's this?" Elan reared back, a low hiss issuing from the big lion. "Since when have you let something that stupid crawl into your head?"

"Since always."

"And always started...when, exactly?"

"Shit, Elan." Max shoved his fingers through his hair. "You know when."

"Father."

"Yeah." He let his arm drop and sighed, feeling more defeated than he ever had in his life. "She deserves better. She deserves... Hell, I don't know. *You*. A king. Whatever she wants."

His brother made a disgusted noise. "Kira wouldn't be a queen if you paid her. She'd hate every second of it, and she and I have never felt that way about each other. She's like my sister—she sees me like a brother."

"I know that." Now, anyway. A couple of weeks ago, he'd have argued differently.

"So, what's the problem? She doesn't want a king. After Seaton was done with her, she probably thinks she isn't worthy of one anyway. It's *above her place*." Elan's voice took on a remarkably accurate Seaton-like English accent. "And even that was bullshit. She's good enough for whomever she wants and so are you. You want each other. It's done. It was done years ago, but the two of you are stubborn asses."

"You're one to speak, brother."

He snorted. "Yeah, well. I didn't say I wasn't stubborn, I said you were."

"I'm a killer." Max swallowed past the huge lump that stuck in his throat.

Settling back in his chair, Elan hitched one ankle onto his other knee. "You've killed people, yes. A few times because I ordered it. Does that make me worse for asking my little brother to do my dirty work for me?"

"You're a good man. A *great* man."

"I feel the same way about you, Max. You left San Amaro and made a life for yourself that was just your own. I just took on the family's issues. Business and government." He gestured down at himself, at his expensive clothing. "None of this is mine—I wasn't the first, and I won't be the last. I admire the hell out of you for breaking out and making your own way."

Max stared blankly at his brother, unable to take in everything he'd said. Max was the screwup. Always had been, always would be.

This was one thing he'd never talked about with Elan. A part of him hadn't wanted confirmation that his older brother—his only real family—agreed with their father's assessment. He wouldn't be as cruel about it, but he also wouldn't lie. And Max hadn't wanted the truth.

He swallowed hard. "She could have died. Like Athena."

"Yes, she could have." His brother pulled in a slow breath, and when he spoke, his tone was considering. "What happens to us in life leaves scars. For Betweens, those scars are just inside. It doesn't mean they aren't there just because the magic heals the outer marks. What happened with Athena, how we grew up with Father, leaving home to make your way among humans, coming back and cleaning up the messes of our entire race...all of those things left their marks on your soul, Max. It doesn't make you a better or worse person than anyone else. We *all* have those marks. We do the best we can from one day to the next. That's all we can do, isn't it?"

"Yeah." A huge weight crumbled away from Max. The relief was staggering. He'd been carrying it around for so long he hadn't even noticed it until it was gone. Elan was right. Kira was right. He'd used his father's opinion of him to color everything around him. He'd let that keep him from getting over Athena's death. It had taken learning to love again to see it.

Elan crossed his arms over his broad chest. "So, is the best you can do running from a living, breathing woman who loves you?"

"No." The best he could do was love her back, hold on tight, and pray he could keep her safe. Though she'd kick his ass for thinking he needed to protect her. He grinned for the first time in what felt like forever.

K ira opened her eyes to a familiar face. "What's up, Doc?"

Her voice was scratchy and weak to her ears, and she realized she was ferociously thirsty. Dead people didn't feel anything, and she felt like shit warmed over, so she was definitely *not* dead.

Josh groaned. "You and Rhiannon really need to find a more original line."

A plastic cup with a straw appeared in front of her, and she latched on to suck down the cool ambrosia. The water flooded her mouth and moistened her parched throat. She drained the glass before she sank back against the pillows, shaking but replete. "I feel like someone took a baseball bat to me."

"Getting shot and almost bleeding out will do that to you." His voice was weary, and she looked at him more carefully. He looked like she felt.

"You helped me to shift."

He nodded, picked up her medical chart, and started reviewing it. "Yeah. We got you here alive, the human doctors got the bullet out and managed to stop the bleeding, and once you'd stabilized with traditional medicine, I got you to shift. If any one of those things hadn't happened, we'd be attending your funeral this week."

The air seeped out of her lungs. "I was pretty sure you would be. I...really didn't think I was going to wake up again."

It was almost disorienting to find she *was* alive. There'd been no question in her mind that she was done. Show over. Time for white light and angels singing.

"Welcome back, then." Josh's smile was as mellow as ever, though there was some tension around his mouth that she'd bet wasn't due to doctoring her up. Genesee. It had to be.

As if on cue, the lynx-shifter knocked softly and poked her head in the door. She flinched when she saw Josh, but a grin lit her face when she looked at Kira. "Hey, you. There are some people who want to see you."

Josh set down her chart, crossed his arms, and pointedly did not look at the other woman. "Are you up for visitors?"

"You two need to work this business out." She glanced between the two.

Genesee rolled her eyes. "Okay, pot. I'll go check if the kettle wants to see you."

"He probably doesn't." Kira glanced down at the blanket covering her legs, plucking at a loose thread. Genesee hadn't heard her—or had ignored her—because she'd already gone to get Max.

"It's rough, this falling in love thing." Josh sighed. "It's an emotional rollercoaster."

"It is, and I'm sorry. I shouldn't have commented. It's not like my love life is anything to brag about." She pushed back the blanket and slid her legs over the side of the bed. "I want to shift again before I see anyone. Then I won't feel like roadkill."

"I'll help." Josh braced her while she stood, his arms beginning to glimmer with silver.

"Are you sure you're up for this?"

He simply nodded in his reassuring way. She closed her eyes and leaned against him, letting his energy spin through her to boost her own flagging reserves. The heat of magic burned within her, sputtering and then flaring to brilliant life.

She flashed into arctic fox form, stretching her front paws into the new shape, twitching her tail. No pain, not even a twinge of discomfort. *»Nice.«*

*»Are you ready to shift back to human form or do you want to stay an animal for a while?«* The doctor's telepathic voice came from the bear before her. The wicked curl of his claws scraped against the linoleum when he moved in the small room.

She cocked her head, considering. It would be easy to face Max as a fox, because what she felt and what she needed to tell him was about very human emotions. No more running, no more hiding, no more lying to herself about what was in her heart. That would be the coward's way out. *»I'll go human, but I think I can do it by myself this time.«*

*»I'm here if you need me.«* The bear grunted and eased back as much as possible to give her some space.

She pulled in a deep breath and shut her eyes, drawing up the energy inside of her. The silver glow filtered through her eyelids as she felt herself swirling into pure magic. She had the briefest moment to wonder if she had enough energy to make the change, but then she was already reforming into a solid shape. When she looked again, she was human.

"Kira?" Rhiannon's voice echoed outside the door.

Josh, also in human form and already clothed, handed her a set of sweats and turned around to let her dress while he went to open the door for the queen.

Kira pulled on the pants and shrugged into her top just as the royal couple strode into the room. She rose to her feet and felt...good. Rock steady. As if nothing had ever happened. Sometimes, it was good to be Between.

Elan and Rhiannon both hugged her, told her how relieved they were. The queen shoved her red curls over her shoulder. "I swear, if you ever do anything like that again, I'll shoot you myself."

Arching an eyebrow, Kira looked down her nose at the other woman. "Taking a bullet for you is part of my job. Suck it up."

Rhiannon huffed. "Fine. Be that way."

"I will." Then she hugged her friend tight. Her father would be horrified at the familiarity with her employer. So what? If she was going to put her life on the line for the woman, it was better that it was someone she actually liked. She realized just how much she'd fallen back into the pattern of her father's mindset when she'd returned to San Amaro. As much as she'd adored the man, she didn't agree with him. She was as good as anyone else, and she could admit that she loved her job. It wasn't about who was destined to be servant and who was destined to be master. If she wanted to quit, she could. She made those decisions for herself, not fate. But she loved what she did. It fulfilled her, and it was important to her to make a difference for her people. It was important to her to keep those she cared for safe. Even if it meant she'd take another bullet for one of them. That was the kind of person she was—regardless of anyone's social class—and she was content with that.

She pulled back, holding on to Rhiannon's shoulders. "How are *you* feeling? Any nausea?"

"Some." The queen patted her still-flat stomach. "I fear I'm going to be living off Saltine crackers for the next few months."

"I'll make sure the Queen's Guards keep plastic bags on hand for you to puke in."

Rhiannon cringed. "Wow, I feel so elegant and royal. This queen gig has so many perks."

The two women grinned at each other.

"All right, we should go and get our transport in order." Elan put his arm around his wife's waist. "I don't know about you, but I'm ready to get back home."

"More than ready." Kira pulled herself up to sit on the side of the bed while everyone disappeared.

They were letting Max have some alone time with her, which was nice, but if he hadn't trampled everyone on his way to see her, that really only meant one thing. She could smell him nearby, could practically *feel* his guilt wafting toward her. A sigh spilled past her lips. She knew the shooting would bring up some terrible memories for him. It was the hardest part of all this. She knew him. She understood him. She understood what made him who he was, but that also meant she knew why he needed to stop punishing himself for things he couldn't change.

*»I know you're there, Max. Come in or leave.«*

*» Which do you want me to do?«*

She closed her eyes. It hurt that he had to ask, that he didn't know. Her mental voice was terser than she intended when she replied. *»Come here.«*

His scent drew closer, and then his big body filled the doorway, blocking the light beyond. "The shooter's dead. I killed him."

"Good." She spoke bluntly, and that seemed to ease some of the tension vibrating through him. "Who was he?"

"We don't know yet. Barrett has our people looking into it and dealing with local authorities." He sighed, his expression haggard and wary.

"You look like hell."

She expected a sarcastic reply, but instead his throat worked for a long moment, he swallowed hard, and it almost looked as if he might cry. "You look beautiful."

Damn. She had to glance away or *she* was going to start tearing up. But she held her hand out and his warm fingers immediately engulfed hers. He set his free hand beside her hip and buried his face in the crook of her neck. The naked need in that gesture staggered her. Moisture burned her eyes as she wrapped her arms tight around him. She dragged in a steadying breath. "I'm all right."

"You were right beside me...and then you were gone." The ragged edge to his voice, the echo of words he'd spoken about Athena, made pain shaft through her.

She ran her palm up and down his back. "I'm not her. I'm Between. I survived."

He nodded and squeezed her tight, all but lifting her off the bed. "Logically, I know that."

"But it brought everything with Athena back."

"Yeah."

"I'm sorry." Was his upset for her, or was it just that she'd dredged up old memories? They were friends and colleagues, and he'd be upset for those reasons alone, but that wasn't enough for her. Not anymore.

His embrace loosened and he braced his hands on either side of her hips. His gaze met hers, open and honest. No masks to hide behind. "I don't know how I can do this, Kira."

Her chest tightened until she couldn't draw breath. A harsh laugh spilled out of her.

Well, that took care of that, didn't it? Did it really matter what she wanted or how she felt if he walked away? She pushed out of his arms and stood, heading for the bathroom door before what was left of her dignity completely deserted her. "I'm going to grab a shower before we leave for San Amaro." She paused and glanced back. "Look, I get it. You don't have to pretend you wanted more than sex. We were friends before and that's what we're back to. It's fine."

"Let me finish. Please." Two strides forward and he caught her elbow. "I don't know how I could live if I lost you now, but it'd be a lot worse to watch you find someone with the guts to hold on to you." He swallowed hard. "I love you."

She felt lightheaded as disbelief punched through her, and she swayed. "Wh-what?"

"I love you. I've always loved you. As a friend when we were kids, and now as a lot more. I've wanted you for years, which I was pretty open about, but...that's not everything." His grip tightened and he met her gaze dead on. "I love you. As in, the kind of love that means marriage and kids and whatever you want. I'm in, I'm yours. If that's what you want, too."

"I...I honestly never expected you to. I thought... Hell, I don't know what I thought." Her legs gave out and she slumped against the bathroom doorframe. "Oh, my God."

A muscle in his jaw twitched. "Is this a no?"

"No! Are you insane?"

He barked out a laugh. "Sometimes it feels that way when I'm around you."

"Are you sure?" Her heart thudded against her ribs, the shock still thrumming through her. Love was one thing, even staying together, but marriage? To Max? She hadn't even let herself go there in her mind. Hell, not even in her wildest dreams. Not really. She realized that was part of her father's training, thinking she wasn't good enough for a prince to actually marry. Time to put that kind of logic away. That wasn't her. She wanted a different life than her father had planned for her. She stared up at Max. "I mean, are you *sure* this is what you want? Because if you change your mind..."

"I'm sure." He took her face in his hands and let her see everything he felt. "Marry me, Kira. Look, I know you'd hate the princess part of this, but I'll do anything I can to make it easier on you. I know I've got a lot of shit to sort out in my head about my dad and my last girlfriend and, hell, everything, but I promise I will. All of this is probably a raw deal for you, but no matter how badly I screw up, I'll keep trying until I get it right, and I'll try to keep you laughing enough that you don't notice you could have done better."

As if she could do better than her own prince charming. "Okay."

He chuckled, pulled her to him for a quick kiss. "Okay, you'll marry me...because you love me?"

"Yeah. Because I'm crazy in love with you." She twined her arms around his neck and pressed herself against him. "Kiss me again."

He kissed her, hot and hard. His tongue filled her mouth, his hands sliding over her until he cupped her ass and drew her up on tiptoe. Passion bloomed inside her, heating her from the inside out. She twisted against him, the soft material of her sweatshirt rubbing over her nipples and making them tighten to stiff points. His hard body, hard arms, hard cock overwhelmed her, made her wet. She could feel everything and nothing. Their clothes kept her from stroking her wolf the way she wanted.

The tension soon became unbearable. Her sex was soaked, clenching on emptiness. Her skin burned with the need for his touch. She'd become addicted to it in the last two weeks. When she jerked away from the kiss, it made him growl, and he nipped at her exposed throat. She choked on a laugh. "I still want that shower."

His fangs scraped the tender spot where neck and shoulder met. "I'll join you."

"*Yes.*" She all but purred the word.

"Mmm, you sound like a cat, my fox." He flicked his tongue over the flesh he'd just bitten.

She shuddered and pulled back, yanking at the bottom edge of her sweatshirt. Tossing it aside, she shoved down her pants and watched Max whip into a whirlwind of light and energy. His clothes fell to the floor and he reformed in his human shape, naked, hard, and ready. His cock curved to just below his navel, the head glistening with a single bead of precum that trailed down the long shaft. The rough spiral pattern that marked him a Between gleamed silver on the muscular slab of his lower abdomen.

She turned and walked into the shower stall, flipping on the water. He came up behind her, his finger stroking down the line of her spine, swirling into the small of her back to trace her Between mark. "I've always loved that this was here."

Glancing back, her heart tripped at the small, soft smile that kicked up the corners of his lips. God, she adored him. Clearing her suddenly tight throat, she grinned back. "Yeah, it was so kind of Mother Nature to land me with a permanent tramp stamp."

A chuckle bubbled out of him, just as she'd intended, but he bent forward and slid his tongue around the edge of her mark. His fangs scored her flesh, and she shivered, reflexively arching away from the hot, sharp touch.

His arm snapped around her waist, reeling her back in. He nipped at the upper curve of her ass. Her breath hissed between her teeth, and heat shimmered through her body, dampening her core even more and pinching her nipples tighter.

She gasped when he straightened and spun her under the pounding rush of hot water. Backing her up against the slick wall, he lifted her off her feet. She wrapped her arms around his neck and her legs around his waist. They both groaned as every inch of them came into contact. "Kira, I need you. Now."

"Take me. Now." Yes, she wanted him to take. She wanted to give him everything. The last barriers of her upbringing fell away, and she gave in to the life she wanted for herself.

She tilted her hips in offering, and he plunged his dick hilt-deep in one swift thrust. Crying out, she arched hard, which only drove him deeper. He rode her against the wall, and the water made their bodies slide together. The beads of moisture trailing down her skin just added to the ecstasy streaking through her body. She wouldn't last long. Already, she could feel orgasm building within her, the muscles in her pussy clenching and releasing in time with his stroking cock.

Her claws dug into his shoulders, and she closed her eyes and buried her face in his neck, drinking in his scent as he fucked her hard. Hot water pounded over her flesh, sent her hair streaming into her face. Too many sensations demanded her attention. Her breath sobbed out, and her body slapped against the slick wall behind her. The water glued their fronts together, increasing the wet friction, and her thighs burned with the strain of moving faster and faster. Gravity would have kept him inside her, but she couldn't wait. Lust and love spurred her onward.

Orgasm broke within her, and stars burst behind her eyelids. The stunning force of it left her gasping. She should be used to how powerful sex was with him, but she wasn't. It would always be better with him than it could be with anyone else.

She loved him. And he loved her. Her prince. Her Max.

Her pussy fisted tight on his cock, milking his shaft in rhythmic waves. Still he ground himself into her, and every time, another wave of orgasm crashed through her.

She threw her head back against the wall, her mouth opening in a silent scream, her fangs punching through her gums. *»Max! Max, please!«*

A helpless groan echoed in the room, and he drove deep one last time before his come flooded her pussy. "I love you, Kira."

"I love you, Max."

Shuddering, he dropped his head to kiss the side of her neck. His arms tightened around her and compressed her ribs, squeezing the breath out of her. "God, how I love you."

And that was all she needed. They brought out the best in each other, and she'd never known anyone who accepted her, valued her, just as she was. Except Max. She knew what had happened in the last day would continue to affect them, but it wouldn't conquer them. They wouldn't let it. No matter what happened, they were strong enough to face it.

Together.

# Epilogue

The helicopters were ready to take them all back to San Amaro. Genesee had shooed the royal couple back to visit Kira when they'd told her they wanted to arrange their transport home. That was her job.

She found Josh first, sitting in a chair outside Kira's door, staring into space. He blinked when she touched his shoulder, then rose to his feet slowly. His obvious exhaustion sent a pang through her heart. How close he'd come to draining himself while he saved her friend's life, she didn't want to know. It would only scare her more to know that she'd come close to losing them both today. She shoved that thought aside and focused on her job, where she could at least pretend to have everything under control.

"Do you recognize this man, Your Majesty?"

With Josh at her heels, she slipped into Kira's crowded hospital room just as Barrett proffered a tablet to the queen. She hadn't meant to see the photo on the screen, but she couldn't help it.

Rhiannon cringed away from the close-up shot of an obviously dead man. "Uh, no. I don't think so."

It wasn't the deathly pallor and slackness in the face that made Genesee's gut clench and her entire body jolt in reaction.

It was that she recognized him.

A choking noise issued from her throat, calling everyone's attention to her presence, and it took a moment to collect her wits enough to speak. "Wh-why do you have a picture of Calvin?"

Absolute silence dropped over the room, and everyone turned in her direction. She took an involuntary step backwards as the force of their sudden interest hit her. She *hated* being the center of attention, hated being stared at. It made the hackles rise on the lynx within her.

Barrett pushed the tablet closer to her face while Josh leaned in to get a better look. His mellow voice broke the tense silence as he asked, "You know this man, Gen?"

The solid warmth of him behind her was the only thing that kept her from turning around and bolting. "Not really. I only met him once, but I knew his sister. Actually, so did everyone who lived on San Amaro about a decade ago."

"What?" Elan frowned, plucking the tablet from Barrett's hand. Several others in the room gathered around to look. The king shook his head. "No, he's not familiar to me. Who was his sister?"

"Alice. She was my mom's girlfriend. She worked for the ferry company with her."

Recognition dawned on several Guards' faces and their gazes sharpened as they looked at the image again, likely picking out a few familiar features.

Genesee gestured to the tablet. "This was her younger brother."

Max straightened to soldierly attention beside Kira's hospital bed and shared a speaking glance with the arctic fox. "I don't think I met her. Did Alice look like Rhiannon?"

Blinking in surprise at the unexpected question, Genesee took a moment to consider. "Not really. She also had long, red hair and pale skin, but those are the only similarities. Alice was shorter than me, very curvy, brown eyes, lots of freckles."

Barrett reclaimed the tablet and waved it before her eyes again. "What was his last name?"

"Um..." Reaching out, Genesee gripped the doorjamb, wishing she was anywhere but here, wishing she wasn't going to have to rip open old wounds in front of her friends and colleagues. So much loss, so much pain. And she'd come so close to more of the same today with Kira and Josh.

Finally realizing that shoving a dead man's face at her wasn't helping, Barrett turned off the tablet but continued to fire rapid questions. "You said you only met him once. When was that, and how sure are you that this is him?"

"Alice's last name was Brawn, and I don't think she'd ever married, so that's probably Calvin's surname too." She let out a shaky breath. "I met him at Alice's funeral."

She watched Kira gesture to Min-ji, who was sitting cross-legged on the floor, and the hawk-shifter began typing into her laptop, no doubt digging up every electronic record available on Alice and Calvin. How legal that digging was, was questionable, but Min-ji never let that bother her. The Guards needed information, and the proficient little hacker could get access to it.

"Wait, when you say Alice was your mom's 'girlfriend'..." Rhiannon tilted her head, trying to meet Genesee's eyes, but she pinned her gaze to the floor. She didn't want the queen to see the turmoil in her expression.

"Mom was bisexual." She wiped sweaty palms on her slacks, bittersweet memories of the two women together swimming through her mind. "They'd only been dating for a couple of months and had just hit a point where they felt comfortable with the girlfriend label."

"Funeral?" Josh asked softly, his hand lifting to cup her shoulder.

"Yeah." Her chin dipped in a sharp nod. "Alice died in the same boating accident as my mom."

"I didn't know." Rhiannon took a step toward her, her eyes deep wells of sympathy that made Genesee's throat close. "What happened?"

She shut her eyes at such a simple question, praying she could keep a grip on her composure. The last thing she wanted was to turn into a sobbing mess in front of a bunch of Guards. She didn't want to answer, didn't want to even think about this. But there was no choice, was there? "They were doing the last run from San Amaro to the mainland around ten that night, and some rich college kid was drunk and showing off his daddy's speedboat to one of his friends. They hit the side of the ferry going almost 200 miles per hour, and that happened to be the side that mom and Alice were on. They both died instantly." She crossed her arms, digging her nails in the opposite elbow, hoping the discomfort would keep the tears at bay. She didn't tell them that Alice had been decapitated by the speedboat, or that it had taken two full days for search and rescue divers to find all the pieces of her mother's body. Those were horrors she didn't need to share. "Most of the passengers and crew on board the ferry sustained some level of injury. In addition to my mom and Alice, one other crew member was killed, along with three passengers, including a two-year-old toddler. The drunk kid's friend died, but he lived."

Her voice broke on the last word, and she swallowed hard, blinking away the treacherous moisture in her eyes.

Thankfully, Elan stepped into the breach. "It was a truly tragic event that harmed so many people. We were just lucky the kid was from a Between family, or that could have turned into an international incident."

"But wasn't that also around the time your fian—" Max cut himself off when Kira elbowed him in the side, but it was too late. Everyone in the room was waiting to hear how that question ended.

Swallowing down the bile flooding her mouth, Genesee forced out a response. "Yeah, that was only a few months after my fiancé died, so San Amaro was down a doctor when the accident happened."

Losing all of them so close together had been devastating. But the worst and most bitterly ironic part for Genesee was that, barely a week before he'd died, Omar had saved that same affluenza-riddled teenager after another alcohol-infused stunt had nearly killed the kid.

The breathtaking unfairness had only added to her pain. She'd never felt so empty, so lost in her entire life. Waking up every single day, alone in the bed she used to share with Omar, wandering through silent rooms that used to ring with her mother's laughter. She'd sit for hours on her patio overlooking the canyons that led down to the Pacific, which used to be her favorite view, but those canyons and that ocean had swallowed up the only people she'd ever loved, her only real family.

"That was also around the time Genesee came to work for me." Elan gave her a kind smile, and she tried to return it but knew she failed miserably.

He said it like she'd applied for the job, but that was so far from reality, it was laughable. The king had walked into her house like he owned the place and issued a royal edict. She had a job to do, and she had better show up for work.

She'd wanted to claw his entire face off.

The bald truth was that he'd probably saved her life. Being his assistant had given her a reason to get out of bed in the morning, given her purpose. If she couldn't have family, then she would throw herself into serving her people.

And it was a very good thing that she'd already been in therapy when, a year later, she found out what her father had been up to since he'd abandoned his wife and daughter. Psychopathic rage, ritualized torture, serial murder.

"I'm sorry." Max's golden gaze was filled with regret, but still incisive enough that he saw far more than Genesee would ever be comfortable with.

"Let's not get sidetracked." Kira recaptured the room's attention. "We need to know about Calvin Brawn. You said you met him at Alice's funeral."

"Yes, her family was human, and they didn't want her buried on San Amaro. So, the day after my mother's funeral, I went over to the mainland to attend Alice's." She rubbed the back of her hand across her lips, trying to focus on anything she knew about the Brawns. "Her family had disowned her when she came out as pansexual, but I remember her saying she was still in regular contact with her brother. I know he was angry that she'd abandoned him with their terrible parents, but he eventually got away from them too and joined the Army. He must have still been serving when Alice died because he came to the funeral in his uniform." She pressed her hand to her throat, remembering that awful day. "He made an ugly scene, screaming in my face in the middle of the service. He said that my mom deserved to die for seducing his sister into our 'cult' and making her 'unnatural,' even though Alice had come out as queer and Between years before she ever met my mother. Then he shouted that his sister would still be alive if she hadn't been turned because she wouldn't have been living on the Between king's depraved island." She shook her head. "It didn't really make much sense, just a lot of Between prejudice mixed with homophobia. Though if that was the way he talked to her when she was alive, I can't imagine why she stayed in touch with him."

"He was the only family she had left," Josh pointed out softly. "Even if he was angry and toxic."

"Yeah, I guess." She dragged in a breath, but it did nothing to ease the pressure in her chest. "All I know is that Alice moved around a lot after her family kicked her out but decided to stay on San Amaro when she met my mom. They were *good* together, and I was glad to see my mom happy for the first time since my dad walked out on us." She lifted her hands and let them drop. "I never saw Calvin or any of the Brawns after the funeral, but that picture is definitely of him. The red hair and ice-blue eyes are unmistakable."

"Huh." Min-ji's fingers paused in their rapid tattoo over the keyboard. "Calvin Brawn was diagnosed with terminal brain cancer two days before Rhiannon and Elan announced their engagement."

A pained sound escaped Genesee before she could stop it, and Josh's hand tightened on her arm, offering comfort she didn't really know how to accept. "So, if his sister hadn't stayed on the Between island because she was dating my mom—"

Kira cut her off. "Then he might have fixated on some person or people besides Elan and Rhiannon, for some other reason. Likely someone who didn't have a security team surrounding them, someone far more defenseless. In this scenario, no one died except him. It could have been a lot worse."

Her friend's reasonableness sent anger spiking through Genesee, and she hissed loudly, the lynx rippling just below the surface. She welcomed the feeling, because anything was better than reminders of her mom and Alice and Omar. She clenched her fists and her claws bit into her palms. "A lot worse? You almost died, Kira! Isn't that bad enough?"

Max made a noise like he'd been punched in the gut and Genesee cringed. Right. That reminder wouldn't have been kind to a man in love with her friend.

"But I didn't die." Kira reached for Max's hand, but her gaze stayed steady on Genesee. "And Josh could have died trying to funnel energy into me so I could live. But he didn't."

That knifed through her anger straight to the fear she didn't want to acknowledge. The terror of nearly losing her friend. The anxiety that hit her every time Josh had to transfer energy to save a life.

It was all just too much. The memories she couldn't escape, the pain, the loneliness, the grief. God, the ugly, bottomless grief that no amount of tears could take away. The way she still walked into her house after work and half-expected to see her mom waiting for her, the sweet smile on her face that had always been just for her daughter. The way she still hadn't deleted the last voicemail Omar had left her, just because she wanted to hear him say he loved her, to be reminded of what it was like to be loved by someone who didn't know she was the daughter of a serial killer. The shame and self-torment of wondering if Omar would still have wanted to have children with her once he knew the unspeakable truth about her murderous gene pool.

"I...I can't..." She took an instinctive step back, which brought her into full contact with Josh's muscular body, and he curled his arms around her in a tight hug. The fit was so perfect, the desire so sharp, that she just wanted to scream or cry or hit something.

Kira continued implacably, her gaze never wavering. "Luckily, we're all safe."

"Luck," Genesee scoffed, moisture burning her eyes. "How is *any* of this lucky? How is a drunk rich kid killing my mom and Alice good luck? How is Alice's death turning her obsessive, cancer-riddled madman of a brother loose on Rhiannon and Elan good luck? How are my friends nearly dying to save each other's lives good luck? How is Max having to kill someone else good luck?"

Kira had the stoic expression of someone who gambled with her life every time she went to work. "Only the madman was killed. Max made sure he'd never hurt anyone else. I kept Rhiannon safe. Josh made sure I pulled through. We all survived to have this little chat. That's what you need to remember."

No, what she really needed was a stiff drink. Not that alcohol ever solved anything, but she wouldn't mind an escape from reality right about now.

She swiped at her eyes. "I'm glad our people are alive. I'm not glad we all had to go through this nightmare."

Sympathy filled Kira's gaze. "I know, hon. I know."

"Yeah." And suddenly Genesee was just exhausted. She wanted nothing more than some privacy to lick her wounds and that stiff drink to wash the bitterness out of her mouth.

As if he'd read her mind, Josh murmured in her ear, "I bet you could use a shot of whisky right about now."

"A shot?" She glanced back at him. "Try the whole damn bottle."

"I've got a fifth of Macallan at my place with your name on it."

"Perfect. Let's go."

## THE END

Want more from Crystal Jordan?

Join her mailing list: https://www.crystaljordan.com/newsletter

# About Crystal Jordan

Crystal Jordan is originally from the San Francisco Bay Area but has lived and worked all over the United States as an academic librarian. After many years of wandering, she returned to her home state and now resides in southern California with her husband. An award-winning author, Crystal has published paranormal and futuristic romance independently and with publishers such as Harlequin, Kensington Books, and Entangled Publishing.

# Also by Crystal Jordan

***On the Prowl series***

Claim Me

Take Me

Need Me

***Twilight of the Gods series***

Reclaimed by the Immortal Viking Wolf

Reclaimed by the Immortal Viking Bear

Reclaimed by the Immortal Viking Shifter anthology

***In the Heat of the Night series***

Total Eclipse of the Heart

Big Girls Don't Die

It's Raining Men

Crazy Little Thing Called Love

***Wereplanets series***

In Ice

In Heat

In Smoke

In Mist

Wereplanets anthology

_Ravencrest Farm, Virginia_

"I need a shieldmaiden."

Bryn was bent over, digging out a rock wedged under one of her horse's shoes. At the sound of that voice, deep and rich and so familiar, every muscle in her body froze. Pain and longing and a million other emotions she refused to feel twisted through her soul. Moving as slowly as a thousand-year-old woman—which was actually how old she was—she carefully set the mare's hoof on the ground and straightened but didn't turn around to face him. "Well, you'll need to keep looking, then."

"Brynhild."

"Just Bryn, thanks. Go away, Siegfried." The gods knew he'd never show up here unless it was to fuck up her life. No, thanks. She might once have been a shieldmaiden, a valkyrie. She might still be able to shift into a raven and soar into the clouds. She might be older than dirt. But all of that meant she had an even lower bullshit tolerance than she did back in the day when Siegfried was the love of her life. Also her betrayer, her tormenter, the man who cost her mortal life. The man she'd betrayed in turn, a blood-soaked vengeance she'd never been able to cleanse from her stained, battered soul.

That was a long time ago, but some wounds never really healed, did they? She tried not to think about it. Ever.

She stroked a hand down the horse's silky neck. Unhooking the cross ties, she snapped a lead line on to the mare's halter, and walked her to her stall.

No sound gave away the fact that he'd followed her, but she was keenly aware of his presence, his nearness, his ability to throw her off-balance. Tingles skipped over her skin, and she tried to ignore the reaction.

His voice came from directly behind her when she latched the stall. "I've used Siegfried as my surname since I came to America. A hundred years ago. Maybe more."

"Okay." She infused as much disinterest into the word as she could manage.

"Erik is what you can call me now."

"I prefer to call you gone." She set off down the wide, concrete barn aisle. The sun would set in about half an hour, so she had to wrap up for the day. One more horse needed to be brought in. She whistled as she approached the paddock gate, and Rogue's Gallery came galloping up. This paddock was designed specially to keep often unruly stallions in—the double fences were several feet higher than normal, for starters, with several other security features that discouraged her boys from trying to get out. Rogue slid to a stop just before he reached the inner fence, rearing up and whinnying.

She snorted. "Settle down, show-off."

The stallion snorted back, shaking his head. The second she opened the gate, he shoved his nose against her shoulder, demanding petting. She scratched behind his ears, and he nickered in appreciation. "Ah, now. That's my boy."

"He looks like my Grani," Erik noted. "Same color, anyway. Gray as stone."

Yes, and she hated to admit that she might have a soft spot for Rogue for just that reason. "Grani was a warhorse who died a millennium ago. Rogue here is a thoroughbred. He had a great racing career, and now I keep him for stud."

She clipped on the lead rope and then had no choice but to face her unwelcome guest.

*Whoa*. Her lips parted, surprise spurting through her. What a change. He was still enormously tall and built like a honed Viking warrior, a berserker who could conquer an army with one hand tied behind his back. It was his hair that caught her attention. Or rather, the lack thereof. He'd shaved his head, and the look was so different she blinked. She'd seen him once or twice over the last thousand plus years, never of her own will, but when Odin and Freya had summoned them at the same time, there was nothing Bryn could do about it.

This was the most dramatic change he'd ever made to his appearance. He'd always worn his hair long, no matter what the current fashion of the time dictated. His silver eyes, framed by absurdly long lashes, somehow seemed even more dramatic, more intense. Before this moment, she wouldn't have believed it possible.

That gaze pinned her in place like a bug under a microscope, and it took effort not to squirm. She wasn't used to that. Most men she met were like spoiled toddlers, and it had been years—maybe a decade—since one had interested her in doing anything other than yawn.

A decade. Shit, she might be regrowing her hymen at this rate.